Haemans

By

Nicoline Evans

Author: Nicoline Evans – www.nicolineevans.com

Editor: Andrew Wetzel – www.stumptowneditorial.com

Cover Design: Martynas Pavilonis – www.whitewhitedog.net

And a big thank you to everyone who has offered me support (in all ways, shapes, and sizes) during this entire process.

Dedicated to those who have come undone

Chapter 1

Darkness covered the space where Sevrick stood, waiting for his fiancée to return. He wasn't scared of her anymore; of what she had become or the knotted wreck she entangled their love into. Everything was ruined, but still he waited for her. Following her new life through the shadows of the city when he knew it was too dangerous to try to see her. She warned him never to return. Told him if she saw him again it would be his end. But no matter how tirelessly she tried to smother his love, she could not stop its beat within his heart. This love belonged to both of them; he knew it was still buried somewhere deep inside her too. Beneath her bones and rotted veins. It was in there and Sevrick would not stop until he found a way to fix her.

The front door to her apartment creaked as it swung open. He held his breath, hidden, watching his love move in the darkness. Her shoulder blades protruded from the skin on her back and her jawline was so sharp that her neck was completely covered in shadow. The weight loss had not ceased. His heart ached as he saw his beautiful fiancée deteriorating before his eyes.

She wore jeweled chains on her head that snaked through her wild red curls. He sighed as he watched; every time he saw her now, she appeared to be more and more a product of Russia's newest fad. Her eyelashes were long, feathered, and fake. She was covered in jewelry devised to cause her harm, and her body was gaunt, covered in scars. She did not try to hide them; no one hid them anymore. People walked around the city, parading their scars to the public like trophies. Rina looked just like the rest of them; all she was missing was the golden spine tattoo. Her lack of that mark meant her immersion into this lifestyle was not yet complete. Every time he saw her without it, he breathed a little easier.

It was hard to place the blame on her, or any of the others who fell victim to this new lifestyle since the media, government, and royals foolishly encouraged it. It was impossible to escape their incessant promotion of the new craze. They pushed it on the public until the masses succumbed. Now, the only people left roaming the streets of St. Petersburg were these monsters.

He still thought she was beautiful though, even if she did not appear to be herself anymore. She would always be lovely through his eyes. He loved her too deeply to ever see her differently.

With a click, she unsnapped her glass stilettos, releasing the small dagger from her skin. The scars around her ankles were alarming; some brown and healed, others red and raw. She flipped the switch on a nearby lamp and carefully picked up her shoe. The heel was filled with blood. Sevrick shook his head, fighting back tears as he watched her face flicker with anguish.

"It's not enough," she whispered. Tears of anger swelled in her dead eyes.

He knew what came next and did not want to watch. It took him seven long years to forgive her for choosing this lifestyle over him, and though her choices hurt him, he could not give up on their love. He was always sneaking off to the city to keep watch over her. His time was running out and she would die along with the rest of the people living like this if he didn't find a way to make her right again. Revulsion and betrayal aside, he focused on saving her.

"Rina," he said, stepping out of the shadows. Her face contorted with fury at the sight of him. She put her shoe down on the counter and stood taller with confidence.

"Do not call me that. She is dead." Her lips pursed together, pulling the skin of her cheeks taut.

Sevrick took a deep breath, maintaining his patience. "Arinadya."

She nodded, placing her hand back onto her shoe. She glared at him with disdain, like they had never been in love. As if he were a stranger, hiding in her apartment to antagonize her. She examined him, visibly contemplating what she was going to do. If she drank the blood in that shoe, she could kill him easily; it wouldn't take more than a flick of her tiny wrist to collapse his esophagus or cause major internal bleeding. She was too strong on her blood. She inched the stiletto closer, slowly dragging it along the marble counter top. The glass screeched as she pulled it closer to her.

"I miss you, Arinadya," he said, trying to stall her from taking a sip. He watched her all day. Normally at lunch, she drank from a raven ring that collected droplets of blood from her finger, but she must have forgotten to put it on that morning. She was weak after a full day without a dose and he couldn't let her drink it until he left. He couldn't risk the unpredictability of her rage.

"Well, I don't miss you," she snapped back callously. She untied the bow holding up the sleek, gray skirt she wore. The heavy, crimson beads at its hem dragged the fabric to the ground, leaving Arinadya standing in the dim room in nothing but her underwear and a sheer blouse. She turned away from Sevrick and he noticed for the first time the long tattoo of small, gold symbols that ran down her spine.

"You let them mark you?" he asked, his voice rising with anger. "What does it mean?"

She ignored him and began running her fingers along the sides of her body.

"I'm not the same girl you used to love."

Her silhouette in the dim light was an enticing sight. She was an exquisitely designed woman. She looked over her shoulder with devilish eyes, daring him to be aroused by her once more.

"No. You're not. But the beautiful, kind, gentle girl I loved when I was eighteen is still in there somewhere. And I am going to get her back."

She shook her head playfully with a sinful grin.

"I already told you, she is dead." She licked her lips, maintaining eye contact. She was playing games, trying to lure him in and knock down his guard. She messed with his head because hurting him was fun. But he continued to fight her.

"Don't look at me like that. You will not tempt me now." But he could not help himself from admiring her barely-covered body. As his eyes scanned the backs of her inner thighs, his insides twisted with desire as he remembered the woman she once was.

"You still want me." She placed her hands between her legs, letting him see only the tips of her fingers caress her upper thigh. Teasing him by touching herself. He took a deep, audible breath. Her words came out like a whisper. "You will want me forever." Then her tone changed into something evil. A voice that came from some other side of her. "Even though I will *never* want you again." She spun around and grabbed him by the neck. She whispered into his ear, "Don't you see how pathetic that is?"

The air in his lungs began to thin. She squeezed tighter, letting the air run out of his body. On his last breath, she released him, letting him fall to his knees. He coughed with pain.

"I *don't* want you," he said with confidence, standing up, "not like this. I want my Rina back."

"I told you, she's dead." She turned again toward her blood-filled stiletto.

"Why do you do this to yourself, Rina?"

"Stop calling me that!" she screamed, losing her temper once more. Her mood was highly erratic and he knew she was beginning to go through withdrawal from a long day without blood. He needed to get her out of the city and begin her rehab before he lost her completely. He could never tell her this, though. The demons that controlled her would kill him without a second thought if his plan to kidnap her, bring her deep into the forest, and rehabilitate her under the watch of his troop was revealed. She picked up her heel of blood and looked at it with thirst; her dependence upon it controlled every waking moment.

"Why do you hurt yourself like this?"

"You don't get it. This is how things are supposed to be. It is how they were *always* supposed to be. Our blood is a hidden gift from God. How could we ignore it once we found it?"

"Tell me you don't really believe that. We all know why the blood works the way it does. It's no secret anymore."

She didn't oblige his accusation. She knew the truth, but could not admit it. She was in the council now; she had been sworn to secrecy. Only the council members, and apparently the damned, knew the truth and it had to stay that way.

Sevrick continued, "What you do to yourself...it is monstrous."

"The only monster here is you." Her voice was heavy with hatred. "Choosing to ignore our body's medicine is blasphemy.

Opting to live a life like our pathetic ancestors is worse than anything I've ever done."

"Really, Ar-i-nad-ya?" He purposefully over-pronounced the use of her full name. "I am worse than you? I don't believe I have ever killed another human being before. What's your count at now? Ten? Twelve?" His words were sharp, cutting right to the point.

Her nostrils flared while her face flashed with wickedness. "It will be thirteen soon if you don't watch where you tread." He quieted; he had made his point. She continued, her words dripping with condescension, "These are new times, Sevrick. There is a new moral code. There used to be a time I felt sorry for you. When the times began to change it was pitiful to watch you fight it. I tried to save you, tried to keep you up to date. But you were always a lost cause and you always will be. I'm glad you're no longer my problem."

He did not believe her. Her words were carefully aimed daggers at the heart of his being. He learned a long time ago these words were empty. All he could trust were her actions during moments of high intensity. He had to break her down, make her emotionally weak. He needed to see his Rina rise from the depths and show him she was still in there; to remind him that this fight was still worth fighting. One day he'd find a crack wide enough to pull her through.

"You do realize drinking high doses of your own blood, for such long periods of time, is like drinking poison, right?" he asked, knowing this was an old argument, but trying anyway.

"Poison? I don't see people falling over dead. Everyone does it."

"Not everyone," he said between gritted teeth.

She let out a laugh, her face shifted with mania, "You and your little tribe of parasites. Thinking you can change the world. Well, you do know that we kill the damned, right? We can tell when somebody isn't using their blood like God intended it to be used and when we see them, we kill them for their betrayal, for their profanity against the human race." She was breathing heavy now, worked up from the intensity with which she spoke. "You're lucky I haven't killed you yet. I do recall the last time you broke in, I promised I would."

"Yet, you still haven't," he retorted.

"Are you testing me? You know that isn't wise. I could crush your bones into dust without blinking an eye."

She placed her fingers around the heel of her shoe. One sip of her blood would shift her judgment and refuel her with enough strength to demolish him. He needed to get her to react without the extra blood in her system.

He threw his hands up and played to her ego, "You're right. My strength does not compare to yours. Not while you are like this."

Arinadya unscrewed the heel off her shoe. She placed the opening to her plump bottom lip, letting a drop of her blood rest upon her skin. Her tongue crept from between her lips, licking the blood off. Her eyes widened, indicating her loss of control, and she inhaled the rest of the blood from the glass heel. After her last sip she slammed her fist on the counter, heel still in her grasp, and gasped with delight.

"You really don't know what you're missing, Sevy." She used an old nickname for him as she began to approach him once more. Her gray eyes were now tinted pink as the blood she re-consumed began swirling through her. Polluted blood seeping back into her veins, contaminating the healthy blood, creating a monster out of the woman he once loved. *No, still loved.* He had to remember she was still in there somewhere.

"This is the fashion now, I'm sorry you can't keep up." She was trying to taunt him, but he had never been so shallow as to care about such things as trends. It was the reason he never joined the rest of the population in this horrendous addiction; he never needed to fit in with them, he never needed to "keep up".

"You look horrible, you know." He pushed back, seeing an opportunity to get Rina to make an appearance. He knew how vain she had become since this addiction took over. "You were beautiful once. But now," he scrutinized her face: what was once beautifully freckled was now dull and gray, "you look so ordinary. Just like everyone else."

The insult hit her hard. He could see he was messing with her high and her mood was nose-diving. "And your beautiful auburn hair, it's a shade of washed-out strawberry now. So dull. You have become so dull, love." He continued, hitting her directly in her oversized ego. This was dangerous but it was working. He wanted to see her struggle. Wanted to test his theory that Rina was still buried beneath this creature somewhere.

"Get out!" Her hands were trembling, "I will kill you if you don't leave now." Something deep inside of her was stopping her outer monster from ripping his head off. It was his Rina.

A shrill howl echoed from her, warning him it wouldn't be long before the internal restraints vanished. That he didn't have much time before Rina lost control of the monster.

Arinadya, or more likely Rina, began shoving Sevrick toward the door. Each touch left bruises, but it was gentler than the death she promised.

She let out a shriek as she gave him one final push, landing him on the outside of her apartment. Her face was crazed with torment and her body continued to shake.

"I still love you, Rina," he tried one last time.

"I told you, she's dead." And the door slammed shut.

Chapter 2

Sevrick could hear her tossing furniture around and smashing glass against the walls of her apartment. Her angry screams were muffled but still loud enough to hit him straight in the gut. He couldn't let it get to him. She could swear that Rina was gone but he knew she wasn't. She was still in there. He would have been killed long before this night if she was truly lost to this addiction.

It was 2 a.m. and he had to get out of St. Petersburg before sunrise. The nighttime shadows would help him slip out of the city unnoticed. Luckily, nobody else was out on the street right now so he was able to make it around the building to a side street without further altercations. The moon over Russia was full and he had to be extra careful not to step into the pools of light it cast upon the streets. If anyone saw him and recognized him as a non-haeman, they would kill him. Though his right hand kept a firm grasp on the Tokarev pistol hidden in his jacket, a gun wasn't always enough protection in these times. Not with these people.

As he turned another corner he saw the face of Prince Mikhail on an illuminated billboard. His eyes were gleaming, his lips were bright with blood, and below his face read: *Russian Power comes from Within*.

Sevrick shook his head in disgust; he hated the prince. Ten years ago, the media found evidence linking a family to the deceased line of the Romanovs, the former royal family assassinated over a century ago. It was long believed their family line was discontinued after the slaughter but the discovery of these people, street rats at the time of their retrieval, proved that notion to be false. Somehow, the bloodline lived on. Mikhail was one of them.

The media made such a big deal of it that President Dobrynin eventually allowed them to take on the façade of being the royal family of Russia again. They had no real power but they quickly became the face of the Russian people. They were looked up to for some reason unbeknownst to Sevrick and people grasped onto the idea of them for hope. He supposed the government had been so overbearing throughout the years that people liked the idea of another source of power having some say in the way the country was run. But Sevrick knew the royals were just delinquents given too much influence in a country desperate for hope.

At first, this new royal family was under President Dobrynin's strict control. The president let the people of Russia believe he was allowing them to take part in the creation of new policies and laws in order to gain back the public's approval. In reality, he had the royals under stringent watch. The government documented their every move, which is how they discovered the epidemic of self-haematophagy. They saw the potential in it and decided they wanted in.

Prince Mikhail was one of the originators of the blood addiction that consumed Russia. As a peasant in Russia, before the media discovered that he, his parents, his sister, a few aunts, uncles, and cousins were descendants of the Romanovs, Mikhail and his ruffian friends would spend the small earnings they made to buy cocaine. A combination of college level chemistry and medicine led them to the discovery of haemanism. They found that drinking their own blood laced with chemically enhanced cocaine caused incredible changes to their minds and bodies. This new drug was a form of self-haematophagy: the practice of getting high by consuming your own blood. It remained a secret from the rest of society for many years, affecting only those living in the underworld of Russia. All of that changed once the spotlight was put on the biggest addict of them all.

After only one year of being recognized as a prince, Mikhail developed a large following. Girls had crushes on him, women threw themselves at him, and men wanted to be him. It wasn't hard for Mikhail to swindle his way into their hearts, and eventually their minds. And it wasn't long before they all began this journey of blood lust themselves. Mikhail's sister, Princess Milena, was an avid user as well and also managed to convert a large following of her own. Mikhail made the addiction desirable for the men and Milena made it fashionable for the ladies. Together they reshaped the country as more and more of Russia's people fell victim to this new way of life.

Within the first two years, President Dobrynin was on board with the Romanov's to make haemanism a national phenomenon. He saw the power, influence, and physical strength the prince had over him and needed to catch up. Dobrynin needed to be just as strong, or stronger. He also reveled in the idea of his people being stronger than the rest of the world's citizens. They had everyone believing the strength and power came from consuming their own blood and recycling it back into their system. No one knew the truth. It wasn't until Sevrick was hiding out in the woods that he discovered the twisted reality surrounding haemanism.

Once he and the other survivors rescued Leonid, a former haeman, they uncovered the secret. What the haemans in power weren't telling people was that they had seized Russia's water systems and placed small traces of the altered cocaine in the water. It was not enough to affect anyone on a noticeable level, but its subtle effects made their blood strong enough to work if they began consuming it like the prince and princess wanted.

Before Leonid was rescued, he was one of the three originators of haemanism. He provided the medical background. Kirill Mikvonski, another originator, was the chemist. He graduated college with a degree in chemistry and synthesized a new chemical that enhanced the cocaine. It intensified the drug, giving users superhuman abilities once it was consumed via their altered blood. This newly invented chemical turned the cocaine powder silver, so they called it silve. Mikhail was the brains behind the whole operation and its takeover of Russia. He put a face to the addiction and cleverly eased it into the lives of all Russians.

Once he had enough power and loyalty from the people, he convinced everyone that this new discovery was a gift from God. He told the public that those who chose to ignore the natural endowment were sinners. It came from within their own bodies, it was a gift from God, so how could it be wrong? They did not know their blood was contaminated by drugs, so they did not realize how blatant his lies were. He managed to brainwash enough people into believing this new power was "natural" and caused by nothing other than God and nature. He hammered this lie into the minds of the masses so devoutly that one day everyone began repeating it as the truth.

Princess Milena changed the fashion to fit the side effects caused by consuming only blood: the scars, the extreme weight loss, the overall dullness of hair and flesh. She began designing jewelry, headpieces, and clothes that fed into the style of the addiction. Her main collection consisted of wearable blood-collecting devices. Princess Milena was gorgeous, walking around like a gaunt supermodel wearing her scars as beauty marks. Somehow, she turned a disturbing sight into something acceptable. It wasn't long before it turned into a trait others envied. The media displayed her as a woman others should strive to be like.

After a few years, the siblings had enough people converted to the haeman lifestyle that distributing the silve became easier to do and slipping it to the masses through their water was no longer the only way to provide the daily dose. A silve pill was created and put into mass production. It was described to the population as a vitamin that "purified" the blood. The truth of the pill's contents were kept secret. The royals feared they'd lose the loyalty of the people who were too conservative to accept that haemanism was fueled by a drug like cocaine and not God. The pill became so popular that all the haemans took it daily. Inside this little "vitamin" was silve cocaine, minimum caloric substance, and a few other regular nutrients. It was their way of making the addiction last. The haemans who were in the council used the real drug and the ones who weren't took the special pill the government had given them.

It only took about three years before half of the population fell into this lifestyle. By the fifth year, more than three quarters of the population were addicted. Once the majority of the population was enveloped in the transformation caused by self-haematophagy, they started referring to themselves as haemans: blood-fueled humans. Rina fell into the trap on the fourth year.

Sevrick's first three years of the new royal regime were salvaged by the love he shared with Rina, but it all went to hell. Sevrick hated the prince and princess for what they did to his people, and especially to his love. Now that the addiction had been around for a decade, the only secret left was that it was natural. The media and the citizens who were deep into the blood lust still spouted that lie every chance they got. Perhaps it made them feel better and helped them justify what they had become. Most knew the truth and were too far gone to worry much about how it worked or the damage they were causing to their bodies and the people around them. All anyone cared about was being better than those around them: stronger, prettier, faster, skinnier. It was a very shallow existence. They all wanted what others had and no one was ever satisfied anymore. It was always about one-upping your neighbor, or beating somebody out of something you didn't want them to have because you wanted it for yourself.

The use of blood had also grown more intense through the years. The first and most common user only drank it. The second type injected it back into their veins through needles rather than waiting for it to absorb into their bloodstream naturally after drinking it. Then there was the third type of user. These haemans were an elite group marked with golden symbols tattooed down their spine. They were nastier than the rest, more hysterical and unpredictable, which also meant they were deadlier. Sevrick and his people were still not sure what the tattoo meant or represented—Leonid escaped before this group had formed—but they knew it was a mark of status, something that showed they were slightly above the rest of the other haemans. Both the prince and the princess had these tattoos down their spines. And now Rina did too. It broke Sevrick in two.

What went unaddressed by the haemans, and was noticed blatantly by all survivors, was the increase in murder since the addiction took over. Death was a daily occurrence, something no one blinked an eye at anymore. People killed each other over trivial things. Their emotions and moods became so intense, and their strength so overwhelming, that people killed one another over common miscommunications every day. People killed their co-workers over missing staplers; they killed their neighbors over a barking dog, usually killing the dog as well. Russia was now a dangerous and volatile place.

Sevrick maneuvered through the shadows, hoping to make it to the edge of the city with enough time to get into the woods before sunrise. He hid in the forests of Karelian Isthmus along with his troop of sixteen other survivors. He enjoyed three wonderful years with Rina before she fell into the haeman addiction. After an additional two years of living with her in the city of St. Petersburg, watching her slowly give in to the addiction and trying to save *her*, he finally realized he had to escape in order to save himself *from* her. She would have killed him eventually; no amount of love could control the beast growing inside her, not if they saw each other every day. So he plotted and planned to save her from afar. The people in the troop he lived with now all had the same two goals in mind: to save as many people as they could and to survive. Over the past five years these people became his family.

The edge of St. Petersburg was in sight and Sevrick paused in order to look back on the city he once called home. Despite the terror within it now, St. Petersburg was still as beautiful as ever. From a distance, the city appeared pure, untainted by the horrors of this new world. The architecture was ancient and divine, and the clear sky was full of stars that shined brightly upon the city below, casting it in a heavenly glow.

From a distance, it still looked perfect. But only from a distance. Sevrick was very aware that its distant perfection was now an illusion. It was a place that used to be his sanctuary, a city that used to hold a special spot in his heart because he loved it so, but not anymore. He shook his head as he turned and continued his path toward the forest. This city held nothing but misery now, home to his broken heart.

Chapter 3

The forest of Karelian Isthmus was deep, filled with mysteries and secrets. One of those secrets was the existence of Sevrick's troop. When he found them after escaping the city five years ago, they had already built their underground bunker. It was a subterranean chamber, made of nature but crafted by man, and was filled with torches for light. Living underground was the best way to stay warm while living outdoors during the long Russian winters.

After Sevrick arrived, the troop took on more people and he helped expand the underground living quarters so there was enough room for everyone to live as comfortably as possible. It was a lot of work to carve out the walls, remove the excess soil from the living space, and craft new rooms but they always managed to make the extra space.

Ruslan and Alexsei were the leaders of the troop. They were brothers in their mid-forties. The troop started out as just the two of them and Isaak, Alexsei's son, now fourteen. Oksana and Pasha joined a few months later. They were an elderly, married couple in their sixties. Pasha was a brilliant electrician. Once the fortress was almost complete, Alexsei and Ruslan stole a solar panel from the city that Pasha helped set up. It brought electricity into their underground home for the laboratory where they needed the power to operate certain medical machinery. The power also ran into the washroom to filter and heat the water they collected from a freshly dug underground well. Together, these five brave souls built a home that had the capability to keep them safe and alive.

For the first year, there was only the five of them. After ten years in hiding, there were a total of sixteen people living in the underground abode, and the number could continue to grow. They never turned away a clean soul looking for comfort from the horrors of the city. There were too few of them left to let any unaffected person wander alone in the woods, open to all kind of dangers.

There were other troops of survivors hidden throughout the forest of the Karelian Isthmus; the space was so large that the amount of people trying to survive away from the city could be endless. Sevrick knew of a troop that built numerous tree huts suspended in the air amidst the thick woods filled with tall Scots pine trees. His troop referred to them as the Scots. Another group they knew of lived hidden within the dense spruce trees off the shore of Lake Ladoga. They were nicknamed the Lads. Sevrick's troop decided to give themselves a nickname as well and began referring to each other as the Clandes, short for clandestine.

There were a few small abandoned villages located at different points throughout the Karelian Isthmus, but most of the people who used to live in them either moved into one of the cities to be a part of everything or they went into hiding as well. From time to time, haemans would travel from the cities and into these small villages just to stir up trouble, killing any person they crossed who wasn't haeman. These occurrences reaffirmed why it was best to stay hidden at all times.

It crossed their minds many times to try and escape the borders of Russia. Life could be normal again if they were able to start over in a new country. But they never bothered trying any of the elaborate escape plans they crafted because the attempt was more likely to end in tragedy than success. Ruthless haeman soldiers guarded the borders with callous force. Nobody got in and nobody got out without proper documentation. It was the only way for Mikhail to ensure the secrecy of haemanism remained within his realm.

Sunrise was steadily growing near and Sevrick could see the white elm tree that marked the underground entrance to his home. Before slithering his way beneath its large roots, he looked around in every direction to make sure he hadn't been followed. He saw no one.

Below the first large root that had grown above ground was a hole the size of a small room with only a small boulder in one corner. Sevrick moved the boulder easily to reveal another opening below it. There were well-crafted dirt steps leading into the world below. He walked down a few steps, slid the rock back into its place, and continued down the manmade stairwell. The only light he could see was a faint glow from a hallway at the landing below. It was dark but he made this journey so many times before that he knew he was at the last step before he even placed a foot on it. At the final stretch the light became brighter and he could see the thick and ornately carved door leading into his home straight ahead. He always wondered how the two brothers managed to get the door down this far into the earth.

Everything was quiet until he turned the doorknob. Instantly, the silent, dimly lit entranceway filled with noise and light from within: voices talking, laughing, singing. The Clandes were enjoying a group breakfast together. He opened the door all the way, smiling from ear to ear, happy to be home.

At the sight of him, Lizaveta rushed over. "Any progress?"

Knocking him back into reality of the night he just spent, gloom washed over his face once more. "No. I couldn't reach her. And I fear she may be using more intensely than before." He paused before adding, "She was marked."

Liza gasped, "Marked? Sevrick, you can't go see her anymore." She was 26, two years younger than him but old enough to understand why he had to go. Then again, he understood why she didn't want him to.

"I have to. Rina is still in there. I almost got her to come out. Arinadya began shaking when I taunted her; Rina was violently trying to escape from within."

"No, Rina was trying to stop Arinadya from ripping your head off," Leonid, who used to be a haeman, joined the conversation. He was deep into the addiction when his girlfriend Nina escaped into the forest of Karelian, looking for help, and found Ruslan. He instructed her to bring Leonid to him and he would do his best to fix him. Somehow she got him to follow her to the white elm tree. From there, the troop restrained Leonid and forced his addiction into remission. He was chained to a table for countless weeks. They slowly weaned him off the blood and introduced real food and nutrients back into his system. It was difficult and took months to complete, but it worked. Nina got her Leo back. It was the first success this troop had at reviving someone from haemanism.

"Yes, I know it was more her holding Arinadya back than trying to escape, but regardless, she was still in there."

Leonid nodded his head, shadows danced upon his gaunt and pale face. They cured him of the addiction, but sometimes, he still looked like a haeman. Nina came over to join the conversation. She held Leo's hand as he spoke.

"I remember fighting against the monster I had become. If she is still fighting it when she sees you, then you should keep trying," Leonid said and Nina nodded in agreement.

"What if she winds up killing him?" Liza interjected. "With you two, Nina got you to cooperate and you willingly followed her into the forest. Sevrick can't even get Rina to come here. And we sure as hell can't go marching into the city to kidnap her. We'd be slaughtered. What if this mission kills him?" She was asking Leo but Sevrick responded.

"Then it kills me and that is that. I will not give up on her."

Liza grimaced, her jealousy clear. Sevrick was aware of her feelings for him but could not indulge her, not even with sympathy. When he first arrived at the white elm, he and Liza formed an instant friendship. They became extremely close and spent all their time together. During this time he was always honest with her: he loved Rina with unwavering loyalty and he never led Liza to believe he had feelings for anyone else *but* Rina. He didn't understand when, or why, she suddenly viewed their friendship as a potential romance. It bothered him that the friendship was lost, but he did not feel the blame was his. Liza shook her head and walked away from the conversation.

Nina watched with a sympathetic look on her face before following after to comfort her. Leonid continued talking to him.

"I am concerned that if she is using more intensely, like you suspect, we may not be able to reverse the damage done. Her body may reject the treatment and she will die in remission," Leonid lowered the volume of his voice, noticing that Sofiya and Agnessa were not too far away, "like the others."

Sofiya had escaped into the forest two years ago with her four-year-old daughter Agnessa because her husband began to use and was becoming violent with them. When Alexsei found the pair and learned of their story, he promised to help mend their family. Sofiya lured her husband into the forest by claiming Agnessa tried to run away and they needed to find her. Once he entered Karelian, the men of the Clandes troop sedated him with a tranquilizer gun, restrained him, and began the treatment. Unbeknownst to Sofiya, her husband's addiction had grown. Instead of drinking his blood, he was injecting it back into his veins. This method of blood use was the second most intense kind. When the troop tried to heal him, his body went into shock and he died during the rehab. Luckily for mother and daughter, during his last few days he became more like his old self. He was dying but communicating more rationally, feeling remorse for the pain he caused them, both emotionally and physically. They were able to say all the things they needed to say to each other before he passed away.

Sevrick did not want this to happen with Rina. Leonid was the first person the troop saved, but he was also their last. Every other person they tried to fix since had passed away. No one could live through the withdrawal. They mostly tried the procedure on strangers; Sofiya was the first person to bring a loved one in for healing since Nina brought Leo. And since Sofiya's husband, there had been two other men that Lizaveta and Elena lured into the forest that the troop intercepted and tried to heal. They both died as well.

No one was sure what was causing the deaths or why it wasn't working the way it did with Leonid, but Sevrick would not give up. He had to get Rina back.

"Welcome back, Sev. How'd it go?" Zakhar crossed toward where he and Leonid stood. Nikolai was with him too. They became Sevrick's closest friends after he escaped the city. Zakhar was 29, only a year older than Sevrick, and Nikolai was 24. The three of them were sub-leaders beneath Alexsei and Ruslan, along with Lizaveta and Elena, who was 25.

"Not how I wanted it to go, but not terrible either. The Rina I love is still in there somewhere," he answered.

"Next time we'll go with you," Nikolai responded. "You've had too many disappointing trips trekking out to the city alone and one day you aren't going to make it back to us."

"He's right," Zakhar agreed. "I know you've wanted to do this solo but it may be time for force. Doesn't seem like she'll ever come here on her own. If you want to save her we may need to physically bring her back here."

"You need to stop refusing our help," Nikolai added sympathetically.

Sevrick let out an audible groan; he wanted it all to happen naturally. He wanted Rina to *want* to quit. He feared if she was forced out of her lifestyle then she wouldn't be ready or willing to heal. But Sevrick didn't know anymore. It had been five years of unsuccessful trips back and forth to St. Petersburg and he couldn't deny that each time he came back without her, it felt like he left another piece of himself behind. It was beginning to add up.

"Maybe. I need at least a week to not think about it again. Next go-round, we'll discuss."

They nodded their heads in acceptance, before Zakhar continued, "Last night, there was a raid on the village of Vyborg. We ran into one of the Scots in the woods."

"A raid?" Sevrick asked confused, "They haven't done one of those in a few years, do you know why they did one now?"

"No," Nikolai answered, "but we want to head out there to take a look and see the damage. The village has been abandoned for a while so hopefully no one took to living there again in the last few years, thinking it was safe."

Zakhar continued, "If so, maybe we will find survivors and we can build up our troop. Maybe going there will also give us some answers. If we discover they were looking for something other than trouble, maybe it will give us a tool to lure more of the haemans into the forest and give us more opportunities to practice getting this rehabilitation process right."

Sevrick was intrigued. If they were able to get more test subjects to try the rehab on, perhaps they'd be able to discover how to make the rehabilitation work one hundred percent of the time before he got Rina to come.

"I'm in. When should we go?"

"I wanted to leave this afternoon," Zakhar said, "Leo, do you want to join us?"

"Sure, I could use a good dose of fresh air above ground."

"Alright then, let's meet back here in two hours."

They all nodded in agreement, then separated to their own personal coves to collect the belongings they'd need to take with them on this journey.

The town of Vyborg was about 121 kilometers away, which meant two days to get there and two days to get back. It was the same distance as St. Petersburg, just in the complete opposite direction. They'd be gone for four days, plus whatever amount of time they spent exploring the village.

Sevrick walked to his own personal nook carved off the main living space. He pushed back the weighted burgundy curtain from the entrance and entered his dwelling. Pulling it closed, the room went dark besides the torchlight filtering through the curtain cracks and the sky light from the air ducts in his ceiling. He took a pack of matches out from his pocket and lit a small candle mounted to the wall. The room lit up with a faint glow and he took a deep breath. Home again.

His bed took up most of the floor space. He managed to scrounge up enough feathered blankets and fleeces to make the old mattress extremely comfortable. Seeing it again after three nights without a comfortable place to sleep made him wish the guys were leaving for Vyborg tomorrow morning instead of this afternoon.

He let his tired body collapse onto the pile of blankets that covered the bed in abundance. A sigh escaped his lips as the soft bedding gave relief to his aching muscles.

"Can I come in?" Lizaveta asked from behind the curtain to his room.

"Sure." He did not move or open his eyes. He was too comfortable. She sat down next to him on his bed and began to talk.

"I'm sorry I walked away from the conversation like that before. I didn't mean to cause a scene."

"You didn't," he said honestly. "Nina only followed you to make sure you were alright. It wasn't a big deal at all."

"Okay," she said with hesitation. The uncertainty of her emotions played out clearly upon her face but he wasn't looking. "I just care about you a lot. You know this. And I don't want you to get hurt," she paused, "I don't want to lose you."

"I know. I care about you as well. I care about everyone here. But we each need to do what we need to do to make it through these hard times. For me, it's rescuing Rina. I can't stop until I save her." He was not reading between the lines.

Tears welled in Lizaveta's eyes. As usual, Sevrick was not paying attention. He did not see the glossy reflection in her gaze. Even if he had, he would not understand why those tears were for him. She loved him for five years now, and for five years she had to watch him try to save another woman who did not want to be saved, a woman who taunted him and tortured him by reminding him how much she did not love him anymore. But he always went back for her. She knew the situation was more complicated than that; Rina was probably a completely different person sober, but it didn't change the fact that she had to watch the man she loved chase another woman who may never love him back. And the worst part of it all was this other woman would probably be the death of him and he did not care. One day, Rina would kill him. With her own two hands. And this was something he knew could happen and openly accepted. He would rather die by her hands than accept the love that was right in front of him. For five years, she stood in front of the man she loved, every day, yet he never saw her there.

"I get it," Liza said, standing up. She was done trying to get him to see past his obsession with saving Rina. Done trying to get him to notice her as someone more than just a fellow troop member. "I'll leave you be." And she left his room.

Sevrick propped himself up onto his elbows and watched her walk out of his room. He knew why he upset her but there was nothing he could do to fix it. The moment he sensed her friendly feelings toward him shifted he warned her not to fall for him; he was always honest with her about where his heart was. He barely had time to let out a sigh before Nikolai came barging in, ready to go.

Had it really been two hours already? Time moved fast beneath the earth with no sun or moon to help indicate time. Sevrick stood and picked up the knapsack he had worn into St. Petersburg to see Rina. Luckily, it was still packed. He grabbed an extra canteen for river water, two more packs of matches, and a duffel bag in case they found anything of value in the village that needed to be brought back.

"Who packed food?"

"Leonid's carrying the food and Zakhar added Leo's personal stuff to his own backpack. Food and flashlights are really all we need since it shouldn't take longer than five days to get back. We've all got a sleeping bag and we'll drink the water from the river. No use wasting water from the well room, better to get it as we go." Nikolai had his own pack strapped to his back and was eager to leave.

"Right. Okay, I'm good to go then."

They headed back out to the main living space where Zakhar and Leonid waited for them. Ruslan was there too. Once the four guys were together, Ruslan addressed them.

"I don't know how much of Vyborg was inhabited or what is left of it from the old days, but check the stores for medical supplies and food. If we can get some of our loot from there instead of heisting it in the city, we'd be better off. I don't know if you'll find anything of value but check anyway. You never know what kind of things the haemans leave behind after a raid, things they find useless might be tremendously helpful for us."

"I've packed an extra duffel bag just in case," Sevrick responded.

Isaak ran up to the group of older men, catching them just in time.

"Uncle Rus, can I go with them?" Isaak pleaded. He looked up with eager eyes.

"Not a chance."

"Please."

"I said no. You're still a kid."

"I'm 14!"

Ruslan glared at his nephew with warning and Isaak's shoulders slouched in surrender.

"Maybe next time, kid," Nikolai said, rustling the hair on top of the young boy's head. Isaak was glum, but nodded with defeated appreciation and walked away.

"Be safe Clandes." Ruslan gave them a small smile and turned back into the living space.

They checked their firearms. Nikolai and Zakhar had semi-automatic VS-121 rifles strapped to their backs and Leonid had a tranquilizer gun locked firmly into a holster on his belt. Sevrick had his own pistol in his jacket pocket. They would be well defended if any animals attacked or any haemans were still lurking in the forest.

Sevrick looked out over the large underground home he and his fellow Clandes made for themselves. He had grown to love everything about it, so he drank it in one more time before they left its comfort. In dangerous times like these, you could not leave your home without accepting the knowledge that it might be the last time you ever saw it.

Chapter 4

The first day of the trip was uneventful. As the sun began to set, the four men found a heavily wooded area and set up their sleeping bags beneath the thick covering of pine trees. The night was freezing cold. Sevrick barely slept. His shivering was too intense and he woke up exhausted.

That morning, the men were greeted by a gray sky and knew snow was on the way. Without delay they continued their journey, attempting to make it to Vyborg before nightfall. They hoped it was truly abandoned. All four men were tired and needed a good night's sleep under the shelter of one of the town's many empty apartments.

Leonid lagged behind; physically, he was not as strong as Sevrick, Zakhar, or Nikolai. When Nina first brought Leonid to their shelter beneath the white elm tree, Leonid could have taken out all three of these men without breaking a sweat. But the transformation from haeman back to his regular self took a toll on his body. He had been weak ever since. Although his body may never recover from the abuse he caused it, his mind remained sharp. It was still good to bring him on missions like this since he lived on the other side of everything in the past. His first-hand knowledge of the haemans was invaluable. It was likely that Leonid would pick up on the small haeman indicators in Vyborg better than the other three would. He'd discover their motive for raiding the abandoned village.

Zakhar took out his map. "We still have about 64 kilometers left. It's 6 a.m. so if we keep a steady pace, we may be able to cover the distance by nightfall."

"Are we stopping to eat at any point?" Nikolai asked, yawning.

"I'd rather eat as we go. It feels like snow is coming and I don't want to risk us getting caught at night in a blizzard. It's safer if we can make it to town. Leonid has the pack filled with sandwiches and water. If anyone gets hungry, take something from his bag."

Everyone grunted in acknowledgment. It was too early and cold to argue about stopping to sit and eat. Plus, Zakhar was right. It wouldn't be smart to stop and risk not making it to Vyborg by night. Last night had been dry and it was still freezing; resting in a wet sleeping bag covered in snow would be much worse.

The men moved at a fast pace: Zakhar in the lead, Nikolai close behind, Sevrick kept a steady pace in the middle, and Leonid trailed behind. Nikolai was the first to break into the food. He inhaled his fresh turkey and tomato sandwich and then tossed a sandwich to each of the other men even though they had not asked for one.

"Everyone eat," he explained, "I'll be pissed if I have to carry any of you because you passed out from hunger." He looked over at Leonid. "Especially you. You look like you're sleepwalking. Eat something."

They all ate quietly and the mood instantly lifted. They were making good time until the snow started to fall at noon. It began as a light flurry but within a couple hours they were trudging through heavy snowfall.

They pressed on in silence. When another hour had passed, Sevrick looked back to see how Leonid was holding up. His eyes were tearing up, his face was bright red, and his entire body shivered from the cold.

"Hold up," Sevrick shouted ahead to the others. He then untied the sleeping bag from the bottom of his backpack and wrapped it around Leonid. Leo gave him a small nod of appreciation before resuming the slow walk through the snow that continually accumulated underfoot. Within another few hours, they were walking through three-meter drifts. The pace they maintained earlier in the day had dwindled into a painstaking trek. The cold water from the snow soaked their boots leaving their toes freezing.

They had about an hour before the darkness of night covered them. The snowfall wasn't slowing down and Sevrick could tell everyone was nervous they'd have to walk through the night in order to reach their destination. They couldn't stop to sleep now; they would die of hypothermia before sunrise if they didn't keep moving.

They found an old dirt road to travel on. Before the snow started, they kept to the depths of the woods where it was safer and there was less chance of encountering haemans. They decided to parallel the old road while remaining behind tree cover, assuming remaining haemans would choose to walk on the path rather than through the woods. But as soon as the snow became too thick to see through, Zakhar led them out to the dirt path. It was highly unlikely any haeman would subject themselves to traveling in these conditions. Plus, it had been a few days since the raid. They were most likely back in the city by now.

There was still enough light in the evening sky to see when they came across an old street sign reading *Vyborg – 16 km*.

Nikolai let out a manic laugh of relief, a feeling the other men could relate to. "Looks like we are going to make it there tonight," he shouted into the howling winds.

Zakhar nodded, his eyes squinting so much they were barely open anymore. "Time to pick up the pace. It's about 6 p.m. We can get there in three hours if we hustle."

There would be no hustling involved, the snow was too thick, but it was great motivation to keep everyone moving forward. The weather was brutal and if they hadn't seen that sign, he wasn't sure how much longer they'd be able to go with no indication of their progress.

The next three hours went by much faster. When they reached the town, the sight of buildings filled the four men with renewed energy. Zakhar began a light jog, Nikolai joined, and Sevrick put an arm around Leonid and followed them into town.

The buildings surrounding them helped block the icy wind. It was a welcome relief from the consistent frigidness that relentlessly whipped across their faces the entire day.

Eventually, Zakhar came across an unlocked door. He cracked it open to look inside, then motioned for the others to follow. The three men followed him up the stoop and inside. No one was there; they could tell from the moment they stepped into the home. They turned on their flashlights and made their way into the living room. The sight of couches was the only thing needed to convince them to retire for the night. They sighed in unison and collapsed onto a plush set of couches framed in exotic wood with gold inlays. As their bodies hit the cushions, a layer of dust rose into the air; no one had inhabited this home for quite some time.

"This place is fancy, huh?" Nikolai said, his eyes taking in all the expensive decorations. He contemplated what he could take back with him to the white elm. "Good pick."

Zakhar shook his head; he only wanted warmth, not a lavish place to loot. Sevrick turned on a porcelain lamp with a beaded shade and light filled the room. Luckily, the power to this town had not been cut off, or perhaps energy still ran into it from the city. Zakhar began walking around to turn on a few more lamps while Sevrick grabbed another blanket for Leonid, who was still shivering. He found a beige throw with golden trim draped along the top of a throne-like dining room chair. The tag on it read '100% Vicuna of Eastern Asia'. He gave the blanket to Leonid.

"We ought to keep an eye out for things that may be of use to us back home, like that blanket," Sevrick said. "Let's put that into the duffel bag before we leave."

Nikolai was sprawled out on the couch and the cushions looked to be eating him alive. "I know it looks like I'm not doing anything," he said, his body appeared to have given up on him for the remainder of the night, "and I may not be moving much for the next few hours, but I promise you, my eyes are already packing things into that duffel bag of yours."

They laughed. Nikolai's good spirited nature never faltered, even after a long brutal day in a blizzard. The home they wandered into really was magnificent. The high ceilings were lined with carefully carved trimmings and the angular architecture of the walls and windows were breathtaking. It had probably been a decade since the owners lived here, but whoever they were, they had expensive taste.

Zakhar disappeared into another room. Nikolai and Leonid were becoming one with the couches, but Sevrick was having trouble relaxing. After a full day of exertion, he should be tired too, but he wasn't. He was restless and couldn't stop pacing the room.

Zakhar reappeared from the kitchen. "Anybody want some hot soup? There are quite a few cans in the pantry."

At the offering of warm food, Nikolai emerged from the depths of the couch with wide eyes and answered loudly, *"Me."*

Leonid was bundled up in a pile of blankets, but he managed to nod his head. Sevrick followed Zakhar back into the kitchen and they began heating up some beef borscht. It smelt delicious as the meat, beets, and tomatoes boiled. The protein and vitamins would do them all good.

"If this snow doesn't stop, we are going to have to stay here longer than anticipated," Zakhar said while stirring.

Sevrick peered around the opening from the kitchen and saw that Nikolai was already vanishing back into the crevices of the couch. He smiled, "I don't think Nikolai will mind."

Zakhar remained serious. "We can't be here too long. For all we know the haemans will come back. Or maybe they haven't even left yet. We didn't have any encounters on the road so maybe they're still here."

"They had at least a day or two to get back to the city before the storm came. I doubt they would have hung around." But the idea that he and his friends were waiting out this storm only to be greeted by an entirely different kind of natural disaster sent chills down his spine.

"When the snow stops, we will be careful," Sevrick continued, unsure of anything else he could say about the pending possibility that there were monsters waiting for them on the other side of this snowstorm.

Zakhar shrugged. "Let's just hope they went right back to St. Petersburg after the raid and we have nothing to worry about. We came here for supplies and more importantly, to see if we could figure out why they came here in the first place. We need the weather to calm down if we are going to succeed in either."

"Well, this place has a lot to offer in regard to supplies."

"Not enough. We have our monthly raid coming up, and I'd like to get as much of it as possible here. The less stuff we need, the less people we will need to send into St. Petersburg to gather supplies, and the less likelihood anyone gets hurt."

Sevrick nodded in agreement. The soup was ready and they set it out on the intricately carved mahogany dining table. Nikolai and Leonid reemerged from the couch and took their seats in the throne-like chairs.

The borscht tasted delicious and its warmth felt fantastic. It caressed their throats as they swallowed. No one talked as they ate; the comfortable silence felt right. They were close friends and words were not always necessary. Once they each finished, they sat back in their chairs and let it digest. Energy refueled them and Zakhar began discussing the plan of action they'd take from here.

"Tomorrow, assuming the snow has ceased, we will go into town and gather supplies first. I'd rather go home with supplies and no information on why the haemans raided versus the counter scenario." Nikolai nodded in agreement but Sevrick wanted to find out how to lure haemans back to the white elm.

"That's fine but ideally we can also figure out why they came back to Vyborg after having left it alone for so long. As far as we know they hadn't done a raid out here in at least five or six years. They came back for something and if we can figure out what, we can get them to come to us at the white elm and learn how to heal them properly."

"He's right," Leonid said, "the more haemans we can practice on, the better chances we'll have to figure it out and get it to work all the time. It may also help us figure out why it *hasn't* worked the last few times."

"We do need to save the human race," Nikolai said thoughtfully. Sevrick smiled but knew Nikolai spoke with all seriousness. "At the end of the day, that has to be our main focus."

Zakhar sighed, "I know all of this, guys, but I figure we can investigate *while* we gather supplies. At least then if we have to return with no knowledge, we're not returning without supplies too."

Everyone else nodded in agreement before Leonid continued, "This all sounds pretty straight forward. My body still seems to be shutting down on me. I'm going to go and find myself a bed to sleep in for the night."

"Me too," Nikolai was quick to jump on the opportunity to depart.

They all dispersed throughout the large apartment, looking for bedrooms to crash in. Sevrick was finally tired too. The food calmed his nerves and he was ready to sleep again. He hadn't slept in days. The previous night's bed on the cold hard ground had been highly unsatisfying. He was exhausted and hoped he was able to finally get a good night's rest.

As he recalled the past few days, he thought of Rina and his most recent unsuccessful visit. With all that was going on, it already felt like many weeks passed between then and now. Maybe it was because she was so distant from him, even when he was near. Her body held great space between him and the girl he once knew who was buried inside the monster somewhere. His heart silently ached.

Upon finding an empty bed, Sevrick laid his body down. The bed was soft and held a comfort he hadn't felt in quite some time. As he got comfortable, he turned his body and wrapped his arms around one of the large feathered pillows, holding it close. The gaping hole within his chest felt ever-present as the idea of Rina lying next to him filled his mind.

What if all he'd ever have was a memory of her beside him? What if this pillow was the closest thing he'd ever have to holding her again? The anxiety that began to fill his body was overwhelming. What if he wasn't able to dig the love she had for him out of the ruins of her addiction? Then he realized in this equation that involved two people, he was the only one working to solve it. The only one still fighting for it. Sevrick sat up with uncontrolled anger and ripped the pillow in half. Feathers scattered all over the room and the remains of the pillow were left in his hands. Suddenly, he felt guilty. Could he have saved her before it had gotten so bad? Should he have taken her away from the city at the first signs that she was giving in to it? Was this *his* fault? No. The blame was not his. For years he felt responsible, like he didn't do enough, and his inconsolable heartache blinded him from reality. It wasn't until he arrived at the white elm and joined the Clandes that he began to see things clearly. Her suffering was not his fault. He spent years trying to save her but she always chose the drugs over him.

The time away from her gave him the space he needed to function normally again. He did his best to cope, but his heart remained quietly broken beneath its unyielding beat.

He was not ready to give up on their love. He needed to separate her from the monster. If he could expose what was left inside, then maybe he'd have a chance at salvaging the parts of her that were still good. He didn't know how yet, but he realized that all this time he had been too passive and that wasn't going to fix anything. Once they left Vyborg, he needed a new strategy. Maybe the guys were right, maybe they had to force her out of St. Petersburg. Sevrick prayed that once they entered the village tomorrow, answers would be waiting.

Chapter 5

7 years earlier

Rina came home from her night class later than usual. The bags under her bright blue eyes were heavy and her wild auburn hair was pulled back into a messy ponytail. She threw her bag onto the kitchen table and then leaned onto the countertop, letting her head collapse into her hands. She was still wearing the daggered bracelet she bought for herself at the new jewelry shop that moved in down the street.

Four sharp pieces of green glass held the bracelet in place on her wrist and the rose gold chains crisscrossed between glass spokes. It was designed for a beginner, someone who was not quite ready to take the leap into haemanism. When Rina took the bracelet off, there would be fresh blood for her to lick off her skin. But for now, Rina slumped with her head down, the weight of life pressing upon her back.

"My love," Sevrick called from the bedroom. He walked into the kitchen to see his fiancée slumped over the counter top. They were engaged for a year but everything was quickly changing for the worse. "What's wrong, Rina?" He hurried to her side and had to take a deep breath to control his anger when he noticed she was still wearing the bracelet. They fought about this many times and she promised to stop.

Tears filled her eyes. "My day was long and horrible and all I want to do right now is take this bracelet off and have some blood." Her breathing was heavy.

"Let me buy you a new bracelet, one that doesn't hurt you."

"It doesn't hurt," she mumbled.

"You are crying because you know it's wrong. You know this will change you."

"But I need it, Sevy. You don't understand how good it feels."

"I don't care how *good* it feels. It's wrong and you know it. If it wasn't so glamorized in the media you would think it was disgusting, too."

"It's natural. It comes from our bodies."

"There is something they aren't telling everybody. There is no way drinking your own blood makes you superhuman," he said.

"You think they've contaminated our blood?" She gave a half smile. "There is no way the government or the royals could pull that off. They'd need to give us shots every day. It has to be a natural phenomenon since it works for every person who tries it."

"I still don't believe it. There is something shady going on and it all started when those pieces of garbage claimed the long abandoned throne."

"You shouldn't talk about the royals like that," she warned. Rina idolized Milena, which made him hate them even more.

"Look what they've done to you and everybody else. They are turning this country into a hellhole."

"I know you don't like the haemanism, or agree with it, but all I can think about is my blood. Now that I know its power, I am consumed by it."

"We need to leave St. Petersburg. Your damn classmates got you into this and now it's time to leave before it gets worse."

"No," Rina exclaimed defiantly, "this is my life!"

Sevrick's heart ached. "This is *our* life. We are engaged, Rina," his voice shook, "I plan to marry you and stay with you for better or worse. And I will do everything in my power to stop this before it devours you."

Rina began to sob, "Can't you just join me?"

"We won't love each other the same if we change. You see how people who are full-on haeman behave. We will hurt each other and cheat on each other and probably wind up killing each other."

"You don't know that. It makes your emotions more intense but it doesn't mean you forget everything you once felt."

"This addiction erases human morals. People become numb and callous, caring only for themselves and killing anyone who gets in their way."

"That isn't true. This discovery is a gift from God. It would never cause people to do that," she said, trying to sound confident even though her voice indicated she was conflicted. She knew he wasn't completely wrong.

"Stop listening to what the media is telling you. You see it happening in the streets. You see the haemans ruthlessly hurting one another. You see them beating on people who aren't using. The media chooses not to report those things so people aren't deterred from haemanism. Open your eyes and make your own opinion. Stop relying on the media and royals to craft your stance on the matter!" He could see she wasn't really listening to him anymore. "This is the royal family's fault. Stop idolizing Princess Milena, she is a disgrace."

"No. It is a gift from God. It *is* natural. They have shown the scientific reports. I've seen them."

"It's a *lie*. One day we are going to find out the truth and when that day comes, it will already be too late. They will be too far gone to save. I can't let you be one of them. There is nothing healthy about drinking your own blood. Not to mention, you barely eat anymore."

"I take the calorie pills."

"–that are issued by the government. I can't even begin to imagine what those pills *really* are."

She slammed her fists against their marble counter top. Her hands were clenched, knuckles white. Her eyes were still wet but the tears had stopped. She disembarked from the conversation without another word. He was losing her to a force bigger than both of them. He was losing her to this new culture the city was adopting. He was losing her to a fad. But worst of all, he was losing her to an addiction that would remain long after the fad passed.

"Why are you doing this to us?" He lost his composure and chased her down. He grabbed her, turned her to face him, and shook her lightly in his grasp as he pleaded with her. "Can't you see it will destroy everything?"

She broke free and slapped him hard across the face. Immediately her hands covered her mouth, horrified with what she had done.

Sevrick touched the side of his face where she hit him; he could feel the deep bruise forming. The blood addiction was already making her stronger; she was already losing control.

Rina took a few steps, backing away from him. Silent and appalled with herself.

"You've only used once. Just don't use tonight and you'll feel better tomorrow. By morning the cravings will have stopped."

She paused before entering the hallway leading to their room. She turned to look at him, her face lined with guilt.

"I lied to you," tears filled her eyes again, "I've been using for two weeks now. I'm sorry."

Sevrick's face went slack. The beating beneath his chest quickened as the feeling of betrayal coursed through his veins. But he could still save her. He ran to her side and held her by her shoulders.

"Run away with me. We can leave this city and start over. What we have is too good to ruin with the sickening things that are happening here. You are the love of my life. I can't let you succumb to this." Rina shook her head.

"This is where our life is. Our school, our jobs, our friends. What would we have if we left?"

"We'd have each other," he said with sincerity.

"That's not enough anymore." Tears rolled down her face as she backed away and disappeared into the shadows of the hallway.

Chapter 6

The snow lasted another day before they were able to leave the fancy complex and wander through Vyborg. The extra day of relaxation was just what they needed to lift their spirits and get their energy back.

The ground was covered with two feet of snow. Walking through it was not easy but they did their best to cover as much ground as possible. Zakhar was hell-bent on finding supplies and Sevrick wanted to learn why the haemans raided here.

Almost every street had at least one torn apart body on it. To their dismay, non-haeman people came back to Vyborg thinking it was safe to live here again. The haemans were not discreet with these murders. Limbs were strewn in all different directions and necks were snapped so hard the skin ripped. On some streets, bodies hung from lampposts and street signs with small lacerations, the kind that would cause a person to bleed out slowly. It was a cruel way to kill a person. The more they saw, the more it appeared these murders had been for sport. The amount of bodies they continued to find at each corner they turned was alarming.

Nikolai moved his scarf up around his face to cover his nose and mouth. "I'm beginning to think they came back here *just* to kill these people."

Leonid looked worried. "I don't know. They definitely have it out for us, anyone who isn't haeman, but to leave the city *just* to kill people in hiding doesn't seem right. They wouldn't care enough."

"The real question is why were there so many humans here to begin with? This village used to be deserted," Sevrick said.

"We've seen at least eighty bodies. And who knows how many escaped. There was a large civilization of survivors here. Maybe the haemans got word of it and didn't want it spreading?"

"No," Leonid said, "There has to be something more to it. These people must have had something they wanted."

Sevrick began examining the bodies more closely, looking for some kind of clue. An old man covered in his own blood sat propped against a stone wall, his eye sockets empty. A woman hung by her neck from a coarse rope strung out of a window. A young man lay sprawled out in the middle of the street, his hands tied and his bare chest revealing the word CONDEMNED sliced into his skin. His worn out jacket lay next to his lifeless body. Sevrick picked it up and noticed the letters H.E.S. stitched to the chest pocket in yellow fabric.

Then Sevrick looked back at the old man propped up against the side of a building; he had the same letters stitched to his overcoat. Then he looked to the woman hanging above them from the window and the letters H.E.S. were sewn onto her dress jacket as well.

The other three men were ahead of Sevrick but he called out to them.

"Guys, come take a look at this."

Once they made their way back to Sevrick, he showed them the letters they all wore.

"H.E.S." Zakhar squinted as he read it aloud, "I don't have any idea what that stands for."

"Well, it appears they were some kind of group. Could be as simple as us referring to ourselves as the Clandes," Nikolai suggested.

"But the haemans came here after them. It must be more than a nickname. Plus, look how many of them there were," Zakhar said. A sinking feeling entered the pit of his stomach.

"We need to find out who they were. We need to find survivors."

All four men nodded in agreement and continued walking forward. They stopped inside more buildings as they went, looking and listening for any signs of human life. Every place they went into was abandoned; no noise was heard except the echoes of their own footsteps.

"Don't forget to keep an eye out for supplies as well," Zakhar reminded everyone casually as they entered another building holding no survivors of the attack. Though his relentless reminders had been annoying, this time, Sevrick was grateful for it; the sight of all the dead bodies in the streets and the fact that it seemed like no one survived had distracted him from the other part of their mission.

The next place they stopped turned out to be a gold mine for supplies. It was a wildlife shop, carrying various weaponry and gear. There was no ammunition for rifles to be found—that supply was likely cleaned out ages ago. All that remained were cases filled with hundreds of tranquilizer darts of every type: sedative, anesthetic, and paralytic. Leonid smashed the glass on the front of the display and began filling his bag. This was a huge score for the Clandes; the more tranquilizer darts they had, the more haemans they could capture for rehab.

Zakhar was throwing heavy fleece blankets into the duffel bag he brought while Nikolai collected some air-sealed packages of beef jerky. There was nothing here for Sevrick and he wanted to keep moving. He had to find survivors in order to find out what H.E.S. stood for.

"I'll be next door," he announced to his friends while slipping out of the building before any of them could object. Wandering alone could be trouble but so far, this town only housed dead bodies and red snow.

Next door to the gun shop was an apartment. As he got closer to the door he saw it was already ajar. As he swung it open and the air from inside hit him, a foul smell assaulted his senses. A few steps into the building and he could see the odor's source: a man and woman lay dead next to each other on the living room floor. The smell of their rotting bodies had been trapped inside the walls of this apartment for quite a few days. While the smell of the decomposing flesh of those who died outside had been carried off by the winter winds, the bodies left indoors only intensified in their decay. The four walls that surrounded them prevented nature from carrying away the rot.

Sevrick immediately wanted to leave. The sight of dead lovers stirred up memories of his own tragic love story, but he heard a sound from somewhere distant in the house that he couldn't ignore. It sounded like crying.

The apartment was huge; another wealthy family once owned this place. Sunrays shone through the large front windows and lit the oversized rooms. He circled the entire downstairs but the noise had not sounded any closer. He got to the large wooden staircase leading upstairs and began to ascend. Halfway up he heard the noise again. It was coming from beneath him.

Sevrick moved down a few steps to check if there was an opening below the stairs. As soon as he began banging on the steps to find the opening, the noise disappeared. He continued searching for the source, slamming his fists and pulling at the steps relentlessly. The wooden plank on the seventh step came off in his hands, taking the next step along with it. There was now a two foot wide opening leading to darkness below the staircase. He turned on his flashlight and let it shine into the opening.

In his light were two little bodies: a girl and a boy. The boy was cuddled into the arms of the girl and the girl was looking up with wide eyes.

"I'm not going to hurt you," Sevrick called down to them.

"Shhh," the girl whispered back. "They haven't left yet. You need to hide."

"What do you mean they haven't left?" Sevrick said, lowering his voice. "The haemans?" She nodded.

Alarm filled Sevrick's entire body. "Stay put. I am going to come back for you but I need to go warn my friends."

"You need to hide," the girl demanded.

He nodded but ignored the young girl's plea. He shut the trap door, leaving the staircase looking untouched and bolted out into the street.

There was still no sign of any haemans, but Sevrick knew they could be watching him from above. Stalking him like prey along the rooftops of this small town with crowded buildings.

Upon reaching the door of the gun shop, he saw three heads, one of whom he did not recognize. Zakhar and Nikolai had their hands raised in surrender as the third person slunk toward them. It was a haeman. The sickly looking man was tall, taller than any of the Clandes, but skinny. So skinny his bones could be seen through his gray dress shirt as he approached his friends menacingly. His dull blonde hair was slicked back against his scalp and his outfit looked expensive.

Sevrick pulled out his gun and aimed it at the haeman's head. Seeing Nikolai's eyes shift, the haeman whipped around and growled, showing off surgically sharpened teeth. He took two long leaps toward Sevrick, covering more than half the distance between them before Sevrick fired. He aimed for the head but missed, managing to only graze the side of the haeman's scalp. As the barely human creature began to recover, Zakhar shouted out, "Sevrick, behind you!"

Sevrick turned his head in time to see a second haeman hurtling toward him. This one was a female with fresh cuts down her arms and a face covered in blood; she had just fed. A loud roar erupted from the depths of her gut when a dart thudded into her neck. She took one more step toward Sevrick before falling to the ground, sedated.

Leonid stood up from behind a trash can with his tranquilizer gun. He immediately went to the woman haeman and began binding her extremities together with ropes and duct tape. Sevrick turned back around to see the male unfazed by the small gunshot wound. The haeman stuck his finger in the bloody injury and then licked it clean. A smile crept upon his face and his chest began to rise and fall slowly with excitement.

"Thanks," he hissed. The extra blood in his system only made him stronger. This haeman was ready to kill all of them and would take pleasure in doing so.

Sevrick aimed his gun at the haeman's forehead, firing once but missing because the haeman was too fast now. Zakhar and Nikolai managed to recover their rifles as Sevrick took one more shot, hitting the haeman in the stomach. Zak and Nik opened fire. Sevrick stepped outside, shutting the solid front door behind him to escape the gunfire. Their semi-automatic rifles would hit everything in the room and Sevrick didn't need to be one of those things.

Zakhar and Nikolai showered the room with bullets as the haeman darted in every direction, climbing the walls, jumping and sliding at such speeds that it was hard to keep track of him. A few bullets hit and splattered blood on the floor. He continued to move around the room like a fly trapped in a jar but could not get close enough to Nikolai or Zakhar to kill them because of the constant gunfire. After two minutes and multiple hits, his reflexes slowed. They took this opportunity to reload. Sevrick heard the ceasefire and tentatively stepped back inside.

The numerous wounds and immense loss of blood made the haeman weak. Sevrick grabbed the dying monster by the neck and slammed his body to the floor, pinning his hands beneath his legs to ensure he did not try to lick up any of his blood that was pooled in large quantities all over the room. Zakhar walked up and placed his boot upon its forehead.

"What did you and the other haemans come to this village for?"

The haeman laughed, sticking its tongue out, trying to reach the floor where his blood lay waiting for him. But every second that passed that the haeman could not refuel himself with his own blood, the closer to death he became.

"Talk now," Sevrick demanded, punching him hard in the eye. The haeman hissed back at him, his sharp teeth bared in anger.

The multiple gunshot wounds he received were bleeding out. The haeman's eyes darted around, looking for any opportunity to get some of his blood back into his system. If he was going to die, he wanted to be able to take these condemned men with him.

Sevrick tried another approach.

"If you tell me why you came here, I'll let you drink some of your blood. Let you regain some strength."

The haeman laughed manically again and Sevrick tightened the grasp he had around its neck. Leonid finished binding up the female haeman and joined the interrogation.

"Why did you come here? What were you looking for?" Sevrick demanded one last time.

Through his last breath the haeman hissed, "Your leader."

"Who?" the four Clandes men said in unison, confused what the haeman meant.

The haeman mouthed a name but it wasn't audible.

"Say it again!" Sevrick shouted, but it was too late. The haeman let out a final, blood-filled gurgle and died beneath Sevrick's grip.

Chapter 7

The female haeman was still tranquilized at the bottom of the stoop outside the gun store. She wore a beaded chain headpiece that hung down her forehead; the back weaved through her light brunette braids. Her outfit was sleek and gray, very professional looking like the male's had been, and she wore devious jewelry meant to draw blood throughout the day. The pearl necklace she wore was stuck to the skin of her neck as each pearl had a small spike on the backside of it.

Sevrick shook his head as he looked the female over. He checked the binds Leonid tied and determined they were secure enough that she wouldn't escape.

"I really didn't think they'd still be here in the village," Nikolai said, shocked at the violent scene they just survived.

"What did he mean when he said they were here for our leader?" Zakhar added. "What leader? What does that even mean?"

"He mouthed a name," Nikolai added.

"Do they think all the survivors live together somewhere?" Sevrick directed his question to Leonid.

"Not when I was still living in the city as a haeman. We pretty much never thought about the people who shunned haemanism and went into hiding. We assumed you'd all die in a few years while trying to survive in the wild. Haemans have always loved killing survivors when they happened to come across them but they never went out *looking* for them. It just wasn't a priority. I don't know why that changed. The survivors pose no threat to the haemans."

Sevrick knew where they would get their answer.

"I almost forgot why I came out to find you guys in the first place. Right before I saw you with the haemans I found two kids hiding out under the stairs of the apartment next door. They were here with their parents, who were both killed. The girl is old enough to possibly give us some answers."

"Let's give it a try. We just need to be careful. Who knows how many more haemans may be hiding out in this little town," Leonid warned.

Sevrick brought his comrades into the apartment next door. They were extra quiet while walking through the streets for fear there could be other haemans lurking about. But none appeared.

Upon reaching the stairs, he removed the top of the secret passage where the children hid. With a small amount of sunlight piercing the gloom of the secret passageway, Sevrick could see the whites of the children's eyes staring up at him with fear.

"We aren't going to hurt you. We want to help you," he called down to them.

"Be quiet," the young girl pleaded. "They will kill us all."

"Come with us and we will protect you," Sevrick said in a softer voice, hoping to ease the girl's nerves. "You can't hide down there forever."

She took a deep breath and nudged her younger brother to let go of her and stand up. The two children climbed a rickety ladder attached to the wall. Upon reaching the open passageway, Sevrick helped them out.

The girl's fire-red hair immediately reminded him of Rina. She looked at them with uncertainty as he pulled her younger brother out of the darkness.

"Everyone we know is dead," she said outright. No tears in her eyes, just a deep pain in her voice.

"Well, now you will get to know us," Nikolai offered from the bottom of the steps. "We will take care of you like family."

The little girl's nostrils flared as she held back tears. Her soft, porcelain skin radiated in the sunlight and presented a severe contrast from the ratty clothes she was wearing. Her little brother immediately ran to her after Sevrick put him down. He clung to her waist; his hair was brown and matted but his eyes were the same intense green as his sister's.

"What's your name?" Sevrick asked. He could tell the girl had been through a lot of trauma and they would need to earn her trust.

"Kira."

"And your brother?"

"His name is Maks," she answered again, looking down the stairs at the other three men with skepticism.

"How old are you guys? We have a few young people at our home base who might be around your age."

Kira hesitated and Sevrick could tell she didn't like the idea of running off with strangers just yet. But she answered him anyway.

"I am 11 and Maks is 7."

"Isaak is 14, you'd like him a lot. And Maks here would get along great with Agnessa who is 6. Would you both be interested in coming along with us?" Sevrick said as sweetly as possible.

"I suppose we don't have much choice," she responded curtly. Catching her own attitude, she continued, "It's not that you seem bad or anything, but this had been our home with our parents for almost a year now and it will be very hard to leave." She fought back tears, "We don't want to have to go on without our mum and pop."

Maks began to cry. Kira pulled him in closer while maintaining her composure.

"I know it is hard, Kira," Sevrick said with empathy. "Perhaps we can all share our own stories with you guys on the trip back. We've all lost people we loved, too. Life isn't easy for any survivor, but you are strong. I can already see that. And I truly think coming with us will be the best option for both of you."

Kira nodded. She already knew this. She knew she could never protect her brother from all the terrors in this world by herself. Leonid cut in.

"Kira," he took a few steps up the stairs so he could talk with her more directly. She looked at him skeptically and Sevrick could tell she initially thought he was a haeman. Leonid did not catch her hesitation toward his appearance and spoke to her with kindness, easing her nerves a bit, "As we were walking here, we noticed the people in the streets had the letters H.E.S. stitched onto their clothing. Do you know what it stands for?"

"Yeah. We are the HESies: the Haeman Extermination Squad." Then a solemn thought came to her. "At least we were."

Sevrick's eyes widened. "What?"

"Well," Kira continued, "I guess we weren't as ready as we thought, but our purpose was to get rid of them once and for all. Lots of people joined us since a year ago and more people kept coming to take part. Word was spreading about our mission and other survivors wanted to help. But the haemans got here before we had enough people, or training, I guess. I don't know how many people survived but my guess is they got most of us."

Maks spoke for the first time, "There were more people coming but they got lucky."

"What do you mean?" Leonid asked.

Kira answered, "There was a group coming from the north to join us in our fight; probably a hundred or so. Our recruiter Demetri went out to find other people hiding in the woods and this new group was going to add real strength to us. They just never made it in time," Kira thought for a moment then added, "Although they'd probably be dead too if they had. That's why Maks said they were lucky."

"Do you think they are still on their way?" Sevrick asked.

"Probably. There's no way they'd have known the haemans came for us."

"Who was the leader of the HESies?" Leonid asked cautiously.

This time Kira couldn't hold back the tears. A single teardrop rolled down her cheek as she answered, "My father."

Leonid nodded but said no more. All four men wondered if the haeman mouthed her father's name in his dying breath but it was pointless to inquire now. They had not heard the name and her father was dead. It appeared to them the haemans accomplished their mission this time.

Sevrick walked down the stairs and indicated for the children to follow. Once the four men and two children were back on ground level, Sevrick immediately remembered the bodies of their parents lying in the next room.

"Close those doors," Sevrick hissed to Zakhar, who looked behind him, saw the bodies, and immediately slid the French doors to the living room shut.

"Our parents?" Kira asked quietly. It was already clear she was much more astute than other kids her age.

Sevrick nodded and Kira took a deep breath. Then, surprising all four men, she made a strange request in times like these.

"Before we leave this place, can we bury them? I don't think I can move on without doing that for them. I know we need to get out of here soon in case any haemans are still lurking about, but my parents deserve respect in death."

"Of course," Zakhar spoke for the first time. He wasn't very good with kids, but believed strongly in traditions of honor and respect. The other three men nodded in agreement.

"Perhaps it's not a bad idea to wait," Nikolai said. "The other group may get here soon and we can let them know what happened. Maybe we can recruit them to build up our own numbers. The Clandes are not a large enough group to defend ourselves if the haemans ever located us."

"Yeah, I can't believe we never thought of that before," Leonid added. "We could get the Scots and the Lads to join in, too. We can all live in our own spots but train together and build up a force."

Sevrick's heart dropped; he didn't want to exterminate the haemans. Rina was still one of them. He only wanted to heal them.

He wondered if he was alone in that sentiment. "What about rehabilitating them?" he interjected.

"Well, I think that would still be the main focus," Leonid answered. "But at some point, we may need to cut our losses and start from scratch. If we can't save them then we need to save ourselves."

"You used to be one of them. How could you say that?"

"Come on, Sev," Nikolai jumped in. "You're only biased because of Rina. If she was healed by now you'd be all for destroying the rest of them."

Anger coursed through Sevrick's veins because Nikolai was right.

"Don't worry," Zakhar continued before Sevrick could say anything else, "We aren't giving up on Rina yet. Or any other haemans we can save. We need a good number of people who are healthy to start over if that's what it comes down to."

Sevrick was breathing heavy, taking all that his friends said seriously. This was too important to him. Rescuing Rina was all that fueled him and he wouldn't let anything get in the way of that.

"We ought to help these kids pay their last respects to their parents," Sevrick said, changing the topic. "You two wait in the other room while we wrap their bodies up. We will find a safe spot in the woods to lay them to rest."

Kira and Maks nodded and went to wait in the kitchen. Leonid looked at Sevrick nervously, knowing he upset him with his previous comment. But the topic was dropped for now. There would be plenty of time to argue about it on the walk home and even more possibilities for debate once the rest of the Clandes were filled in on what the men discovered in Vyborg.

The burial of Kira and Maks's parents turned out to be an invigorating moment for all six of them. Despite the manner of their death, it was refreshing to honor the life of someone who fought back.

The men wrapped both of the parents in satin and chiffon sheets and dug the 6X6 hole prior to the children walking out to the burial site. Digging through the frozen ground was trying but they made it work. The kids only had to see their parents' dead bodies wrapped in sheets for a few moments before they ceremoniously covered them in dirt, one shovelful at a time.

Kira kneeled before the hole her parents were in and began to sing. Her tiny voice sang a song about survival. A song Sevrick could tell the HESies must have sung together often. It was a song about strength and endurance, but this time it was meant only for her parents. After she finished the first verse, Maks kneeled beside his sister and sang the chorus of the song along with her. Their small voices were loud as they sang in perfect harmony:

Take our city, take our lives
But you will never take our pride.
We will not run and we will not hide.
We shall endure these evil times.

They repeated the chorus three times before Zakhar and Sevrick finished filling the grave. Kira and Maks held each other close for a few moments in silence. Eventually, Kira placed her right hand upon the dirt covering her parents' bodies and shut her eyes. Tears rolled down her cheeks as she sat silently. Sevrick wondered if leaving goodbye unsaid would keep them with her a little bit longer.

Kira then stood up and grabbed Maks's hand to help him stand too. She looked at Sevrick and nodded to indicate she was finished, and without another word, the four men escorted the children back out of the woods and away from the burial site.

They walked through a small open field, then through an alleyway. Upon reaching the street they exited from earlier, noise erupted from the village. Zakhar quickly put out an arm to stop the others from walking into the unknown. Paused, they crouched down in the shadows to determine the source.

It didn't take long before they realized the noise came from normal humans. They deduced these fellow survivors were the ones who came here to meet up with the HESies. There were more than a hundred of them. The Clandes prayed they killed off the last of the haemans that remained in Vyborg.

"If we can get up to that balcony across the street, we can address them all," Sevrick said, indicating an apartment overlooking the group.

The group of six made their way through the crowd and broke into the apartment building. They went up the stairs and onto the small balcony facing the people. Their appearance caught the attention of the crowd and as Sevrick began to speak, the people below hushed in order to hear him.

"I know you all are looking for the HESies. I am burdened with the task of telling you they were slaughtered only a few nights ago." A low murmur of discussion resonated through the crowd; they saw the dead bodies strewn throughout the village and assumed the worst already. Sevrick continued, "The good news I can give you is the cause is not lost. I am Sevrick. My friends here are Zakhar, Nikolai, and Leonid. We are from another group called the Clandes. We came to Vyborg after the raid and found exactly what you see now: a slaughter of our people, the other survivors. The HESies were fighters and defenders of the human race. We did not know the HESies but we would have certainly joined forces with them if we had known of their mission in time. In our home, we have been attempting our own process of saving the Russian population. We have been practicing the art of rehabilitation on haemans. When we are able to capture them, we make attempts to restore them back to their normal selves."

Another low murmur of shock ran amongst the crowd, this time a large man with a thick beard in the middle spoke up.

"That's not possible, they'd murder you before you even got the chance to heal them."

"The trees we are surrounded by offer great hiding places and we knock them out with tranquilizer darts before they can attack."

"Does the rehabilitation work?" a woman cried out. The desperation in her voice indicated that she had someone she wanted to save.

Sevrick motioned to Leonid.

"Leonid here used to be haeman. His girlfriend found us and we offered to try and help heal him. As you can see, he is no longer haeman."

Leonid was still pale, much more pale than Sevrick and Zakhar on either side of him. And although he was healed and had been for quite some time, he still maintained the gaunt look he had as a haeman. The sunlight shone upon Leonid's skin and the scars all over his neck were visible to those in the front of the crowd.

A collective gasp came from the individuals below.

"It can work. It doesn't always work, but we are experimenting and doing our best to save as many people as possible. The HESies may have been slaughtered but they still managed to bring us all together. If we join forces we can unite and be stronger than ever."

"How would we help though? We came down here to fight, not to be doctors," the same man with the grisly beard shouted.

"Well, maybe we can teach you how we do it. Or if you relocate your group closer to ours, we can keep training to fight together in case the day comes that we need to defend ourselves. If all the survivors are located hundreds of kilometers apart, there is no way for us to help one another."

"We already know of two other large groups hiding out near ours. I'm sure we could convince them to join us," Zakhar spoke. "Until we heard what the HESies had been organizing, we never thought to have all the survivors band together and form one strong united force. They were definitely onto something. If we combine that with our idea to heal a large number of the haemans, we may be able to outlast the haemans in the city and then rebuild the Russian race. They are strong but they are unhealthy. They won't survive as haemans forever."

The whispering in the crowd below sounded to be approval but no one spoke up right away. After a few moments of discussion amongst one another, the bearded man spoke once more. A proud smirk crossed his face as he shouted.

"We are with you!"

And the crowd erupted into cheers.

Chapter 8

The phone rang: it was her mother. Rina was alone in the living room. Sevrick was at his night class and his mom was sleeping in her bedroom. Rina moved in with them after her parents left for the United States to follow her brother, Adrik, while he attended college there. They now lived in New York City and Adrik attended Columbia University. She was *supposed* to be living in her old family home, but that house no longer felt like home. Her parents found strangers to rent out the top half of the house and left her with only the basement. Rina found it uncomfortable to live in a place she once called home with people she didn't know, so she left. Sevrick and his mother happily took her in.

Her parents' plan was for her to move to the United States after she graduated high school. They wanted her to attend college there too, but Rina had no interest. She was angry with them; betrayed that they left her in Russia all by herself. She was grateful every day that she had Sevrick's love to help her through this, but it didn't erase the hardship of her parents' abandonment.

Her cell phone continued to ring. Rina sighed and finally answered it.

"Hello mamochka."

"What took you so long to answer? You've ignored my calls the last three times I tried to reach you. You never call back."

"That's because I know why you're calling and I don't feel like arguing with you anymore."

"You graduate in two months. Have you gotten any letters back from the colleges you applied to in New York City?"

"No."

"They should have come by now."

"I haven't gotten any letters back from those schools because I never applied," she admitted. There was silence on the other end of the line. Rina took a deep breath. "I lied about it a few months ago so you'd stop hassling me. I don't want to move to New York. I got accepted to St. Petersburg State University. That's where I will be attending school next September."

"I forbid it," her mother protested. "The plan was for you to come here after you graduated high school. Russia is no good for you, or anyone. America will provide you with opportunities you cannot get anywhere else."

"There is nothing that country can offer me that I don't already have here."

"That is not true."

"I have a life *here*, in Russia. The love of my life is here with me and I will not leave him to follow a family who left me all alone to fend for myself."

"Have him come with you."

"How could you even suggest that? You know he cannot leave his mother. I won't leave her either. They are my family now and I won't abandon them like you abandoned me."

"You are being too sensitive."

"Do you realize how much it hurt me that you and dad couldn't wait one year before you left? Do you know how hard it has been on me to work and attend high school? You didn't even leave me with enough money to pay for food."

"You know how badly we struggle financially, and America is very expensive. We can only wire money to you when there's enough left over after our monthly bills are paid."

"You even had the rent those strangers were paying to live in the house go toward your expenses in America. I saw none of that money."

"We needed it here," her mom tried to explain.

"Okay, but I needed it more. The first month after you left, I was lucky if I ate one meal a day." Rina was getting worked up; she was shaking. "And how about the fact that you left your young daughter to live with complete strangers? What if they were pedophiles or serial killers? Did you even run background checks on these people before you let them move in with me?"

"Don't be dramatic, Arinadya," her mother tried to shush her accusations but Rina could not bear the unjustness of the situation.

"I am not being dramatic, I am being realistic. You were only thinking of yourself when you made the move. And until you can admit that to yourself and apologize for being awful to me, then we will probably never be able to move forward from this."

Her mother sighed, tired of an argument they'd had many times before.

"I am sorry it was hard on you, but if you listened to me and got accepted into a college here, it would have been worth it in the end. They have great student loan programs for foreigners and you would have graduated with a degree that would set you up with a job that would ease our financial woes forever."

"Any money I make isn't going anywhere near you or dad. Not after this, not after you left me alone for a year instead of waiting. I understand you *thought* you were doing this for us, and that you think we have a better shot there, but you don't abandon your youngest child in an attempt to get out sooner. I can't describe how betrayed I feel."

"We've been over this already. Your father and I are both sorry it happened this way, but you need to stop being stubborn and see the future we have arranged for you. We have established residency here. You will be set up for success once you arrive."

"I am never going to live with you there. Despite the hardship you placed on me by leaving, I am happy here. I have a man who loves me and I will earn my college degree here. I will get a job here and I will make my life here. Sevrick and I already have it planned out. I will graduate high school in a few months and with the money we saved, student loans, and the money we continue to make, I will pay my own way through college. I don't need you anymore. I have Sevrick."

"You cannot trust this boy. He may love you now but what about in a year from now? How about five years from now? Young boys are fickle; their emotions and desires change with the weather. When he leaves you one day you will call me crying, begging me to let you live with us in New York."

"That will never happen."

Her mother laughed. "You are young and naïve. You don't understand the devastation of a broken heart. When it happens, you will wise up."

"Don't tell me how things will go with Sevrick and I. You don't know what we have gone through together and you don't know anything about the love we share. This isn't just young love; this is the real thing. If you cared enough to stay with me here, you would have seen it for yourself. But you didn't stay, you didn't wait for me, and now you don't get to be a part of this chapter in my life."

"You are foolish. I cannot believe I raised such a stupid girl."

"I love Sevrick more than I ever thought I could love another person," Rina's eyes filled with tears. "More than I love myself sometimes. He means the world to me and I will never abandon him the way you abandoned me. I have a good thing here and if you loved me at all you would support me."

"Of course I love you, don't be irrational. I just cannot stand to see you making life choices that are setting you up for failure."

"I don't believe I will find any failure by choosing to follow my heart. I don't care if you disagree."

"I guess it doesn't really make a difference what I say. You didn't even apply to the schools here. It's too late for you now so I hope you don't wake up one day and regret this idealistic choice to remain in an oppressive country for love."

"I won't. I can promise you that." Rina was confident; she was positive this decision was the only option for her. She was certain of her feelings for Sevrick; she had never felt an emotion stronger than what she felt for him and she knew he loved her just the same.

"Goodbye then. Call me once in a while to let me know you're alive," her mother conceded.

"I will." And then her mother hung up. Rina sat on the couch with her phone in her hand. She didn't care what her mother thought. She knew she was meant to be with Sevrick. Her heart pounded as she thought of him.

She went back into the kitchen where she had been preparing dinner. She didn't usually have time to cook between school and work, but she had the night off and wanted to do something special. The beef stroganov smelt delicious and the aroma filled the entire house. She kept it covered on the stove to cool while she finished the final touches on the knishes. She spread shredded cheese over top of them and placed them in the oven.

Rina heard the front door open and close. She left the kitchen and wrapped her arms around Sevrick's neck. He buried his tired face into her hair. After giving him a dozen kisses on the side of his neck, she spoke.

"I missed you." She gave him a final kiss on the lips and looked up to see him smiling at her.

"I missed you too. I learned a lot in class today and they gave us a list of criminal justice internships in the area that can lead to great jobs. Hopefully I can get one of those for next semester."

"I hope so too." She smiled back at him and grabbed his hand, leading him to the small kitchen table. "I have a surprise for you."

"Does it have something to do with how delicious the house smells?"

"Yes," Rina laughed, happy he thought it smelt good. She didn't get to cook much so every time she made food it was a learning experience.

The knishes were done and Rina prepared a plate for him. She placed it on the table and Sevrick dug in. Rina covered his mother's plate, placed it in the microwave, and then sat next to him at the table.

"I think this is the best meal you've ever made."

"Thank you, I'm glad it came out well."

"I am so lucky to have you."

"It goes both ways," Rina smiled back. "I have never been happier than I am when I'm with you."

He planted a kiss on her forehead.

"Thank you for making me this wonderful dinner."

Rina took a deep breath of relief, everything felt perfect in this moment.

"I love you."

He smiled. "I love you."

They finished their meal in blissful silence.

The phone rang. Its ringtone was loud and jarring. Arinadya rolled over on the couch, trying to remain asleep but the noise continued. It was impossible to continue her nap with the earsplitting chimes. Was it her mother again? Arinadya tried to open her eyes. No, her mother hadn't called her in years. She hadn't called in years? But she just talked to her a few hours ago.

Arinadya sat up and rubbed her eyes. They fought about college and she told her she was dumb for choosing a boy over New York City. Sevrick? Arinadya's heart began to race. She was dreaming in memories again. Her subconscious was messing with her; this hadn't happened in years.

She slammed her fist against the coffee table, cracking the glass surface. The phone stopped ringing: missed call from Boris. She laced her fingers into her hair and tugged it tightly as she slumped over and shook her head, trying to shake the ancient memory away. Recollection of that memory felt so good in her dream but it wasn't her reality anymore. She no longer lived a life filled with love. She chose haemanism over Sevrick years ago, ruining any chance of a future where she truly loved another person. She could not let these happy memories infiltrate her life now; it was dangerous to think fondly upon reminiscences that were impossible to recreate.

The phone rang again: Boris.

She answered it, irritated. "What do you want?"

"I've called you four times in the past two hours, why aren't you answering your phone?"

She realized she must have heard it ring while she was napping; it must have triggered the memory.

"I was trying to take a nap," she answered, annoyed that he was calling her after working hours. "What is so goddamned important that you are calling me at 7 p.m.?"

"I just got an email from Prince Mikhail's PR team. They are moving the campaign's deadline to tomorrow at 2 p.m. I thought you'd want to know, considering the team hasn't produced any useable material yet."

"Jesus Christ. Alright." She tried to refocus on the issue at hand, burying the unsettling memory for a moment. "When you get into the office tomorrow, get the team together. I want functional ideas presented to me when I come in at 10 a.m."

"Okay, got it."

"You're in charge of this. Don't let me down."

"I won't, boss." Then they both hung up their phones.

Arinadya tossed her cell phone on the floor and threw her body back against the couch. Stupid Sevrick, still haunting her after all this time. Every time she believed she finally erased him for good, he showed up in her apartment, reversing all the work she had done to bury his memory. It was infuriating.

Arinadya could not handle this extra stress, not with the most critical deadline her company has ever had coming up tomorrow. She had to be focused. The royals were a new client, her biggest client, and she could not fail on the first assignment they gave her.

She walked to her kitchen and grabbed a steak knife from the drawer. Her subconscious put the aroma of beef stroganov back into her nostrils. As the memory tried to come alive inside her mind again, Arinadya screamed and stabbed the knife into her wooden cabinet. She could not take this anymore; she had to erase Sevrick's presence from her mind.

She took the weekly allowance of silve given to her by the council and laid out four silver lines of the powder. This was more than she normally would take in one sitting, but she had to get through this night and she couldn't do that without a higher dose. She would still have enough to last her through the weekend if she rationed it out carefully the next few days. She snorted all four lines and then waited ten minutes before pulling the steak knife out of her cabinet and making a deep incision in the back of her wrist. She drank the silve-laced blood as it poured freely from her skin. She lost track of time as the high took over and erased her surroundings. She was lost within herself now; no awareness for who she was or where she was. Every worry she had disappeared as the drug took over.

She let her demons do the thinking for her now, and all they thought about was blood. Her vision was covered in a red fog and she stumbled into her bedroom where she passed out. She knew her dreams would not haunt her tonight; her demons kept the memories suppressed.

Chapter 9

Arinadya woke up in a foul mood. She drained too much blood before falling asleep. Although it gave her an incredible high and eased her mind from the ghosts of her past, she was paying the price for it now. Her head throbbed and the circles beneath her eyes were an ominous shade of purple. She had to be more careful or she'd accidentally kill herself. It was part of the rules of haemanism: You were to control your blood intake otherwise the consequence was death. Many fell victim to this fate because the power of the blood was so irresistible, but Arinadya knew better. She was part of the council; she was of a higher social standing now. She had to hold herself to a certain standard of grace or else she could risk being shunned from her new group, a fate she deemed worse than death.

She slid out of bed. Her silver satin nightgown clung to the bare skin beneath. As she went to brush her teeth, she deliberately used as little toothpaste as possible. A few years back, the government took over that industry and began placing slight traces of silve into all toothpaste distributed within Russia. She was still hung over from the night before and did not want to overdo it before her day started.

In the kitchen she took her morning pill. It was mandatory, another rule. Besides having a small quantity of silve in it, the pill also contained 500 calories. A side effect of being haeman was the loss of appetite. If the citizens did not take their pills they could die of starvation. Arinadya always remembered to take it in the morning. Her afternoon and nighttime pill she often forgot about.

After tossing the pill down with a glass of faucet water, she routinely pricked her finger on the sharp needle trunk of the elephant statue she kept on the counter. A smile steadily crept upon her face as she sucked on her finger. The blood lessened her headache and filled her with renewed strength. She skipped her usual line of silve on this particular morning since she had overdone it the night before. The small trace of drugs in her morning pill, the toothpaste, and the faucet water would fill her veins and suffice until suppertime. She ran her fingers along the jeweled tin that held her weekly supply of the narcotic; being in the council had its advantages.

She stripped naked in the kitchen, throwing her satin slip on the floor. Her head pounded with pleasure as the blood seeped back down her throat, absorbing through the tissue lining her stomach, and eventually entering back into her veins. The world around her was moving faster than she was and it filled her with wonder. She ran her hands along her bare torso as the lightheadedness of her recent consumption left her dizzy. She had work today. She had to focus.

Quickly, she went back to her room and dressed. She wore a black lace bra covered with a sheer beige button down shirt. The sheer top was covered in red beading on the shoulders that dripped down the shirt like splattered blood. She put on a pair of black shorts that clung tightly to her body and showed off her long skinny legs. Her scars were plenty, canvassing her skin like a tragic portrait. Arinadya looked at her reflection.

Her pale blue eyes were wide from lack of sleep. She blinked twice with intention, trying to snap herself out of her revelry. The first few minutes after consuming were intoxicating. She needed to level off before leaving the house. She hastily smeared a coat of red lipstick over her purple-tinted lips and tied her strawberry blonde hair into a messy bun on top of her head. She stared herself down in the mirror.

Her mind spun around how easily she transformed into a beautiful, perfect haeman. It had been easy. When she first started she thought she would never be able to look like the girls in the media. But here she stood, looking like a supermodel. She had been beautiful before but suddenly, once everyone started shifting into haemanism, the desirable look changed and she no longer fit it. The perception of beauty was altered and she had been left on the outside looking in. The choice was to be an outcast or adapt. So she adapted.

A light buzz filled her skull as old thoughts began to creep toward the surface. Sevrick. He thought she was beautiful before. She didn't need to change to keep his love. *No.*

She slammed her fist into the mirror, shattering it into a thousand tiny pieces. Her knuckles bled but she couldn't consume any more blood right now. Her heart raced and her cheeks flushed with heat at this sudden emergence of anger. He was dead to her. Arinadya growled from the depths of her stomach as she grabbed her bag and went to the kitchen to rinse the blood off her hands.

As usual, the streets were crowded and everyone was highly agitated. People shouted nasty things at one another as they bumped shoulders. Arinadya knew how easy it was to receive a hard punch to the face when running into a foul-tempered person. And if she was in a bad enough mood too, they'd get punched right back. When this happened, it often started a fight to the death. It happened to her twice before; once with a teenage boy and another time with a woman her own age. Obviously, she emerged as the victor both times. As exhilarating as those battles had been, Arinadya didn't have time for that kind of pettiness today.

A man slammed into her as he walked by. "Watch where you're going, you stupid whore."

Maybe she had a moment for that kind of pettiness.

The man barely finished his sentence before Arinadya was upon him, squeezing the sides of his face together and slamming him against the brick wall of a building.

"A stupid whore?" Arinadya asked tauntingly. With her free hand she grabbed the man's crotch so tight he squealed in pain. Then she leaned in closer.

"If you ever degrade me again, I will rip your dick right off your body and shove it down your throat. Do you understand me?"

The man immediately lost his bravado and succumbed to her threat. She was stronger than him. She was stronger than most. She was marked and one reward for being a part of that elite group was an allowance of direct access to the ingredient that made the blood so powerful. There were only a select handful who earned this status, hence why there were only a select few with strength like hers.

She let go of the man's face, punched him hard in the eye, and sauntered away like her day had not been interrupted. Her high heels clicked confidently against the concrete sidewalk as she left the grown man cowering against the wall.

The office was loud. People were arguing over Prince Mikhail's new campaign to expunge the condemned. There were many names for the non-haemans: the damned, the condemned, the others. Like Sevrick. Arinadya let out an agitated groan as the idea of him popped into her consciousness again. She no longer cared but she did not wish to see him dead either. She enjoyed the fact that he still desperately wanted to save her, wanted to win back her love. The idea that someone in the world still loved her unwaveringly comforted her on a deep and unconscious level. It was selfish because she knew the end to their tragic love story came with Sevrick on the bladed end of the sword. But she also knew she would never be loved by anyone else ever again. Not in this world. Not by another haeman. Love no longer existed. You screwed who you wanted and then moved on. When feelings became involved, people died. Ex-lovers, new lovers, the person being fought over. One or all wound up on the receiving end of death when one of the parties became too attached. Extreme emotions such as jealousy and possession could not be controlled; they were too intense for the haemans to manage and such feelings led to murder. This was why Arinadya numbed herself to all emotions. This was why she knew she would never feel love again. Any emotions from her past were now distant memories she was calloused toward and there was no room left in her heart for feelings. In this new world, there was nobody worth loving anyway.

The office was loud with arguments. The prince was coming in later that afternoon to hear the new pitch and nobody could agree on the slogan. Arinadya rolled her eyes; her employees used to be her best friends. A lot of them had been her classmates at the

University who initially got her into this lifestyle, but now she was beyond them and couldn't stand their infantile bickering.

Arinadya's golden spinal tattoo shimmered as the sunlight found it.

"Enough," she demanded, though the cacophony of quarrels did not abate. Her rage was rising. She didn't like to be ignored. The noise in the open office grew louder inside her head. The blood pulsed angrily against her skull.

Faster than a blink, she grabbed her assistant Veronika by the neck and slammed her against the wall; her feet kicked in the air as she struggled for oxygen.

"I said enough," Arinadya shouted. Everyone went quiet this time. She glared at her subordinates and scanned everyone in the room as she effortlessly continued to hold her assistant up against the wall behind her. More time must have passed than anyone realized because a hush covered the room as the woman went limp in Arinadya's grasp.

"Damnit," she whispered as she lowered her coworker's body. "Get back to work," she commanded. She was their boss. She had once been in Veronika's role as an assistant to the CEO, but times changed and Arinadya found herself now sitting in the CEO's seat.

Veronika's body was crumpled in a heap. Her thick brown hair covered her pale face and her bones stuck out in weird angles from her skin as she lay dead on the floor.

Arinadya called out to an eager young man she just hired. "Aristarkh, take her body downstairs. Leave it at the street corner. The city maintenance crew will collect it later tonight."

He nodded and effortlessly lifted the limp body into his arms. Veronika's lips were a shade of purple and her dead hazel eyes were open, staring at Arinadya, who shooed Aristarkh away with a flick of her wrist. He left without question.

23.

Five years ago she made her first kill and now her count was at 23. This twenty-third was an accident. She underestimated her own strength, but it still counted toward her tally. It was the slam against the wall that did it. Or maybe she held her throat closed for too long. Or maybe it was both. Either way, she had not meant to kill Veronika. She sighed. She'd have to let the council know at their next meeting. They would be thrilled and would update her tattoo. Arinadya shook her head; she was trying to keep her number low. A long life still lay ahead of her and she did not want to lose touch with her humanity too fast. Though it seemed the more time that passed the less grasp she had of where she was headed, and the short moments in which she cared passed by quickly, leaving her cold and numb, unconcerned with what she had become.

The prince was coming at 2 p.m. The pitch for his new slogan had not been finalized.

"Luca, Tanya, and Boris, come with me into the conference room. Bring all the ideas you've gathered from the team so far."

They would have to work diligently if they were going to finish this project before Prince Mikhail arrived. Arinadya wondered if Princess Milena would be accompanying him. She only saw her in person once and it was surreal, a true out-of-body experience. There were very few people who impressed Arinadya, but the princess had been her idol when she initially embraced haemanism. The princess inspired her choice to pick this lifestyle over everything else. Her goal was to look as beautiful as Milena, and seeing her in person proved she accomplished it. Realizing she was on her level physically diminished the admiration she once held for the princess, but she remained fascinated and eager to know the woman behind the crown.

Being in the council meant you could be trusted. It took hard work and dedication to be inducted. It also took loyalty and a sense of confidentiality. Arinadya had proven herself worthy after a year of tracking her progress and submitting her application to the council. It was a great goal but now that she achieved it, she found herself feeling lost. Six months passed since she was accepted into the council and her purpose in life seemed to have vanished. There was no new objective she sought, nothing to keep her focused or entertained. It left her with too much time to think and reflect upon the things she had done to get to this point and all the memories she buried along the way.

The conference room was sunny but cold. They were a few floors up and the sun shone through large glass windows that surrounded the table, but no warmth traveled with the light. The glass was too thick and the air outside too cold.

"What ideas do you have so far?" Arinadya demanded immediately. She stood tall in her glass stilettos and the way her hair was pulled back made her cheekbones appear razor sharp. None of the people that worked for her crossed her. She was as strong as she looked; Veronika's death was a testament to that.

"Well, first we thought to play on the word *condemned*," Tanya said. She was small with short black hair. It was pin straight and stopped right above her shoulders. Her eyes were ocean blue and she wore dark black makeup that enhanced their color. She wore three silver armbands: one on her bicep, one on her forearm, and one on her wrist. This was how she collected her blood. Each band was connected by small hollow chain links that slowly pooled her blood into a large ring she wore on her middle finger. It was already half full. Tanya continued explaining her idea in a small, calculated voice. "Something like: *Condemned to death: by God and by Us.*"

Arinadya scrunched her nose, creasing her faded freckles that had become less visible over the years.

"Good concept, awkwardly phrased."

"Well, my group came up with a different approach," Luca chimed in. He was tall with lean muscles. His eyes were bright green and his dark brown hair was buzzed close to his scalp. He was handsome but he also had a terrible temper. He did not mess with Arinadya but in the past year she had to reprimand him for killing three of her best workers over dumb fights. He was a grenade with a loose pin and she was tired of cleaning up the fallouts from his explosions. Arinadya had to deal with him like she would an annoying younger brother: with delicate force. "My guys came up with *Your veins hold the cure. Be with us, be pure.*"

"We aren't trying to recruit them." Arinadya closed her eyes and squeezed the bridge of her nose. "Those days are over, they are a lost cause. We are trying to make all of Russia aware that Prince Mikhail is planning to find wherever they are hiding and exterminate them. We need every able body to fight alongside him. We also want to instill a bit of fear into the condemned once they catch wind of this slogan."

"Why has Prince Mikhail taken a sudden interest in exterminating the outliers?" Boris asked. He was an enormous man. Somehow the process of becoming haeman didn't have the same slimming effect on him. He was pale and his face was chiseled like the rest of them, but his body was a heaping mass of muscle. He got along well with the others and he was the person to go to if things ever got out of her control in the office. He worshiped the ground

Arinadya walked on. Boris kept talking, his deep voice calm but serious, "I don't get what the point is. No one ever seemed to care before. So why now?"

It was a good question. No one knew why the prince was suddenly so hell-bent on killing anyone who wasn't haeman. He had his reasons but very few knew what they were.

"We aren't paid to ask questions," she said, cutting his inquiry short before the topic took their conversation off track. "We get the big bucks for our catchy ads and flashy billboards. Now, what other ideas do we have?"

"How about something simple like *Extermination of the Condemned*?" Luca suggested. His green eyes were focused, determined to come up with the winning idea.

"Or maybe switch the words around: *Condemned to Extermination*." Tanya beat him with a witty rearrangement of words.

"I like that. Boris, jot it down. Add a colon and *It's in your veins to fight*." Luca's face went dark as Boris took out an electric pen and scribbled onto a black metallic pad. As he wrote the words, they appeared in green font on the large white wall of the room.

CONDEMNED TO EXTERMINATION: IT'S IN YOUR VEINS TO FIGHT.

It was already noon. "We need at least one other idea to present to him. Even if this first one is good enough. I like the idea of veins or blood, and I like playing with the word condemned."

"*We fight with our blood, they die by theirs,*" Boris said out loud.

"*Condemned to this war by choice,*" Arinadya added. Luca and Tanya both nodded and Boris added it to the list.

WE FIGHT WITH OUR BLOOD, THEY DIE BY THEIRS.

CONDEMNED TO THIS WAR BY CHOICE.

"Should we go with the scripture?" Tanya asked, referring to the verses cited within the Haeman Russian Orthodox doctrine. She quickly batted her long black eyelashes toward Luca before continuing. "*Blessed be our veins by which we thrive.*"

Arinadya nodded.

"But change it to *Blessed be our veins by which we rid this world of misuse.*"

Everyone mumbled in approval as Boris wrote it onto the wall.

BLESSED BE OUR VEINS BY WHICH WE RID THIS WORLD OF MISUSE.

"Alright, that's good enough. Leave and clean the rest of the office. I want it presentable for when the prince arrives." The three subordinates left and Arinadya took a deep breath. She was relieved that they came up with a few good options for this new slogan. But her migraine was returning and her mood was gradually worsening. She knew the prince was a pompous jerk and she had to make sure she was as fake and pleasant as possible in his presence. She worked too hard to gain her new status to have it taken away from her because of one bad encounter with the crown.

There was already commotion beyond the glass doors of the conference room. How much time had passed? Were they early? Arinadya did not know why she could not get a solid grasp on this day.

The prince stepped into the office with a small group of trusted advisors. He barged through the glass doors to the conference room. Arinadya immediately shifted her face into the smile she had practiced in front of a mirror for weeks. Despite the fact that it was entirely fake, it was dazzling.

Prince Mikhail paused in his stride and squinted at Arinadya.

"I remember you." They were both in attendance at the most recent event the council held for its members. Since she was still new, she had only been to one so far. Arinadya was shocked he had seen her there; at the time she felt invisible.

"Yes. I am in the Council."

"Right," Prince Mikhail said slowly. "You are quite striking. Your face is not easily forgotten. I thought of you once or twice as the beautiful redhead without a name," he said bluntly, waiting for her to drool at this compliment. She was flattered but not impressed; he had a new girl on his arm every weekend.

"My name is Arinadya," she reached out to shake his hand, "Nice to meet you, Prince Mikhail. We have three possible slogans prepared for your viewing."

Prince Mikhail stared at her in bewilderment. Her lack of response to his compliment baffled him but he quickly replaced his confused look with a stoic façade; trying to prevent her from seeing him falter.

Prince Mikhail continued his brisk stride to the chair at the head of the table. The sunlight hit his brown mop of short, loose curls. His eyes were sunken deep into their sockets but their piercing dark stare was still mesmerizing as he glared at Arinadya.

"Show me your ideas."

She tapped the black metallic drawing board and the three slogans appeared on the white wall before them. No one else entered the room, though his posse watched intently through the glass walls.

"No and no," he said as he read the first two pitch ideas inside his own head. When he got to the third slogan, he leaned his body back in the oversized chair and read it out loud. *"Blessed be our veins by which we rid this world of misuse."* He then shifted his stare curiously toward Arinadya. "Who thought of that one?"

She wasn't sure if he liked the slogan or hated it, but maintaining her fake expression was becoming tiring. Her smile faded; if she was being honest with herself, she didn't care at all what he thought.

"Tanya and I. It was a combination of our ideas."

"But the words?"

"Me."

Prince Mikhail nodded then looked back at the slogan on the wall, reading it again in his mind.

"It's perfect," he finally said aloud.

This pleased Arinadya. She did a good job and this day would soon be over.

"Schedule a photo shoot for me." Prince Mikhail stood up. "My team will instruct your team the details of what I need from this session. I want this slogan on every billboard in Russia by the end of next week."

"Next week? Do you understand the logistics required for something like that?"

He walked right up to her, so close their bodies almost touched. He moved so fast he blurred from her sight for a moment. One day she'd move like that too.

"I have no inkling of what it requires." He looked down on her with a wicked smile. His breath was hot on her skin, running all the way down her neck. He glanced over her shoulder at the golden tattoo on her spine that peeked out from the top of her blouse. "But you are truly one of us now and I trust you will manage." He quickly wrapped his arm around her lower back slamming her body against his then whispered into her ear. "I'll be seeing you again."

Then he let her go and walked out of the room. Arinadya was furious. Who did he think he was to grab her like that? To imply anything other than business with her? She didn't care that he was the prince, she wanted to rip the skin off his face.

Tanya walked into the room.

"You okay, boss?" Her eyes were mischievous, glimmering in the sunlight.

"Of course I am. He liked the slogan."

"He also liked you," Tanya added, her face twisted into an evil grin. Arinadya could feel her heartbeat quicken.

"Get out of here before I lose my temper."

Tanya quickly retreated, knowing what her boss was capable of. All Arinadya could see was red. She had to leave. She needed to go home before her uncontrollable mood got the best of her. She thought of Veronika; it already did. She grabbed her purse and bolted out of the conference room.

"Boris!" She shouted as she headed toward the elevator. "Get in touch with Prince Mikhail's PR team. Find out what he wants for his photo shoot and then schedule it." Boris nodded and Arinadya flung the doors open to the hallway outside her office. She waited for the elevator and counted down the minutes until she could find

peace in the solitude of her tiny apartment.

Chapter 10

Prince Mikhail had his limo driver initiate the sirens on their car. He needed to get home to Milena. She was sick and he did not trust the nurses.

Sunset was upon them and he could see the Winter Palace down the road glowing in the day's fading light. Mikhail loved having this majestic fortress as his home; they moved there when they were discovered to be royals. It was extravagant, it was opulent, and it was what he deserved. As the city grew dark from nightfall, the garden lights went on, illuminating the property.

As the car crawled up the long entranceway, Arinadya popped back into Mikhail's consciousness. She was lovely. Resistant toward him *and* pretty as a flower, but he did not know her last name.

"Viktor," Mikhail called up to his driver through the glass that separated them. "Page someone from my team and tell them to find out the last name of the girl I just met with at Arkline Advertising."

Viktor grunted in acknowledgment and paged in the request. It was only a few seconds before somebody responded.

"Arinadya Tarasova," an anonymous voice answered over Viktor's pager. Mikhail shut the glass divider and sat back against the warm leather seat of his limo. He shut his eyes and thought of all the ways he wanted to have that girl. She smelt like a fresh summer day and her body had been warm and alive against his. He had to have her; she would be his. Though he had many other lovers, he needed a woman with a fresh face, a look comparable to the beauty of Milena's. He needed one woman like this to stand next to him in public, one woman like this to call his own. The others would remain, but strictly confined to the shadows. Arinadya would be put on display and worn like a crown.

His limo pulled up to the front door of the Winter Palace and Viktor opened the car door for Mikhail. His pace was brisk but not quick enough to prevent a few snowflakes from landing in his brown curls. He shook them off after getting through the front door, knocking any melted snow from his hair, and immediately headed upstairs toward Milena's bedroom.

He burst through the large mahogany doors leading into her room, startling the two nurses that sat beside her bed. "I have found the girl."

Milena moaned. Both nurses looked at Mikhail with annoyance but said nothing. Milena took a few moments to catch her breath before speaking.

"What do you mean, brother?"

"Don't you remember me telling you," Mikhail sat down at the end of her bed and shooed the nurses away. They left the room, leaving the siblings alone to speak. "I told you I needed to fix my image. With this attack on the condemned about to start, I need to present myself to the public as someone who values loyalty.

Someone they can trust. And the best way to do that would be to take on a wife."

"You can't just *take on a wife*," Milena laughed while coughing. "That's a terrible idea. You'd be horrible to her."

"Regardless, a steady female companion is the only thing I can think of that would fix my playboy image. The rest of the women can stay, in secret of course. This girl, I am going to make her my steady. She will be the only woman the media sees me with from now on."

"I pity her," Milena said harshly. She shook her head and the jewels she refused to take off jingled in her light brown hair.

"You shouldn't. She will live lavishly."

She looked at her brother skeptically.

"And she has agreed to this? This lavish, loveless life with you?"

"No. She knows nothing of it yet. But who is she to refuse?"

"Good luck with that," Milena let out a small fit of laughter. "What is this poor girl's name?" She took a sip of the blood medicine concoction the nurses were trying out on her. It was meant to heal her but she kept getting worse.

"Her name is Arinadya."

"Arinadya what?" Milena asked.

"Romanova," he said slyly.

Milena shot her brother a nasty look.

"She's not your wife yet. I may know her, what's her full name?"

"Arinadya Tarasova. Owner of Arkline Advertising."

"I've heard of her," Milena grinned. "She's a wicked little thing. Just joined the council a few months ago and there are already stories being spread about her strength. And her temper."

"She sounds even more perfect than I had already thought," Mikhail said, aggravated with his sister's petty opinions, then continued. "Keep your gossip to yourself. I have no patience for it."

"What else am I supposed to do while I'm trapped here dying in this God forsaken bed? All I have are the stories the nurses tell me." She was offended but Mikhail was not going to argue with her about it. Milena had always fancied being the first to know each budding rumor. Mikhail changed the subject.

"It doesn't matter. How are you feeling? Have the nurses been able to make any progress?"

"No," she said, her voice was hoarse. "I actually feel like I am getting worse."

Mikhail took a deep breath, trying to maintain his composure. He could not lose his sister; she was the only person in this world he truly loved.

"Well, this war on the condemned is for you."

"What?" Milena was confused. "I thought you heard rumors that the condemned were forming armies of their own in order to try and take us out first. I thought that is why you decided to get rid of them once and for all?"

"That is one reason. But it's also so we can find Leonid. Apparently, he was cured."

"Leo? He isn't haeman anymore?" This was news to Milena. They had known Leonid forever; he was Mikhail's best friend for years and was part of the reason they discovered haemanism in the first place. He disappeared years ago and after an extensive search brought back nothing, they assumed he was killed and his body lost. She would have never guessed he turned his back on haemanism. "How did you find out?" Milena asked, appalled.

"His neighbors came forward a few weeks ago and turned him in, years after the fact. They said he came back to try and 'save' his sister, Lara, who refused to leave with him. In confidence, Lara told them that it was Nina's doing. She brought him someplace to be cured and after it was done, he was dumb enough to come back to try and get others to follow his lead. This all happened about five years ago. His neighbors kept it to themselves until recently. Once I made my speech about exterminating the condemned they came forward with the information. Said they didn't think it was of any importance until now."

"That makes no sense. Of course we'd have wanted to know of a traitor the minute it was realized."

"Yes. It turns out timing was key in this situation. If I had found out then, I would have had him killed. Now that you are sick, I need him alive to find out how they did it so I can save you."

"I don't want to be cured! I want to stay haeman." Milena's hazel eyes grew wide and her voice was lined with hysteria.

"I know, sister, I know," Mikhail stroked her light brown hair. "We'd tweak the cure so we could heal you without having you revert back completely. Don't worry. Kirill and I have been strategizing how to move forward with this endeavor properly. We will make sure it all works out."

Milena nodded but her face was worried. She could not go back to how she used to be; she had become too powerful to ever allow herself to feel weak again. Never again did she want to be the sad and hopeless girl she was while living in the underworld of Russia.

"This girl you were speaking of," Milena changed the topic, "Arinadya. How do you plan to win her over?"

Mikhail's face became puzzled with insult.

"Win her? I don't need to win her. Or any other female."

Milena rolled her eyes at her brother's arrogance.

"Then how are you going to go about getting her to agree to be yours? She won't be easy."

"I just plan to take her. How can you deny the courtship of a prince?" He gave Milena a conceited wink and smirk before kissing her on the forehead. "I must go. I have to make arrangements for my bride."

"Do you have time for a line?" Milena asked before he left.

Mikhail paused.

"You were told to stop until you got better."

"But it helps the pain."

"Stick to your blood. The chemicals flowing through the tap water you've been drinking are enough to keep you going for the time being."

Milena rolled her eyes.

"Whatever. Just leave."

As he got to the door he turned and looked at his sister once more.

"Start healing," he commanded, then left Milena's bedroom. She let out a wheezing cough as the door slammed behind him. A single drop of blood ran down her face from her nose. She licked it off her lips and let the chemicals take over. It would soothe her pain for a little while. Her vision blurred as the blood seeped into the skin of her tongue and she fell into a sleep as deep as a coma.

Chapter 11

Arinadya was finally home. She took off her robe and was ready to submerge into her bathtub when her doorbell rang. She ignored it.

The water was steaming; she let it run at its hottest temperature. The numbing heat would soothe the uncomfortable feeling growing beneath her skin. Restless and achy, she dipped her body into the water, letting it cover her. She closed her eyes and held her breath, submerging beneath the waterline. Disappearing from the world.

Through the muffled space underwater, she could hear the doorbell ring again. She ignored it. The scalding heat of the bath stung the delicate skin on her face but it was exactly what she needed. Pain. She could no longer feel anything except pain and she craved the sensation. The air in her lungs began to tighten, crying out in warning. Sirens demanding oxygen.

She rose from the water, taking in a deep breath of air. The cool contrast of it flowing down her throat and into her body sent tingles down her back. The doorbell rang again. Arinadya desperately tried to hold onto the soothing feeling this bath had finally given her. She struggled to ignore the doorbell as it rang for a fourth and fifth time. Her rage was building and she submerged herself beneath the water once more, hoping to erase the noise of the bell.

It rang a sixth and a seventh time. Even through the water she could hear its faint chime. She let out a submerged scream, bubbles erupting all around her when the bathroom door swung wide open.

A man she didn't know broke through the lock. He was in uniform, a man of the royal militia, but Arinadya did not care. All she could see was red.

So fast she barely made a splash, she pounced from the bathtub onto the man, snapping his neck instantly. Her heart was pounding so ferociously beneath her frail ribcage she could see it beat when she looked down at her naked body.

24.

This man was number 24. A guttural howl emerged from the depths of her soul, so loud the strength of it made her collapse upon herself. While sitting on the ground, she used her foot to push the man by his head out of the room. His dead body moved easily and she maneuvered him into the shadows and out of sight.

She stood up, tightly wrapped a towel around herself, and then leaned over the steaming hot bath. To breathe. To regain her composure. To remember where she was. Everything was blurred. Her hands gripped the hot porcelain as she took deep breaths, trying to escape from her own wrath. Trying to wipe away the red fog that still filled her vision.

"Have you calmed down yet?"

She knew the arrogant voice coming from the doorway but she did not dare look up yet. She still felt murderous.

"I wouldn't try what you did to him on me. The outcome would be very different for you."

The prince. Arinadya looked up, moving only her eyeballs. Her glare was lethal.

"What are you doing in my home?" she demanded.

"I am beginning our courtship, of course," Mikhail smirked. He placed a hand across the frame of the door and shifted his weight as he examined Arinadya soaking wet in nothing but a bath towel. His eyes revealed nasty thoughts.

She stood up, unafraid of his presence.

"How long have you been standing there?"

"Long enough to see that I want you even more," his face twisted with desire. "You are a fine specimen my dear." He grazed her body with his hungry stare.

"I have no interest in you," she said flatly. Mikhail laughed.

"Oh, really? I like a challenge."

Arinadya's bright blue eyes widened in defiance at his suggestion.

"I am no toy. I am not a game to be won. Do not insult me."

"You truly are fascinating. " His comment almost seemed genuine, like she overwhelmed him in some small way. But she did not trust any misgivings in his façade.

"I believe you know where the front door is, considering that's how you broke in. Please feel free to see yourself out," Arinadya said. "And take your dead bodyguard with you."

Mikhail laughed again; her confidence was rattling him. She walked right up to him.

"Leave."

He grabbed her by the small of her back and pulled her in tight. "You'll find that you love me long after it's snuck up on you."

"Unlikely."

"You'll see." He smiled and let her go. He grabbed his dead guardsman by the foot and dragged him toward the front door.

She took a deep breath, the red fog still lingered in her vision. She shook her head to clear the last of it and he was gone.

The rage inside her was so strong that her memories were beginning to feel like imaginings, even the recent ones. She popped her head out of the bathroom, but it was too dark to see. She listened for footsteps, but heard nothing. Not a sound. Maybe it was a hallucination, a nightmare she'd wake up from.

Then from the other side of the apartment his voice rang out loud and clear.

"Our first date will be this Friday at 8 p.m. Wear something sexy."

Chapter 12

The sun was warm on Sevrick's skin in the field where he and Rina had picnics when the weather was nice. In spring, the field filled with wildflowers, covering the landscape in color.

Rina smiled at him. The light from the sun made her blue eyes radiate. Her full cheeks made little apple bumps beneath her eyes when she smiled at him. He loved her so.

A brisk breeze passed over them and Rina shivered. Sevrick took off his wind jacket and placed it over her shoulders. She gave him a sly smile then kissed him tenderly on the lips.

"I love you," she said, her voice was calm and sure.

"You know I love you too."

She nodded happily and held eye contact with him. There was no one in the world but them, Sevrick would have sworn on it. They were so connected to one another that she felt like an essential part of him. A vital organ he could not live without.

"I went to the candy shop and got you some chocolate jelly." He smiled as her eyes lit up.

Rina opened the small box of chocolate jellies and began devouring them.

"Thank you," she managed to mumble through a mouthful of sweets. She smiled as she said it, teeth covered in chocolate, and Sevrick let out a laugh. Everything was perfect.

"Sevrick, wake up!"

He rustled under the blankets and slowly opened his eyes. Lizaveta was standing in his doorway, shouting at him.

"It's nearly noon. I know you had a long journey but all the other men are up and they need you." She gave him a small, sympathetic look before shutting the heavy curtain to his room as she left.

He did not want to wake up; his dreams were the only place his memories felt real again. He choked down the pain rising beneath his chest and got out of bed.

They made it back from Vyborg with all the new recruits. When they went to retrieve the female haeman Leonid tranquilized, the new group of recruits had already killed her upon their arrival in Vyborg. They put her out of her misery before she got a chance to attack them. Nikolai and Zakhar didn't care at all, but it upset Sevrick and Leonid because they were looking forward to another opportunity to try the rehab. They all agreed, though, that their journey home was much easier without the extra deadweight to carry.

The Clandes had been a small group of 14. Now with Kira and Maks there were 16 people living in their underground home with an extra 300 or so recruits sleeping in the surrounding woods above ground. Lizaveta woke him because they needed to find, or make, shelter for these new people who agreed to follow and fight with them. These new recruits went by the name Primos, since their initial hiding place had been in the town of Primorsk of Karelian Isthmus.

Sevrick made his way out of his room and down the dim hallway toward the open living space. He could hear voices already discussing how to move forward with this endeavor.

"We could easily help you make shelter amidst the trees at the border of the neighboring forest. The white elm is out in the open, but the forest line begins again less than forty meters away. I think that would be a good spot," Alexsei suggested. He and Ruslan were back in charge, heading this conversation with the leaders of the Primos, who journeyed below ground to discuss this matter.

"I want to be underground like you. It is safer. We are much too close to the city here," said the bearded man that had spoken up in Vyborg.

"We understand that, Vladimir," Ruslan spoke. "But it will take time for us to expand our underground fortress. And much more time to begin digging new living quarters for your people. You will need someplace to stay in the meantime." Vladimir grunted but did not object.

"What about the Lads? Or the Scots? Can they take some of them in until we have someplace more suitable for them?" Sevrick asked as he entered the room.

"That's not a bad idea," Alexsei said. "We need to fill them in on this plan and get them on board."

"They don't already know what you have going on with the rehab? And the idea of fighting back?" asked Oleg, another bearded Primos member.

"No. We hadn't thought to share what we were doing with the others until Vyborg opened our eyes to the power in numbers," Zakhar answered. "I don't see why they would oppose it, though."

"Because not everyone is cut out to fight. My people are warriors," Vladimir said proudly. "Seems like your people are a mixture of scientists and soldiers. These Scots and Lads or whatever you call them, if they aren't made of the right stuff then we are better off without them."

"Time will tell," Ruslan said, stopping the momentum of Vladimir's unwarranted conviction.

"Alright," Alexsei said. "Zakhar and I will go with Oleg to Lake Ladoga to speak with the Lads. Ruslan, you go with Sevrick, Elena, and Vladimir to the Scots pines and see where they stand. We will meet back here tonight to see the options we've got."

"What about tonight? Where will the rest of my people sleep tonight? You can't expect them to sleep out in the open again. The haemans have been leaving the city at random lately. I will not tolerate another night of that. We used to live much further north, many kilometers away from Vyborg in the safety of a dense forest.

We followed you here with the intent to help your cause but we cannot stay if suitable living accommodations cannot be provided." Vladimir's face grew rosy with frustration beneath his grisly beard.

"Of course," Alexsei said, realizing he missed this crucial element in the plan for the day. "Leonid will begin building temporary forts within the safety of the tree lines that surround our field. Though I do believe our comrades will agree to house your people after our meetings with them."

"That's fine," Vladimir grunted. "We will make sure to help you speed along the expansion of this underground fortress as well. With all my people helping, it should not take long."

"Great," Alexsei said. "It will all work out in due time."

Sevrick made his way with Ruslan, Elena, and Vladimir toward the Scots pines. Ruslan and Vladimir walked ahead of Sevrick; Elena walked right by his side.

"Liza said it was hard to wake you this morning. Like you were in some kind of unconscious struggle," Elena said, breaking the silence.

"I was tired."

"Are you okay?" She looked at Sevrick with genuine concern.

"Yes." He did not want to talk about how when he slept he no longer dreamed. That he only saw old memories and they haunted him. He did not want to reveal that everything that once made him happy now tormented him.

"Fine. But I'm worried about you. Everyone is," she paused, "especially Liza." He took a deep breath. He knew where this conversation was going.

"There is nothing to be worried about. I've been with you all for five years. I am the same now as I was then."

"That's the concern. You are still stuck in the same place you were five years ago. You can't let go. She will be the death of you."

"So be it."

"Can't you see the good life you have all around you? You even have a good woman who has fallen in love with you!"

Sevrick shot Elena a cautionary glare. "She should not love me."

"Well she does. You made her."

"I did not. I told her a long time ago that I could never love her back."

"Just because you were brutally honest with Liza doesn't mean you still didn't lead her on in your own weird and twisted way. I agree, she should have never fallen for you. But she did. And you didn't stop it."

"She was my closest friend when I got here. When I realized she saw it as more than that I tried to stop it. She knows she can't have my heart. It belongs to Rina."

Elena let out a heavy sigh. "You are so messed up."

"Exactly. I'm no good. And Liza is. She needs to move on."

"No, *you* do. From Rina. You are in love with a woman who would kill you because *she* was in a bad mood. You are in love with a woman you can never see because she's deeply addicted to a murderous lifestyle. You are in love with a woman you don't even know anymore."

"She is still in there. I've seen her struggle. You don't know what we used to have and you don't know how wonderful she was before all of this."

"I'm sure she was the love of your life," Elena said sympathetically. "But she is no longer that woman. She is a ghost of who she once was. She destroyed the girl you fell in love with a long time ago. If she'd do that to herself, she'd most certainly do that, or worse, to you." Sevrick's heart was racing, his blood pressure rising.

"Stop it. You don't understand. You never lost the person you loved the way I did, to a filthy addiction. The loss of control, the intangible barrier it put between her and I."

This was not entirely true but Elena did not mention her own loss. Her eyes became watery.

"I just want you to be happy. You are my friend and I can see how deeply you are suffering. There are so many good things in this world that you stubbornly remain blind to."

Sevrick swallowed back his own tears. "I can see only her."

"Well, I don't know what you need. Maybe it's her, the old version of her, or maybe it's closure. But either way, I can help you try to find it."

"I think it's something I have to do on my own."

"That's ridiculous. This is far too big to do alone. I know the guys just want you to get over it. And Lizaveta is clearly too in love with you to give a fair assessment. I'm neutral. Let me go with you next time."

"Into the city?"

"Yeah. I won't go in to see Rina with you, of course. She has no loyalty buried beneath her haemanism for me, she'd kill me instantly. Probably you too for bringing me. But let me go with you and I can be your sounding board on the trip back. Help you dissect whatever goes down. Maybe you just need to talk about it out loud to someone while it's fresh in your mind."

Sevrick nodded. He never made the trip with anyone before. The journey home to the white elm always left him distraught and tangled in his own thoughts. The guys offered to go with him before but Elena was right, they just wanted it to be over. They wouldn't be as understanding as Elena might be.

"Alright. Let's go tomorrow night. We can just observe her, see how she is doing. It's too soon to let her see me again. It's been barely two weeks since I last made contact with her and that's not long enough. The anger, sadness, and confusion won't have settled yet. I can't see her again until she misses me."

"You want to go all the way to the city just to watch her? Why?"

"To look out for her. To see how she is doing. Make sure she's okay."

Elena looked skeptical.

"Alright," she said, thinking the whole thing was slightly over the top. "If that's how you do this, then I'm with you."

"Okay. Good." Sevrick began breathing more quickly as excitement slowly crept its way through his nerves. He had something to look forward to again, and with Elena there, maybe it would keep him in a better frame of mind.

Scarlov of the Scots greeted them; he led this group. They did not know the Clandes referred to them as "the Scots" but when he heard it, Scarlov let out a hearty laugh and adopted it on behalf of his group.

They lived in the part of the forest where the Scots pines grew, sheltered by the elaborate tree houses they built throughout the densely wooded area. The houses covered the trees, connecting to one another so they formed even larger homes while still remaining camouflaged in the forestry. From a distance, they were invisible. It was likely you'd walk right beneath them, never noticing they were there. But when you knew to look for them, the sight was a work of art. Using what they could find in nature, they built detailed cabins that bent and curved along with the natural flow of the woods surrounding them.

Sevrick admired the craftsmanship of the architecture as Ruslan filled Scarlov in on why they were there.

"Why didn't you come see us sooner about this? We don't like living in hiding any more than the rest of you," Scarlov said, his tone playful but serious.

"We honestly just thought to combine forces about a week ago when a few of our men traveled into Vyborg and came across Vladimir and his people," Ruslan motioned a hand toward Vladimir, introducing him.

"And what name do your people go by?" Scarlov asked Vladimir.

"We are the Primos," Vladimir said. "Our first home in Karelian Isthmus was Primorsk. We went to Vyborg to meet up with the HESies but they are all dead now. Besides those two kids."

"Yes," Scarlov nodded, "Well, you and your people are more than welcome to stay here with us until proper shelter can be built. We can hold an extra hundred or so up in our tree homes."

"Great. Alexsei and a few others went to see the Lads. Hopefully they can hold the rest of Vladimir's people."

"The who?" Scarlov asked.

"The Lads of Lake Ladoga. You know, the people living in those dirt caves out by the lake."

"Oh," Scarlov laughed again, "*those* Lads. These nicknames you've doled out are ridiculous, did you think we were Scottish?" he asked playfully. Everyone laughed.

Ruslan continued, "We don't know much about them but Alexsei is approaching them just as we approached you today. Besides housing the recruits until we can put up more shelter, it's really just a proposition for your alliance. I don't see why they wouldn't be on board."

Everyone nodded. It wouldn't make sense for them to deny the chance to team up with a large group of people. Having numbers meant they'd be better protected.

"They'd be fools not to align. I don't want to live in hiding for the rest of my days. If we can train and get the numbers to fight, then we ought to," Scarlov proclaimed. "Vladimir, come back with some of your people tonight. I'll have my own people start making room for them now."

"Until then, my new friend," Vladimir said.

The Clandes waved a farewell to Scarlov and began to head back to the white elm. Their trip was a success and they could only hope the Lads had been as eager to join them as Scarlov was.

The next day, after finding out from Alexsei that the Lads were on board as well, the Clandes began to teach the Scots, Lads, and Primos about their methods for rehabilitation. Leonid led the large lecture lesson from a tree branch of the white elm while the mass of students sat beneath. They had a million questions for him.

"How can we possibly cure enough haemans if it takes months of constant supervision before they are able to operate normally again?" a lady of the Lads asked. "There isn't enough space or time for that kind of endeavor. There are thousands of haemans in St. Petersburg alone. Hundreds of thousands throughout the rest of Russia."

"Well," Leonid began, "We are now much greater in numbers, so we have more people to act as nurses. More hands to care for the healing."

"Fine," a man from the Primos spoke up, "but where will they stay once they are healed? There is barely enough room for us as it is."

"This is true. But we will find a way. It is too important not to. We can push deeper into the woods if need be."

"When was the last time a session of rehabilitation was successful?" Vladimir asked. Leonid paused before answering.

"I am the last successful case. And I will not lie to any of you: I am the only case that has been successful so far. But the more we practice, the easier it will get. The last woman we had in our custody was a few days away from being released when she relapsed and went into a convulsive seizure." A look of defeat crossed his face. "She almost made it."

"But it was a health issue, not an issue with the woman's will," Nikolai stood up and shouted out to the crowd. "She was happy and ready to be saved. She was looking forward to getting her life back. Nobody had any control over what happened. Her body just shut down."

"I am hoping that with further trials we will be able to figure out what is going wrong," Leonid concluded.

"What about fighting? What if the haemans attack again and find our homes? I want combat training to be the other main focus," Oleg said with unmasked ferocity lining each word.

"Of course," Ruslan agreed from beside the white elm. "We want to be ready too. I think we ought to train in the field between the white elm and the Scots pines each and every day. The haemans have superhuman strength, great speed, and a complete lack of compassion. No amount of training will ever be enough, so we ought to drown ourselves in it. A day shouldn't go by that we aren't readying ourselves."

The entire crowd nodded at this. Sevrick felt the need to speak up.

"But we mustn't go looking for a fight. Our goal is to heal the population and be ready to fight if they attack us first."

"Agreed," Alexsei said and the rest of the crowd did not argue.

The questions continued to flow and Leonid answered every single one. But as the sky began to darken Sevrick got antsy to leave. Elena promised to go into the city with him to see Rina and he intended to take her up on that offer. He caught her eye at the far edge of the crowd and nodded for her to meet him on the other side of the white elm. She carried her small body confidently as she rounded the tree toward him.

"We ought to head out now. It takes two days to get there and I want to arrive around nightfall. We can't sneak around the city without any shadows." He gave her a smile; his deep blue eyes were bright with the pink sky behind him. Elena took a deep breath.

"Alright, let's go then."

They retrieved their backpacks from their home below ground and were ready to go. Elena tied her blonde hair into a ponytail, pulling the skin over her high cheekbones tight. She looked serious and Sevrick was glad; there was no time for revelry on a trip like this.

On their way out, Sevrick made sure to tell Zakhar they were leaving for the city. He looked at them skeptically; no one ever went with Sevrick to see Rina, but he did not verbalize his confusion. It would be good for his comrade to have company. Zakhar demanded they return safely and pick up whatever scraps they could gather on their way back. They did have quite a few more mouths to feed now.

This was the first time Elena would be back in the city of St. Petersburg since she escaped six years ago. She found Ruslan and Alexsei at the white elm a year before Sevrick showed up. Her older brother Pavel began using his blood to get high like everybody else, and Elena convinced him they needed to escape before it got worse. He left with her, hoping to escape from the addiction that continued to lurk inside every nerve in his brain. They found the white elm and lived there for about six months before Pavel left in the middle of the night. He scrawled Elena a note saying he had to go back to the city because he could not live a life in hiding. But she knew he never really kicked the blood habit. She caught him trying to drink blood out of the cuts and scratches he got "accidentally" while working in the woods. But his blood did not work the same here as it did in the city; it did not transform him, did not give him the strength and power the people in the city were getting. It did not turn him into a haeman. So he left.

That was when the Clandes began to suspect the blood wasn't creating the haemans naturally. If it were a gift from God, it would work no matter where a person was located.

Sevrick arrived six months after Pavel abandoned his younger sister. Lizaveta told him what happened but he never asked Elena about it and she never brought it up. She kept her feelings toward what happened with her brother locked up tight.

As they walked he could see Elena's mind was someplace else.

"Are you alright?" he asked.

"Yeah. I'm fine. It's just been a long time since I've been to the city."

"It's not the same. The roads are the same and the buildings mostly, but it doesn't *feel* the same. The darkness pours out of the haemans and into the streets. The whole place is completely contaminated with despair. After being there, you're left with a heavy feeling, almost as if the city wants you to take some of its burden with you as you go."

"That sounds horrible."

Sevrick shrugged. "It is."

Elena laughed. "So glad I volunteered to accompany you into this tragic kingdom."

"I'm just being honest. There's no need to be worried. It's not your home anymore. The second you step foot onto the streets you used to know, you'll see what I mean. You won't feel the nervous attachment and anticipation you're experiencing right now. All of that will be sucked right out of you and replaced with a feeling of great loss."

Elena nodded but said no more. They kept walking, mostly in silence. She was focused on the trees and strange, new environment she was getting to see. Sevrick was worrying about Rina.

It wasn't until halfway through the second day of their journey that Elena finally asked him about her.

"So what have I gotten myself into?" she asked brashly. "I know we are only spying on her this go-round, but what are you hoping to get out of this?"

"I'm not sure. It's different every time."

"Is this just so you can see her?"

"Sometimes. Sometimes I get clues about things I should bring up the next time I let her see me. I find out what she's interested in now and try to let her see we can still have things in common."

"You do realize how pathetic that sounds, right?"

"Oh, I know, but I don't know what else to do. And it doesn't mean it'll be like this forever, just until I can heal her and get her back to normal."

"Alright. I'm here to observe, but I'll let you know now, I'm not going to sugar coat my thoughts. I care about *you* first and foremost. You're worried about healing her, but me and everyone else who is part of our chosen family, we're more concerned with healing you."

"Be honest, fine. But don't try to fix me. I'm not broken."

Elena rolled her eyes.

"You're right. You're not broken. You're shattered."

It was 6 p.m. when they reached the suburbs surrounding the city. It was easy to sneak through the area in the hazy shade of twilight. Most haemans did not leave their homes much once they retired from the city for the night, and since it was winter, no one was outside enjoying the weather. They easily crept through the backyards of numerous houses, ducking behind trees, fences, and shrubbery. As they walked, Sevrick attempted to cover up the tracks they were leaving in the light dusting of snow that covered the ground.

They crossed through two neighborhoods before the tall buildings of the city were upon them. The new and modern skyscrapers stood in front of them like a tall glass wall hiding intricate mazes beyond its surface. Sevrick picked the street he always used and Elena followed him onto the dimly lit sidewalk.

To Elena, being back in St. Petersburg felt like walking onto another planet. The surroundings appeared mostly the same, but the feeling it gave her was entirely foreign. It was dark and foreboding. The streets reeked of corruption and the air felt stale. Elena understood now what Sevrick tried to explain before. This city had no remnants of the home she once loved.

Sevrick continued to lead them through the seemingly abandoned back streets. The sky was darkening now and there were plenty of shadows for them to maneuver between. It wasn't long before Sevrick slowed his pace and led Elena toward a rickety fire escape in the alley between two apartment complexes.

He climbed the ladder slowly. Halfway up he whispered down to her, "Skip this step here." He pointed to a rung as he stepped over it. "It makes a loud creak."

Elena nodded and avoided that particular step. They reached the second platform and Sevrick stopped. He took a deep breath and moved in closer toward the small window. He placed his large hand against the beige brick wall and peered into the apartment.

"This is where she lives," he said to Elena without looking back at her; he was focused intently on seeing Rina. "But she's not in the kitchen, or the living room."

"Maybe she's in her bedroom?" Elena offered.

"Or she's not home." He finally turned to look back at her. "It's best to wait here, though. No one will see us on the fire escape. Plus, she always returns home at some point. It's a little after 7 p.m., maybe she had a long day at work."

Elena nodded but was skeptical. She didn't like that Sevrick was making excuses for Rina and trying to predict her whereabouts. He was too concerned with a life he no longer had access to, and a person who no longer wanted him to have that access.

The sound of objects being dropped onto a counter came from inside the apartment. Rina stood in the kitchen. He ducked instinctively, even though she hadn't seen him. He was on his knees with the windowsill at eye level. Elena got down on her knees next to him and watched Rina hustle about the living space of her apartment.

She was in a slinky black cocktail dress that accentuated her breasts. Sheer red lace ran down the back of the dress right to the bottom of her lower back. The dress was promiscuous and Elena was confused.

"Does she always dress like that?" she asked but was ignored. Sevrick's expression answered her question. *No.* He looked just as perplexed by her outfit as Elena was.

Rina seemed agitated. She was pacing the kitchen, picking up random objects, and throwing them against the walls. After throwing a teacup and watching it shatter, she finally stopped pacing and sat on the high stool at the small bar in her kitchen. Elena noticed her shoes. They were clear glass. She could see the very slow collection of blood pooling in the heel. Nausea filled her chest but she contained it. She was here to support Sevrick, not to judge the woman he loved. She did not want him to have to go through this on his own anymore.

Rina's doorbell rang and Elena's heart immediately tightened. She now realized why Rina was dressed the way she was: she was about to go out on a date. She looked over at Sevrick but his expression appeared to be even more confused than before. He was in denial. Or maybe he was fighting hard against the inevitability of what he knew was about to happen.

Rina continued to sit on the stool, not moving. The doorbell rang a second and third time before she finally got up and walked toward the door.

As she opened it, Prince Mikhail stood on the other side. Elena quickly grabbed hold of Sevrick's arm for comfort and possible restraint. She didn't know what his reaction was going to be to this new development but she did not want him lashing out and revealing their location. Surprisingly, he remained calm, though she could feel his arm shaking beneath her grip.

They could not hear what the prince was saying to Rina, or what she was saying back. Their exchange was short and Rina's shoulders sagged like an imaginary weight rested on them. She switched off the lights and left with the prince, locking the door behind her.

Sevrick crumpled to the floor of the fire escape platform with his knees to his chest and his face buried between them.

"Are you okay?"

"She is being courted by the *prince*, the most foul, decrepit human being alive. How did he even become *aware* of her?"

"I don't know," Elena shrugged. "But if it's any consolation, she looked miserable."

Sevrick took a few deep breaths. He thought she seemed unhappy about the arrangement, too. Maybe she had no choice, maybe he pursued her and she couldn't say no.

"We will need to come back sooner than I normally would to follow up on this," he said after a few moments of considered silence.

"Okay. But let's go home for now. Don't let this stew inside your head until we come back again. It is out of your control, making yourself sick over it won't change anything."

Sevrick heard her but did not say anything. He could not control how the sight of Rina with the prince made his stomach roar with disgust, how it made his heart buckle beneath the grave implications. Of all the men in this world, he could not lose her to him. If this date was any indication of how much further her addiction had progressed, Sevrick feared the woman he had been fighting for all this time might be lost forever.

Chapter 13

Arinadya locked the front door behind her and turned to face a gawking crowd and flashing lights. The paparazzi followed Prince Mikhail to her apartment and were now taking thousands of pictures of them walking down her stoop and into his limousine. She thought they'd be safe inside the car but the crowd of haemans pressed their bodies and faces up against the side of the vehicle and rocked it back and forth violently.

"This is normal. You'll get used to it," Prince Mikhail said to her. "Viktor, drive."

His limo driver hit the gas and they escaped the crowd.

"They will be outside the restaurant too," the prince continued. He looked Arinadya over. "Your face looks nice." His expression twisted with disapproval for her outfit. "What did you pay for that dress? 3,000 rubles?"

"I paid 1,500 actually. What does it matter how much it cost?"

He shook his head. "We will work on your wardrobe."

"I don't need to change for you. *You're* the one pursuing *me*."

"I am the prince. You will adapt to my lifestyle. Plus, you'll be happy when I buy you a whole new wardrobe. Once you see the pictures from tonight plastered all over every magazine, you'll be grateful to have better options in your closet."

Arinadya looked at him skeptically. A whole new wardrobe? Was he being serious?

"Do you actually like me? I assume I am just another pretty girl for you to have on your arm for a short period of time until you find another."

Prince Mikhail narrowed his hazel eyes at her.

"I'm not sure what I think of you yet. But I've decided I need to portray a more serious image to the public. I need a consistent woman by my side and I've chosen you for that role. You are the most stunning woman I have seen in quite some time and I can't have anything less than the best."

His arrogance outweighed the flattery. "And what if after our date tonight, I decide I can't stand to ever see you again?"

"Then you'd be setting yourself up for a miserable existence. You see, you have no choice in the matter. You're mine now." He saw her outraged expression. "Don't worry, you'll grow to like this life."

"Doesn't mean I'll ever grow to like *you*," she spat back.

"If you keep fighting it, then you're right. You'll hate me and be miserable. But maybe if you stop being so hostile you'll find I'm not so bad."

She didn't want to trust him or let her guard down, so she chose to end the conversation instead; she had nothing left to say.

The limo sped through the streets of St. Petersburg. It whipped around corners with no regard for pedestrians, running through red lights and stop signs along the way. But this was nothing out of the ordinary. Everyone drove like maniacs, so much so it was unclear why they even had street laws anymore.

They arrived at the Kompinski Hotel where the prince escorted her up to the Bellevue Brasserie. She always wanted to try their cuisine but never had because the prices were outrageous. Upon walking into the fine dining room, she immediately regretted her choice of wardrobe. She subconsciously shrunk into herself, trying to hide in a situation where there was no place to hide.

"Wishing you had better dresses now, huh?" he whispered into her ear and she stood up straight in defense.

The hostess sat them at a table near a window with a view of the entire city below. The lights from the buildings lit up the cityscape like stars in the night and Arinadya couldn't shake this new feeling of power coming over her. Being with the prince meant a variety of new experiences and opportunities would be available to her. She needed to stop being so stubborn and try to see his courtship with an open mind. This could be her ticket to bigger and better things. Maybe this would get her out of her slump.

"Thank you for getting my photo shoot scheduled so quickly," Prince Mikhail said as a bottle of wine was delivered to their table. He poured them each a glass.

"Of course. The billboard should be up by Tuesday. We've orchestrated the campaign to run through the entire length of Russia. Everyone will see it."

"Excellent. Hopefully the leeches hiding in the outskirts will see it too. I want them to be afraid."

Arinadya thought of all the times Sevrick had snuck through the city to visit her and knew they would get word of Prince Mikhail's new billboards. She nodded but did not mention it to the prince.

"So now that you are forcefully courting me," Arinadya said trying to sound playful even though it still annoyed her, "what should I expect in the upcoming months?"

"Lots of dates. Lots of publicity. I need to show you off. I will have Milena's stylist take you shopping. She will pick out the start of your new wardrobe. I need you looking your best at all times. Eventually it will get more serious but we can deal with that as it comes."

He left out the mention of emotion or love, but she did not bring it up. She wasn't too interested in those things anymore; romantic notions no longer existed. Not amongst the haemans anyway.

"Sounds hectic. You do realize I own a company, right? Arkline Advertising still needs me at the helm and I do not intend to let that slip by the wayside."

"Of course not. You represent a strong independent woman. I want you to stay that way." He smirked. "Even if behind the scenes you belong to me."

"You are starting this entire thing off on the wrong foot. I do not belong to anyone and I never will."

Prince Mikhail smiled like he knew something she didn't. "Whatever you say, my dear."

Arinadya huffed in frustration; she wouldn't let him take control over her. Even if she tried to be open to this experience, she refused to lose herself to him.

Two golden plates, each with three silver lines of cocaine, were delivered to their table. The drugs shimmered in the candlelight. Arinadya then realized this must be a council member-only restaurant; none of the haemans outside the council knew about the drugs or that the chemically altered cocaine was the only reason consuming their blood had the effect it did. This was why becoming a member required a certain level of loyalty and discretion; this knowledge had to remain confidential. Sharing this secret with every haeman was too great a risk. If the knowledge of this forced addiction somehow spread beyond the Russian borders, Mikhail's entire realm could be ruined. The world discovering this indiscretion would be catastrophic if it did not happen under Mikhail's strict and strategic watch.

They also didn't want to gamble with the possible backlash once haemans found out they'd been lied to. Especially the very holy individuals who began new religions based off haemanism and the notion that it was a gift from God. It was crucial everyone continued believing it was natural; it was why the phenomenon had grown so big in the first place.

Prince Mikhail took a small golden cylinder out of the napkin folded neatly in the middle of the table, then inhaled his first line. There was a second skinny tube of gold for Arinadya to use. She took it and snorted her first line as well. The silve hit nicely behind the backs of her eyes and filled her with renewed strength. She let out a sigh of relief. Lately, she had been craving a good hit outside the water and pills.

"It's nice to have the real stuff at your fingertips whenever you want it," Prince Mikhail said as he snorted his second line. "The stuff the public gets is so watered down, it's really only good for keeping their blood functioning properly. It doesn't give them a high like this."

"Nothing compares to silve in its true form. There aren't enough chemicals in the water, vitamins, or toothpaste to let anyone outside the council feel this kind of high. This is completely different."

Prince Mikhail smiled and sat back in his chair, relaxing before taking his last line. Arinadya did her second then put her cylinder down for a break as well.

"I do like you. When you stop being so hard-headed, you're quite pleasant to be around."

"Thanks," Arinadya said with hesitation, trying to receive his half-compliment without anger.

"Do you like dessert? Or would you rather they just bring us a calorie pill? I usually get the chocolate jelly here. It's superb."

"Sure, I haven't had chocolate in years."

Prince Mikhail smiled and waved their waiter over. He ordered the chocolate jelly that came with an assortment of fruit and small sandwich cookies. Arinadya took her third line as they waited for their dessert to be served.

The prince's bodyguards remained stationed around them, giving them space, but still present. The paparazzi were not allowed inside the restaurant so they were spared from that annoyance until they finished and left for the night. Talking to the prince wasn't as terrible as she anticipated. As long as they were off the topic of the arrangements he had planned for her, she found him to be tolerable.

The dessert arrived and it felt amazing to have real food in her stomach again. She couldn't remember the last time she ate solid food instead of relying on the pills for calories. The prince dipped a blueberry into the chocolate jelly and fed it to her. Once, this flavor had been her favorite. There was a memory tied to it that she destroyed a long time ago. Its shards lay deep within the creases of her mind and though she was too high to piece them back together right now, she felt it struggle for life inside her. She took another bite and swallowed the old feeling along with the dessert.

They finished and the prince escorted her through the crowd of flashing cameras and back into his limo.

The door to the car closed behind him and he sat so close to Arinadya their bodies touched. He put an arm around her shoulder. "Your place or mine?"

Arinadya shot him an icy glare. "Mine. You can drop me off. I don't have sex with any man on the first date."

The prince laughed confidently and instructed the driver to bring them back to her apartment.

They drove out of the nicer side of town and into her middle class neighborhood. She owned her own company but the royal's campaign was a recent acquisition. Arinadya suspected it would make her rich but not for some time. Though now that the prince intended to make her his wife, she could not begin to imagine where her life was headed anymore.

They pulled up in front of her apartment; there were no paparazzi here now. They all expected the date to end at Winter Palace where the royals lived and where Prince Mikhail normally took his dates.

"Don't expect this to be how every date ends," the prince said with a smirk.

Arinadya rolled her eyes; her mood worsening.

"If you want the public to respect me then you are going to have to respect me as well."

Prince Mikhail shrugged and maintained his devious grin.

"In public, at the very least. The things I want to do to you in private aren't very respectful at all."

"Well, enjoy your wet dreams about me. I'll be going now." Arinadya opened the door to the limo, eagerly wanting to escape his presence.

Before she could get away, the prince grabbed her by the arm and yanked her back toward him. She fell back into his arms and he flipped her around so she was straddling him. It happened so fast and effortlessly, Arinadya was left stunned. Her heart raced and desires she tried to keep suppressed began to surface.

The prince kept his grasp firm upon her thighs so she could not escape.

"Kiss me," he demanded.

"I thought I told you that you had to respect me."

"What harm is there in one small kiss?" He held steady eye contact with her, his longing for her was intense and she could feel it radiate off him. His passion felt contagious and it was hard not to let it affect her feelings. But if a kiss was how she would get to go home and be alone in her apartment again, then she would do it. She had kissed a thousand men, and worse, for pleasure or purpose, since Sevrick left. The prince was no different than the rest of them.

She leaned in and gave him a kiss he wouldn't forget. One that let him know she was in control. A kiss of authority. Their lips touched and she let his desire for her smolder. His guard dropped and she escaped his grasp.

She was outside the limo door before he regained full awareness.

"See you when I see you," she smiled at the prince. His eyes glowed and he smiled as Arinadya slammed the door on him, putting a physical barrier between them. Separating whatever this night was from the reality she knew. She took off her stilettos and walked barefoot to the front of her apartment building, sipping her blood from the glass heel as she walked back into the safety of her own home.

Chapter 14

Sevrick didn't talk the first few hours of their trip back to the white elm and Elena did not pressure him. She let the silence linger as they made their way through the suburbs and back into the forest. Sunrise was quickly approaching; they hadn't stopped to rest at all, and it looked as though they weren't going to anytime soon.

Elena yawned but did not complain; this was Sevrick's journey and she had volunteered to tag along. She was going to do things his way. It's what she signed up for.

His face remained serious through the silence and the skin between his eyebrows was constantly creased in thought. They were making great time getting back to the white elm but Elena could tell Sevrick didn't even notice.

"We might make the trip in a day and a half at this rate," Elena finally offered, half way into the afternoon.

At the sound of her voice Sevrick stopped dead in his tracks. He turned around and looked at her incredulously, like he forgot she was there. As he regained awareness of the world around him, he crumpled to the forest floor and placed his hands over his face.

"I'm sorry," he said, his voice muffled through the barrier he created. "I forgot I wasn't alone."

"It's okay. I need a break anyway." Elena sat down on the ground too, relieved to let her body rest.

She gave him space, sitting a few feet away from him. He curled up on the ground, keeping his face covered. His breathing was quick and heavy. He was having a panic attack.

Elena repositioned herself onto her back and stared at the clouds through the trees. She did not watch him. She did not ask him if he was alright. She let him have his moment, let him feel like he was alone for another minute. Let him go through his grief without worrying he was being watched or judged. After a few minutes she snuck a glance over at him and saw that he was staring up at the clouds now as well.

"That one looks like a rhinoceros with a balloon tied to its horn," she said aloud. Sevrick said nothing so she stole another peek at him and saw that she made him smile. That was all she wanted.

The silence remained for the next hour and Elena took this time to rest her body. Eventually, Sevrick broke the quiet company they kept.

"Let's move slower. I'm not ready to be back with everyone yet."

"That's fine," Elena said. She sat up to face Sevrick again when the sound of branches and sticks cracking came from a few feet away.

Immediately, everything went tense. Sevrick's eyes darted around the entire forest looking for the culprit while Elena held her breath, trying to become invisible.

"Were we followed?" Sevrick asked, unable to recall his own clouded memory from when they left the city.

"I don't think so," Elena hissed back, petrified they might have made some crucial error and were seen by a haeman as they snuck back into the forest. "If it was a haeman, wouldn't it have killed us by now?"

"Probably," he said, unsure.

The air around them began to settle and the intensity of what they felt for a brief moment began to pass.

"I take back what I said. I'm ready to be home again," Sevrick said and Elena agreed with a nod. They got up and continued their walk toward the white elm. Sevrick took out his tranquilizer gun and kept it in his hand as they continued.

A few hours later, as the sun began to set, they reached the section of the forest's end and crossed over the tree line that landed them in the field with the white elm. The tree was still about three kilometers away but they could see their people outside practicing combat moves and talking in small groups. They were gone for almost four days and Sevrick was glad to see the forward progress had not stopped.

Lizaveta was teaching an older man karate moves when she spotted Sevrick and Elena approaching the white elm. She paused her fight to wave to them only to receive a swift side kick in the gut from the old man. She hunched over in pain but applauded the man on his good technique and refocused back on the training. Leonid noticed them when they were 500 meters away, but his face was fixed with a grim expression. He began running toward them and shouting, but neither Sevrick nor Elena could understand what he was saying. Leonid began pointing somewhere behind them, his voice loud but the sound of the words got lost in the open air.

He then pulled out his tranquilizer gun and pointed it right at Sevrick. Alarmed, Sevrick's heart tensed. Was he trying to shoot him? But the brief moment of confusion disappeared as fast as it came when Elena grabbed him by the arm and spun him around to face the forest they just exited. A ravenous looking haeman was darting toward them, occasionally running on both its feet and hands, and its face twisted with murderous rage.

Sevrick quickly raised his own gun and aimed for the haeman. He waited patiently until the haeman was a few feet away. As the haeman made its final plunge to pounce, Sevrick took his shot and hit the monster right in the neck.

The haeman roared and landed on Sevrick, holding him down to the ground by his throat. Leonid shot the haeman two more times in the shoulder. As the sedatives were released into its neck, its grip loosened and Sevrick was able to break free. Leonid reached them and together they flipped the haeman over onto its back and held it down with their knees until it was knocked out completely.

"Elena, go grab some rope," Leonid instructed and Elena ran off to find something to bind the haeman with. "This actually will be our second test subject this week."

"You've already captured another?" Sevrick asked.

"Yeah, Liza, Nina, and I went for a walk the other day toward the city, and we came across one. It was a female. This one is a male, so it will be nice to see a comparison of the rehabilitation process between genders."

Sevrick got an uneasy feeling in his stomach.

"It's not good that they are wandering out into the woods now. They never did that before."

"Yes. But we are getting prepared," Leonid said. "If they only come in small numbers for a while we will be alright."

"So long as we catch and tranquilize each one that sees any of us out and about around the white elm," Sevrick added. "The worst thing we could do now is give away our hiding location."

Leonid agreed and when Elena returned with the ropes, they tied the haeman's hands and feet together. They wrapped another rope tightly around its abdomen, tying its arms down to its body. They carried the haeman back to the white elm and everyone stopped what they were doing at the sight of this monster being brought into their home.

"We've never done two at one time before," Nikolai said.

"Isn't one enough? At least until we get the process right?" a lady from the Scots shouted out.

"Did that one follow you guys back from the city?" Vladimir asked, appalled.

"It's alright everybody," Ruslan spoke up before more inquiries could be shouted out and chaos ensued. "Go about your training and lessons. We will handle this."

Most of the crowd went back to their business, but Scarlov, Vladimir, Oleg, and Lyov, leader of the Lads, gathered around Sevrick, Leonid and Ruslan before they brought the body in.

"How did we come to capture another haeman so soon?" Oleg asked with suspicion.

"It came out of the woods behind Elena and I," Sevrick explained before Lyov cut in.

"They followed you back from the city?" He was outraged. "We can't be leading them here."

"He's right. If they learn where we hide they will come for us and it will be a slaughter," Vladimir added.

"This is true," Ruslan said. "But we can't rule out trips to the city. It is how we get food and certain supplies we need for survival. And with all these new mouths to feed, those trips are even more essential."

"Perhaps we can set up a scouting crew that patrols the forest's border. We give them tranquilizer guns and they make sure no haeman ever crosses into the field. If they never see us all around the white elm, then we have nothing to worry about," Sevrick suggested, eager to figure out a solution because he could not be banned from going to the city.

"Alright, not a bad idea," Ruslan said. "Get this haeman contained before it wakes up. We will brainstorm on how to protect our home."

Sevrick and Leonid continued carrying the haeman into their underground home. It was much harder to get the deadweight of this unconscious body through the small spaces of the intricate entrance, but they managed.

They brought the body into the room designated as the laboratory. They put the male haeman on a bed next to the female haeman that was caught while Sevrick and Elena had been in the city. Both were sickly, skinny, and dressed in fancy jewelry and expensive clothing, but no amount of money or style could disguise the illness they both carried. They were addicts who would die if they were not healed.

The female looked weak under sedation.

"How long has she been here?" Sevrick asked Leonid.

"About two days."

Sevrick's eyes widened.

"And she's not off the anesthetic yet?"

"Nope, her addiction is the strongest one we've faced yet." Leonid went over to the unconscious haeman and raised her shoulder just enough so Sevrick could see the golden tattoo that trailed down her spine. "She's marked."

"Do we know what those markings mean yet?"

"No," Leonid responded, disappointed. "Whatever it is, it started after I was already here. All we know is that it means they are stronger than the other haemans and they are somehow deeper into the addiction than the others."

Sevrick then lifted the male haeman to see if he was marked too, but he wasn't.

"Well, I guess this will be a good test to see if healing one versus the other is easier," Sevrick said, thinking of Rina and how she was now marked.

"We haven't been able to make any new progress. What they did to heal me isn't working on them. It hasn't worked on any haeman we've brought back since. Weaning them off isn't enough and I cannot for the life of me figure out what needs to be different."

"Why did it work for you?"

"I think it was because deep down, I wanted to be healed. I didn't fight the process. I wanted to be with Nina again. But that was over five years ago. Things have changed. The disease has only progressed and intensified. I think these haemans we are capturing now and trying to rehabilitate are too far gone. They don't want to be healed."

"Right. And that's a variable we cannot control," Sevrick said, resigned. "There was that one female haeman that died who seemed excited to get her life back. She wanted to be healed but still wound up dying."

Leonid shook his head at the reminder, frustrated that nothing seemed to line up and help him find a solution.

"I don't know. I haven't been sleeping. I can't stop trying to figure out what I'm missing or what I need to do differently." Leonid had large circles of exhaustion underneath his eyes.

"We will figure it out, Leo, stop making yourself sick. We can't lose you, you're the brains of this operation."

"It's just frustrating." Leonid let out a heavy sigh.

"It'll be alright," Sevrick gave him a supportive pat on the shoulder. "I have faith that good will triumph. The human race can't go on living like this forever."

"It's only Russia."

"I know. I meant us Russians can't go on like this much longer. If we can't solve the problem, the problem will eventually solve itself. How the haemans live is unnatural and I do not believe it can last forever. They are sick and they will die." Sevrick had another thought. "They also do not reproduce. There's an issue those haemans haven't thought of yet. It's only been a solid five or six years with the majority of the population on this kick. If they don't find a way to repopulate, I am positive this dark time in our history will fade away. If we can wait it out until the majority come to terms with how unrealistic it is to live their entire life this way, it will eventually bend in our favor."

"Very true."

"I just hope I can get Rina out of there so she's on the right side of things when it all begins to spiral out of control for the haemans."

"I hope so, for your sake and hers. I'd be lost without Nina," Leonid said. But Sevrick did not want to talk about it anymore.

"Alright, I'll let you get to work on this guy," Sevrick said as he placed a hand on the sleeping haeman. "I'm going to see how Kira and Maks are adjusting. Haven't seen them much since we brought them here."

"Good idea." Leonid continued his work on the sedated haemans and Sevrick left with only one thing on his mind; he had to see Rina again. He would go within the next two weeks, without anyone to accompany him this time, just to watch her. He had to make sure she was safe. If he tried to bring Elena, or even Leonid, they would try to convince him to wait longer. But he couldn't wait; he had to go as soon as possible. Every cell in his body would explode if he didn't. He had to discover what was going on with the prince; he needed any kind of clue to indicate where Rina stood with that monster. And most of all, he had to start strategizing a way to end whatever it was the prince wanted with her because he could not lose her to him.

Chapter 15

Arinadya was exhausted. It had been a week and a half since her first date with the prince and things were moving too fast. He wanted marriage as soon as conceivably possible. Not because he loved her, but because she looked the part he needed her to play. She was his perfect wife. He wanted to fix his image so he could rally a better following for his army and making her his bride was his approach. It seemed to be working for him. The tabloids became relentless, following her everywhere, stalking them on their dates, putting pressure on them to have the marriage soon. It was becoming too much for Arinadya to comprehend. Since she now had even easier access to the silve cocaine, she numbed herself to the madness with drugs and blood. She thought this new change in lifestyle might ease her restless heart, but it was only suffocating her and causing her more unease than she felt previous to Mikhail's sudden entrance into her life.

Some of Princess Milena's stylists took her out on a shopping spree the day after her first date with the prince. Thankfully so, because her wardrobe would not stand up to the level of criticism the media had prepared for her. But besides the few cruel remarks on her debut wardrobe, the public was embracing her, as the prince wanted. They loved her and their love for her transferred over to Mikhail, making him seem like a decent guy for a change. She did not want any of this though. It was too much. Patience was always her weakness, and this newly forced attention and pressure from everyone around her was testing it.

In the past week and a half she had been on a wardrobe replacement spree and two dates with the prince. The second date went alright; he was still putting on his gentleman façade. But by the third date he no longer had the will to pretend. When she protested his touch he forced it upon her; raped her and called it love. Since that date she was battling whether to give in to his pressures and desires or whether to keep fighting. She knew she could not win and being resistant to it would only make it harder on her. She was losing her will and it didn't seem like there were enough narcotics in the world to numb the deafening defeat she felt.

She had another date with him today. He would be at her apartment to pick her up at any moment. It was meant to be a daytime date in the park, so the public could see them together in the light. She had not heard from the prince in a day and a half but this was normal; he only called her to set up dates, never to see how she was doing or to express any kind of feelings toward her.

He showed up at 1 p.m., an hour later than he told her he'd be there. He smelt of whiskey and perfume.

"You are late," Arinadya said annoyed. Her tolerance was at an all-time low; she didn't want any of this, it was being forced upon her.

"I slept later than I intended." He stepped in closer to kiss her. Arinadya grabbed his collar; another woman's lipstick was on it from the night before. She averted his kiss.

"Why bother with this charade if you still have a thousand other women at your beck and call?" She wasn't jealous, she was embarrassed. His actions made her look like a fool.

"You already know why." He tried to kiss her again but she pushed him away and took a step back.

"You think I want you near me after I know you've been with others? Those dirty women you have lined up at your bedroom door, who probably have a multitude of diseases?"

"Don't worry, so far I've been saving the main event for you." His breath reeked of alcohol, indicating he was still drunk. He took a step toward her again and she pushed him back once more. Without hesitation he backhanded her across the face, so hard she could already feel the welt forming.

She slumped over from the impact then looked up at Mikhail incredulously. His nostrils flared; he was not sorry. He grabbed her by the shoulders and made her stand up straight. He examined the right side of her face unsympathetically.

"Great. Now we cannot have our date in the park. People cannot see you like this."

He threw her onto the couch and lifted the skirt of her dress. She struggled to break free but he held her down firmly. He had her panties off and was inside her within a minute. As defeat overcame her again, her muscles relaxed and she let her mind go blank; trying not to collect any memory of this submission.

The prince gave her a hard kiss as it ended, snapping her back into reality. He stood above her, zipping up his pants. She lay there frozen, unable to process how to act now.

It didn't matter though. The prince wasn't fazed and carried on normally.

"Do not leave this apartment today. I'll have someone come by to help heal your face and get you looking pretty again," he said, making no attempt to hide his condescension. She refused to look at him. He gave her another forced kiss on the lips as she lay there motionless. "Until next time, my bride."

He left a small, jeweled box on her coffee table that held a nice portion of silve in it and then left, as quickly as he came.

The door slammed and Arinadya sat up once she knew it was safe that he wouldn't return. She carefully laid out two lines of the silver drug on her glass coffee table and snorted them using a 10 ruble bill from her clutch. It was amazing how fast she went from using golden tubes to dirty rubles. Nothing really changed; now she just lived in the shadow of a royal. She was still the same middle-class nobody. If the prince ever chose to forget about her, so would the rest of the world.

The drug filtered through her nose seamlessly and in a matter of seconds, it hit her straight in the back of her brain, shifting the chemical balance of her mind, making the day easier to deal with. In a few minutes she'd drink her blood and everything would feel right again. At least for a little while.

The time passed slowly, every minute dragged on as she anticipated her dose of blood. She put on her fake ruby pendant necklace, inserted the small needles into the skin of her neck and let the blood drip slowly through the chain links and into the hollow piece of costume jewelry. After twenty minutes, the glass adornment was almost full. She detached it from its chain and began to sip the blood slowly.

The blood seeped into her tongue and through the skin lining her throat. It made its way back into her system and she began to feel the initial euphoria. It cancelled out all the pain she felt and allowed her to bury the emotions she did not want to carry.

Though it helped, she still needed to get out of her apartment. She needed to get away from the couch she had just been used upon. She needed a new landscape to fill her sight, something she had never seen before. Unaware of the bloody mess that covered her neck, she put on an oversized knit pullover, a pair of ballet slipper shoes, and yoga pants. She grabbed her wool-lined red pea coat from her closet and let its large hood engulf her. She exited her front door without locking it behind her and began walking. She did not know where she was going; she just had to get far away for a while.

She walked through the back alley behind her apartment complex to avoid the wandering eyes of the public. As she walked beneath the old fire escape attached to her building, she heard the loud creak of someone climbing down.

Her heart jumped at the thought of being discovered so soon into her journey but when she looked up, no one was in sight. Arinadya groaned in aggravation at this momentary fright and continued on her way. Upon reaching a busier street, she avoided making eye contact with anyone she passed; too many people knew who she was now and if they recognized her they'd take pictures or try to talk to her. She did not want to be bothered; she wanted to feel invisible.

Although it was winter, the temperature was warmer than usual. She let the cool, fresh air whip across her face beneath the hood of her coat. As soon as she made it out of the city and into the suburbs, she removed the hood and let the wind dance within her hair. It swirled around her head like fire, each red strand being carried however the wind blew. Her face out in the open, the air stung a bit as it caressed the fresh wound on her face. She placed her malnourished hand upon the welt that had formed on her right cheek and winced at the slight touch; he really hit her hard.

She refocused her attention on her high and the steps she took toward the unknown. She reached the end of the development she had walked through. Two options lay ahead of her: go right and wander through more of the suburbs or go left and eventually reach the forest line in the distance. Naturally, left was the way to go if she truly wanted to escape. So she headed toward the forest and listened to the frozen grass crunch beneath her feet as she walked forward.

Her mind was fuzzy from the cocaine-laced blood and she let the sensation of nothingness carry her all the way to the forest. Upon reaching the first layer of trees she lifted the hood of her coat and placed it back over her head. She walked through the woods for hours. When she finally considered the time that passed, afternoon was long gone. It was not dark yet but the calmness of twilight was settling into the sky.

Without meaning to, she reached a body of water. She had walked a substantial distance and knew she was somewhere north of the city. She figured this lagoon was part of an inlet off the Gulf of Finland, which bordered St. Petersburg and the wilderness above.

She removed her hood again and took in the scenery. The ground surrounding the water was bright green and mossy. On one half of the lagoon the trees were tall and close together, their leaves and branches cast a full covering over the area. On the other side was a large jagged cliff. The rocks were sharp and gradually built up in layers to a wall nearly thirty meters tall. There was a small opening of sky between where the treetops ended and the cliff began that would let in sunshine on a nice day.

Arinadya took her coat off and placed it on a dry rock near the water's edge. She knelt down and placed her hand in the water. Despite the fact that it was winter, the water felt comfortable. The trees and rocks kept it sheltered from the frosty winds. Or maybe it was just that Arinadya was numb from all the chemicals coursing through her veins and she couldn't feel the water's true temperature. Either way, it felt delightful.

She began to strip down, taking off her yoga pants and knitted top, leaving her exposed to the world in only her black lace bra and panties. She took slow steps into the bank of the water. It came up to her ankles and she continued to move further into the lagoon letting the water rise up her body and cover her skin. Once it reached her stomach she stopped. Her hands rested lightly upon the surface of the water as she looked around with no feelings other than tranquility. It was a strange kind of peace that ran through her now, a feeling she had not experienced in years. If she had the choice, she would stay in this moment forever.

She took a handful of the clear green water and splashed it on her face. It ran down her cheeks, kissing the wound that still ached. Her bright blue eyes watched the setting sun peek out from beneath the clouds for a few seconds before it quickly hid away again. Its brief warmth spread across her body like an intoxicating tidal wave. In the water, she fell to her knees, letting it rise up to her neck. Her head floated at the water's surface and as she hovered, a small pool of blood surrounded her neck. It came from the fresh scabs her cheap necklace left. She cleaned off the excess blood from her skin and let her high resume. The view felt even more overwhelming from this vantage point. The greenery, sky, and cliffs appeared to completely encase her now. She let herself submerge beneath the water, bubbles of air escaped from her nose, tickling her ears as they made their way back toward the sky. The water was clear as she tried to look around beneath its surface. She saw small fish and beautifully colored rocks of all shapes and sizes. Upon reemerging from beneath the water, the brisk air hit her lungs like an electric shock, reminding her she was alive.

Her light red hair was now dark with wetness and slicked back against her scalp. She twirled around in the water once, enjoying how it brushed against her skin before laying back and letting herself float for a while. With her ears below the water but her face above, everything was silent and everything was calm. In this moment, she felt invisible to the rest of the world, like she finally found a way to disappear. The silence the water gave her soothed her aching soul. It let her believe for a moment she was the only person in this world. It gave her the solitude she was craving.

She wasn't sure how much time passed but the sky suddenly shifted from cloudy pink to dark purple. It was late. The stormy sky cleared and the moon shone brightly onto the lagoon below, giving her light to guide her out of the water. She made her way back toward her clothes, accepting that this was all the escape she could have for today.

As she began to redress herself, she heard a slight rustle come from the darkness within the woods. Was someone watching her? Or was it an animal? The noise happened a second and third time. Her gut suspected it was another person lurking in the woods. How could she have been so naïve not to realize the prince would have someone on her trail at all times?

"Who is out there?" she called into the shadows. She got no reply and her anger began to rise. "I will hunt you down if you do not reveal yourself."

The sounds of twigs crunching beneath footsteps approached where she stood. She finished dressing and was putting on her warm red pea coat when the source of the noise revealed itself.

"You?" Arinadya said in disbelief. She quickly moved her wet hair to hang over the right side of her face, covering the large bruise on her cheek.

"I was coming to see you in the city and when I got there, you were leaving your apartment. So I followed you," Sevrick said, keeping his distance from his ex-love. She was stronger than him and one false step could be his last.

Arinadya's gaze bore into him.

"You need to stop stalking me."

"It's not stalking, I am just watching out for you. I don't think you realize how far gone you are and it worries me."

"Well stop. Stop 'watching out for me' and stop worrying. I don't need you."

"I've seen the tabloids all over the city of you and the prince." He tried to mask the desperation in his voice. "Is it true?"

"Yes. We are to be married."

Sevrick took a deep breath.

"Is that what you want?"

"It doesn't matter what I want." She shifted uncomfortably as she answered him. Her gaze moved from Sevrick to the shadows of the trees.

"Yes it does. Come with me. I will help you escape."

The word "escape" echoed inside her mind a few times before she regained enough composure to put this silly man she used to know back in his place.

"Who said I needed to escape? Especially with you. You think I want to live your dirty life in hiding? *You* chose that life, not me."

Her sudden outrage was a meager attempt to mask her own desperation. It was a futile form of self-preservation; Sevrick could not save her and she would not let his offer to try break her down. She had to stay strong to safeguard her sanity. "I am marrying the prince. End of story. You need to stop being pathetic and move on." As she spoke again her voice cracked, revealing a fragment of uncertainty. "It's what I want."

Sevrick picked up on the battle raging inside her mind and body. "I don't believe you."

Furious with herself for showing weakness, Arinadya took a deep breath and recovered her self-control.

"You are a fool."

"I'd rather be a fool than a quitter."

Arinadya did not know why she was lying to him. She did not want to marry the prince, but she could not go away with Sevrick either; she ruined that possibility a long time ago. She didn't want either of these lives. All she wanted was to disappear from it all.

"Be a fool then. Be whatever you want," she said. "But what comes of it is on you now. I will not carry the burden of you any longer. I punished myself enough when I forced myself to forget you. And all these times I have fought my rage to spare you. This is your last warning; I won't do it anymore."

Sevrick looked at her shocked, never having thought of any of this from her perspective before. Did she really have remorse for their love at some point after he left? Was she aware and remorseful about the pain she caused him?

"It can be salvaged—" he tried to explain but she cut him off.

"No. Stop." Her breathing increased. "It was ruined years ago. It could never work. And I don't want it to." The tiny voices of her demons shouted different things inside her head. The loudest one repeated monotonously, *You need more blood.*

Without thinking, she swiftly sliced her arm down the sharp side of the rock her clothes had been on and drank the blood that poured out of the wound. Sevrick stared at her in horror.

After swallowing a mouthful of blood she looked back up at him.

"I'm too far gone. If you keep trying to save me you'll only lose yourself too."

Tears of anger filled his eyes.

"I already lost myself the day I lost you."

The chemical-laced blood flooded her mind and she no longer cared. Her nostrils flared as she took a few menacing steps toward him. She breathed her bloody breath into his face.

"Chasing after me will be your demise. I can promise you that."

She put her hand up to his cheek but did not touch it, the heat from his face radiated onto her hand. She looked into his eyes and a feeling deep within her gut began to scratch and claw its way out from under the weight she placed on it years ago. It was fighting the restraints that kept it buried, trying to resurface for air once more. She took a step away from him and swallowed any remnants of the returning feeling she had worked so hard to erase.

"Goodbye forever," she said. The evil gleam returned to her eyes and she sped off like a blur into the woods, leaving Sevrick alone once again.

Chapter 16

Princess Milena burst into Mikhail's bedroom to find him atop a strange woman, kissing her neck. Milena clicked her tongue in disapproval.

"Already Mikhail? You've barely been with Arinadya two weeks and you are already cheating on her? What about the wedding?" She didn't care about Arinadya, just her role as party planner.

"The wedding is a done deal," he said as he held the other woman down by her shoulders and sensually inhaled the fragrance coming off her neck. "No one else needs to know of my indiscretions."

Milena's patience was wearing thin.

"Get rid of this whore. I have matters to discuss with you." Her tone was serious and Mikhail reluctantly obeyed. He shoved the woman off his bed and she stumbled out of the room. Milena closed the door behind her and walked toward her brother. She sat in an embellished armchair with velvet cutout designs in red and purple. The ruby jewels she wore in her hair jingled as she cautiously sat her frail body down. Mikhail plopped himself onto his bed across from her.

"How are you feeling, sister?"

"Not so great. My bones feel brittle and my heart is working too hard. We need to hurry this wedding up. I'm too excited about it to risk dying before it happens."

"Stop thinking like that. I am going to find a remedy for you. I have carefully selected haemans scouring the country for Leonid. One of them is bound to find him."

"Perhaps, but I want to make sure I see all my plans and ideas play out on the day of the wedding. If I die before then I swear on my grave I will haunt you and this whole damn city for robbing me of this one small request."

"Fine. We can hurry the process along. When do you want it to happen?"

"Give me a month and a half. I do need time to get all the plans in order." The wedding was a perfect distraction, a way to forget about her sickness.

"Whatever you wish, but you may need to work on Arinadya. She is terribly difficult and I doubt I will have her eager to participate in that short time span."

"Maybe you should try a little harder then," Milena said harshly.

"What more can I do? I bought her a whole new wardrobe, I bring her jewelry all the time, and I take her out on expensive dates. She should be putty in my hands."

"Perhaps if you stopped fooling around with other women she may learn to trust you more." Mikhail huffed but Milena continued.

"Women can always sense when their man is being unfaithful, no matter the way, shape, or form. Physical or emotional; it doesn't matter. It's a sixth sense we are born with."

"I am offering her a new and better life; I am giving her fame and riches, she shouldn't care what I do in secrecy. This was never meant to be about love."

"I doubt she cares much for love. I've heard stories about her; she doesn't seem the type. But I would bet she doesn't want to look like a fool, even if it is only to the few of us who know what you do behind closed doors."

Mikhail slammed his fists against the plush top of his bed. He groaned in frustration.

"Fine. I will behave until the wedding. But I cannot make any promises after that. I am a man and I have needs."

"You are a spoiled brat who thinks he needs more than he truly does."

"Do not anger me."

"If you keep cheating on her she may wreck everything. I doubt she takes kindly to those who make her look like an idiot. You will not ruin this wedding for me, brother, it is all I am living for."

Mikhail wore a scowl as he surrendered to this explanation. Milena rested her head against the back of the chair as she remembered where Mikhail should be on this night.

"Weren't you supposed to be with Arinadya today? The public proposal in the park?"

"Yeah. It needed to be rescheduled."

"Why?" she demanded, sitting up in the chair.

"I hit her in the face and it swelled up fast. I couldn't bring her out in public like that."

"You can't do things like that before the wedding. She needs to look perfect in the pictures."

"Obviously."

Milena paused to think.

"You are right. You are going to need my help to dig yourself out of this hole. I'll befriend her. Try to get her to trust at least one of us."

"Thank you," he said with relief. "Try to get her to like me. The sex would be much more enjoyable if she participated."

"You are disgusting. Stop forcing yourself on her until I get a chance to mend things. You will only make it worse."

"You expect me to stop fulfilling my needs with these other women *and* with her? You truly overestimate my will power."

Milena rolled her eyes. "Just behave yourself. I will go to her in a few days, once her face has healed, and take her out on the town."

"Fine." He stood up from the bed and walked toward the large window that went from the floor to the ceiling. "Have you seen my new billboard?"

"Yes, it is quite impressive."

"I think it is going to serve its purpose. I need all of the haemans in Russia to join my army, to join the cause. I have a creeping suspicion that one day, the continued existence of the condemned will be my downfall. They know too much and since they aren't aligned with us, they must be eliminated. I want their annihilation to be swift and effortless."

"Even if you only got half the haemans to move into the forests with you, you'd still wipe them out easily."

"I know, but I want it to be epic. I want it to be so easy we get a good laugh in as we murder them."

"Do you plan to find Leonid before or after this raid takes place?"

"Hopefully before. I still have my people scouring the forests for him. Kirill has been training men to search the outskirts for Leonid's face. They don't know why they are looking for him—nobody except Kirill, the nurses, and I know of your sickness—but these men have been instructed to return him to St. Petersburg unharmed. I am hoping he will turn up before I infiltrate the rest of the condemned."

"I hope so, too."

"Don't worry, I am going to have you healed." He walked to her side, "This will not be the end of your reign."

Milena looked up at him with her wide, hazel eyes and gave him a small smile. Her chapped lips cracked and began to bleed. She licked her lips, cleaning the tiny trickle of blood off them, then returned to her normal somber expression. Mikhail offered her a hand and helped her stand. The dress she wore was a heavy duvetyn and weighed more than she did. He gave her a light kiss on the cheek.

"I have arranged a session to have pictures taken of me in front of my new billboard. I must go, but please rest. I do not want you getting any more fragile than you already are."

"Of course. I will plan my day with Arinadya from the comfort of my bed."

"Don't plan more than you can handle."

"I can save up enough energy for one day out of this suffocating palace."

He kissed her again on the forehead then left. Milena returned to her bedroom and removed her weighty dress. The slip beneath felt light as air on her skin. She laid her tired bones upon her bed and the small dose of blood she licked off her lips snuck into the corners of her brain. She fell into a deep nap laced with terrifyingly magnificent dreams.

Chapter 17

A few days passed since Arinadya left her temporary prison for the night and found the lagoon. It had been glorious, minus her unexpected and unwelcomed stalker. She managed without much difficulty to push Sevrick back into the recesses of her mind and regain her normal composure. The wound on her face was healing with the help of some medicine the royal doctors delivered to her. There was still a faint bruise around her right eye but it was vanishing at a steady pace.

Finding the lagoon was a blessing in disguise. She needed to escape in a terrible way and that little adventure was just enough to get her through the next day without doing anything drastic. Seeing Sevrick was a slight set back but nothing she wasn't used to recovering from. He always popped up unannounced and probably always would. And although she was growing accustomed to dealing with him now, she knew the time was coming that she'd need to find a way to truly make him stop forever. He could not show up unannounced once she lived at the Winter Palace with the prince. If he did, he would be killed. Though she tried to tell herself she did not care whether he lived or died, deep down she did not want the burden of his death on her hands; she already hurt him enough. If there was any sliver of humanity left in her, it was that she did not want to destroy him any further. Perhaps for selfish reasons or perhaps for his benefit, she did not know; nor did she have the energy to dissect her intentions.

The sun came through her living room windows as she sat on a high stool at her kitchen counter top. She enjoyed the past few days with no interaction from the prince. Things were almost beginning to feel normal again.

Then a knock came from her front door and Arinadya's short reign of peace came to a screeching end. She took a deep breath then opened the door.

"May I come in?" Princess Milena stood at her doorstep sporting a dazzling smile.

Shocked, Arinadya nodded and stepped aside. Milena strolled into her apartment in her stilettos and sleek dress, then stopped upon reaching the kitchen. Arinadya closed the door behind her and the princess removed her large floppy black hat. Jewels of green and purple cascaded along the sides of her hair through chains of gold. Her light brown hair beneath was wavy and gleamed in the sunlight.

"It's nice to finally meet you Arinadya," she smiled, brilliant white teeth exposed and eyes glowing.

"You as well, princess." Arinadya was at a loss for words. She always knew she'd meet the princess eventually but she never expected to be caught off guard like this. Princess Milena stood in her humble and untidy apartment looking like a supermodel while

Arinadya was in pajama shorts, an oversized t-shirt, and had her hair in a messy bun. "I have been looking forward to getting to know you," Arinadya maintained her composure. "I'm sorry I'm so disheveled, I was not expecting company."

"My apologies. I should have called but I knew you were confined to your home the past few days." Milena looked with intention at her wounded eye. "So I thought a little company might do you some good."

"Yes, well, it is almost healed. I am looking forward to being out and about again," Arinadya lied. She loved having a few days with minimal social interaction.

"Well, if you want, I can help you cover up the remnants of that bruise and we can have a day out on the town."

To anyone else, she'd decline, but a small part of her was excited to spend the day with her former idol. Plus, she couldn't say no to the princess.

"Of course."

Milena reached into her crystal-covered clutch and pulled out concealer and powder. She sat Arinadya down on one of the kitchen stools and got to work.

The princess's fingertips against the skin of her wound caused her some discomfort, but it didn't take long before Milena was satisfied with her work. Arinadya looked in a mirror and was amazed how thoroughly she covered the remaining bruise. While she was happy the makeup disguised it like magic, it also concerned her that the prince had a right hand "man" who was very good at covering up his dirty work. Perhaps this would be the routine she was destined to live for the remainder of her life; Mikhail beats her, Milena covers it up.

"Let me pick out an outfit for you and we will go." Milena headed into the bedroom while Arinadya waited in the kitchen. She came out with a dress made of sheer silver fabric. Rhinestones covered the area over her breasts and the hem fell above her knee. She also carried out her normal blood stilettos and a thick white headband covered in pearls and diamonds. Arinadya changed into this outfit. Milena helped her tie the headband into her red hair and they headed out to the car Milena had waiting for them.

As the driver began to head away from Arinadya's apartment, Milena placed her floppy black hat on the seat next to her and rested her head against the leather headrest. The two women sat in silence for a while as the driver headed toward Milena's favorite shopping destination: Alexander Strip.

"Why did you choose to become haeman?" Milena asked, breaking the silence. "Everybody has a reason, something that convinced them. What was yours?"

Arinadya looked at the princess skeptically; she did not want to reveal too much. If Milena found out she chose to become haeman in order to be more like her, she would lose complete control in this new friendship. She could not let Milena have the upper hand on her like Mikhail already had.

"The fashion," Arinadya finally answered. "It was new and beautiful and exciting. It was overwhelming and I wanted to be a part of it."

A wicked smile crept across Milena's face, like she was on to Arinadya and detected the previous fascination she once had with her.

"I love that answer." Milena placed a hand on Arinadya's shoulder and whispered in her ear. "You have succeeded. You fit the role perfectly. It's why Mikhail chose you out of thousands to stand by his side." There was something very mysterious, and slightly devious, about Milena, but nothing Arinadya couldn't handle.

An old feeling from her early days as a haeman arose inside her chest. She felt pride and accomplishment. The woman she once aspired to be like was recognizing her as one of them. Though she did not let any of these juvenile feelings show on her face, a small part inside of her couldn't help but feel giddy.

"Now, I have heard you and the prince are not hitting it off as smoothly as he hoped. What is the problem?"

"He is very difficult to be with."

Milena smiled. "He says the same of you. Why can't you love him?"

"Love?"

"Yes. Love. You do know what love is, right?"

"Of course I do, but you speak of love like it still exists."

"You don't think it has a place in our world?"

"No. It vanished along with the condemned. It no longer lives in this city."

"Interesting," Milena said thoughtfully. "Well, if you cannot love my brother, then you must find some common ground. Some way to tolerate him. Otherwise you are in for a long and torturous life."

Arinadya took a deep breath. She had no retort for this. She knew it to be true.

Milena continued, "Perhaps if you place your focus on something else, the whole process will be easier. Maybe even enjoyable."

"Like what?"

"Well, you got into this lifestyle for the fashion, so why not embrace that part of this new life? Focus on the fame and the admiration you are receiving from the public. They all love you, revel in it. The attention is intoxicating. It's a whole different kind of high and I am positive you'd enjoy it if you let yourself take part in it instead of hiding out in your apartment when you aren't on dates with Mikhail."

Arinadya was unsure. She liked her solitude and couldn't fully understand how people prying into her everyday life would feel like a good thing.

"Let me show you," Milena said, recognizing Arinadya's uncertainty. "Today will be the first step. I know Mikhail is your new partner but we can be a fierce duo as well. I am gorgeous, you are gorgeous, together we could draw in millions," Milena smiled, her beauty radiated. "You will see."

"Alright," Arinadya said. She was intrigued by the proposition, but thought it best to keep her guard up in case.

"And perhaps my company will be more tolerable than Mikhail's."

Arinadya laughed. "It already is."

The car pulled up to the corner of Kronverkskiy Road at the edge of Alexander Park. Arinadya could already see the herd of haemans beginning to gather around Milena's limo. She looked at the princess with trepidation and saw that Milena was already putting on the façade she wore for the public. Her usual scowl melted into a stoic smile, one that made her appear elegant yet unreachable. She was sitting up straight and looking at a mirror to make sure the chained jewels upon her head fell within her hair as she liked. She then took a tube of red lipstick out of her purse and handed it to Arinadya.

"Red is your color. Put this on." Arinadya carefully spread the lipstick across her plump lips. Milena continued, "Remember, it's all about confidence. You are with us now. Make sure to carry yourself with an air of unattainability."

Milena led the way out of the limo and into the madness. Even in the daylight, the flashes from the paparazzi cameras were blinding. A few times, the light reflected off all the gems and jewels Milena wore, causing Arinadya to squint in pain.

"Excuse us," Milena shouted as she pulled Arinadya through the crowd. People shouted and screamed for their attention but they ignored them all. Milena held Arinadya's hand and dragged her forward until they escaped most of the crowd. Eventually, they gained enough distance and the paparazzi got the hint to photograph from afar. Despite the space, they were still being watched and people approached them occasionally. Milena was always gracious if the individual was respectful. But overall, the madness ceased.

They walked along the outer edge of the street where it curved. Years ago it had only been a park, but since the Romanov's reclaimed their status as the royals of Russia, Princess Milena began to reshape the city. Kronverkskiy Road bordered one entire half of the park and Milena transformed it into a small fashion district. The shops were plenty and varied in different haeman styles. Arinadya was very excited to look into some new jewelry because the scars around her ankles weren't healing as fast as they used to.

"Where to first?" Milena asked.

"I need a new device to collect my blood." She stuck her ankle out for the princess to see.

"Yes, I see. Let's try Avilov's. He has the best assortment of beautiful blood devices. They keep to the traditional Faberge style, so all his pieces have a royal flair to them," she smiled at Arinadya. "We will find you a new place to collect your scars."

Arinadya smiled back. She was thinking her neck, or maybe her thigh. She wasn't sure but was looking forward to seeing some new options.

They walked into the store and were greeted by Mr. Avilov himself. He was a short, old man with a red tint in his light brown eyes. His cheeks were hollow and his gray hair was thinning. He wore a rose gold belt with a bejeweled glass bottle attached to his hip. This was similar to what the prince and other rich men wore to collect their blood. The belt cut into the skin around the hips and the hollow tubes along the inside of the belt collected the blood and drained it into a small opening at the back of the bottle. He approached them with a wide smile and kissed the back of Princess Milena's hand.

"Welcome back, princess!" His voice was old and squeaky. "What do I have the pleasure of assisting you with today?"

Milena retracted her hand from his grip and maintained her pleasant yet distant composure.

"This here is Arinadya. She will be added to our account and can come anytime she wishes to purchase some of your fine jewelry."

"Of course." Mr. Avilov grabbed Arinadya's hand and kissed it. "I have read all about you in the papers. Your beauty isn't given full justice in the paparazzi's pictures." His eyes shimmered up at Arinadya who was taller than him in her heels. She followed Milena's lead and remained cool and collected.

"I need to find a new device to collect my blood. I have gathered a sufficient amount of scars around my ankles and they are no longer healing as they should. They are reopened too often." Mr. Avilov glanced down at Arinadya's ankles and tightened his lips.

"You are right. Follow me and I will show you some of the new pieces that arrived earlier this week."

They followed him to a glass showcase counter filled with cuff bracelets covered in different kinds of gems.

"This is the newest thing in from Moscow. They are cuffs fitted to wrap around your wrist perfectly. When you need blood, you simply twist the cuff slightly, it makes small incisions, and you have a dose of blood that can be licked right off your wrist."

"I can't walk around like the average haeman anymore with blood dripping from random places throughout the day and staining my clothes. I need something a bit more discreet," Arinadya said.

"She is right. We conduct our blood intake with style and grace. We have a standard to live up to. Scars are fine, visible blood and clothing stains are not," Milena added.

"Okay," Mr. Avilov said, self-consciously gripping the bottoms of his own blood stained sleeves as he led them to a different case. "Here we have earrings that cuff the entire earlobe." He took out a pair that were clear diamond with gold trim and showed the women the mechanics. "The earring goes in as any normal earring would, but these blades along both sides of the top make incisions into the skin. As the blood drips out, it is collected into the concave base of the earring. Same concept as letting water drip into a bowl. What's nice about the diamond pair is by the end of the day they look like crimson rubies." Arinadya held both earrings in her hand, each the size of a 50 kopeck coin. She really liked them.

"These are nice. They are inconspicuous too. Can I see what else you have?"

He led them to a third glass case filled with shining necklaces that sparkled in all different colors. Arinadya immediately held her breath so she did not appear too awed, but she had never seen so many jewels in one sitting before. Being escorted through a jewelry boutique and actually being able to purchase and take home some of the finer pieces was a new feeling. She usually shopped at the mid-level stores that carried the knock offs, so this experience was a treat. One she could certainly get used to.

Mr. Avilov pulled out a simple egg pendant covered in sapphires.

"This one is a nice piece to store blood in. You put a small dose in a vile," he twisted and tilted the egg so it opened, "store it inside the pendant, and you have a backup supply in case of an emergency." He placed the necklace back into the case and pulled out another. "This one operates quite differently." The necklace he now held was two strings of pearls held together with diamond encrusted vertical bars and a large garnet jewel at the center. He placed it around Arinadya's neck and it fit like a choker. "This necklace works only when you activate it. May I demonstrate?"

"Yes, proceed."

Mr. Avilov pinched the top and bottom of the garnet stone, activating a secret trigger that caused small spikes to pop out of the back of the large gem. He firmly pressed the jewel into Arinadya's throat and she could feel the blood begin to flow. She was about to protest for fear it was going to cause a mess, but the blood did not drip down her chest like she thought it would.

"The spikes behind the jewel have small holes in them. As long as they are securely inserted into the skin, the blood will continually filter into the pearls. The pearls are hollowed out and connected by little tiny tubes." His aged eyes lit up as he excitedly explained the science behind this particular device. "So when you feel like drinking, you just carefully remove the necklace, unclasp it, and let the blood inside the pearls drip into a cup, or your mouth if you are alone. Whatever suits you, of course," he smiled at her. "This device is not always the cleanest; when you remove the garnet from your skin you'll need a handkerchief to absorb the residue that is bound to drip out, but it is a lovely piece. And it is very clean until its removal."

"What is the maximum amount of blood it can hold?" Arinadya inquired.

"Up to three ounces."

That was more than enough. She quite liked it. It was simple enough to wear every day and could collect enough blood to keep her satisfied.

"There is one more item I would like to show you. I saved it for last as I think it is the best in our shop at the moment." He led them to a vertical case with rows and rows of dazzling watches. He pulled out a thin watch with a band made of solid emeralds. At the face of the clock were two serpent heads with ruby eyes.

"I know watches are untraditional as blood collection devices, but when I heard of these, they were so spectacular I had to get a supply shipped to my boutique."

"How do they work?" Milena asked.

"They each collect blood in different styles but the overall concept is the same. The wearer of the watch programs it and picks the times at which it draws blood. This serpent watch is a clever one. Let's say you set it for noon. At that time, both snake heads will rise and strike down upon your skin, piercing it and drawing blood. Every 15 minutes for one hour the heads will reposition their bite to continue the flow of blood. You can change this setting to be more or less frequent depending on if you have it set to hit a vein or not. The blood is filtered through the teeth and into the hollow band. This particular watch can also hold up to three ounces. My variety of watches can hold anywhere from one to seven ounces."

Milena was intrigued as well. "Show me your smallest watch."

He handed the emerald snake watch to Arinadya then took out a yellow gold chain that was covered in tiny amethysts. The face of the watch was a small oval framed by slightly larger amethysts. He handed it to the princess.

"This works similarly to the serpent watch except there are no snake heads," he explained. "This watch has small prick points along the inside of the band that draw and filter blood into the inside of the wristband."

Milena's eyes glowed with greed. "I'll take that one." She looked at Arinadya. "Do you like the emerald snake watch?"

"Yes, very much. It's my favorite one here."

"Wonderful. We will take both watches, the earrings, and the necklace." Arinadya could not hide her shocked facial expression this time; she was getting all of the jewelry? But no one else blinked an eye at this exchange.

The shop owner smiled, happy to benefit from such a large purchase. He took the earrings out of Arinadya's grasp and the necklace from around her neck. He handed her a handkerchief to clean her skin, then dipped the used necklace into the sterilizing device out of habit. Once it was clean, he brought all the jewelry up to the register.

Milena ran her fingers down Arinadya's golden spine tattoo, which was visible due to the low back of her dress, then whispered into her ear, "Follow me."

She took her to a dark corner of the shop, a place Mr. Avilov had not pointed out before. Princess Milena spoke slowly, appearing to choose her words very carefully.

"Before I was put on a special diet, I used these." She picked up a solid gold ring that was melted and bent to have a very sharp design on it. She placed it upon her finger. "For those of us in the council, the golden tattoos marking our kills are our trophies, but so are the scars we collect. And I used to enjoy making my own, unique scars." She swung her arm downward and violently slashed the ring a few centimeters away from her leg. She made no gash but Arinadya got the point. Princess Milena liked to make her own incisions; she liked to collect blood however she wished. "I never liked being restricted to specific jewelry to get my blood because there are only so many locations the jewelry can leave its mark. If you want original scars, unlike anybody else's, you need to make them yourself." Her eyes glimmered with deep-rooted mischievousness that Arinadya had not seen in the princess until this moment. It only lasted a second before it vanished and she slipped the ring off her finger. "Let's go. We've had enough fun in this shop for the day."

Mr. Avilov billed the expensive pieces to the royal account and they left his store. They continued walking along the edge of the park and Kronverkskiy Road, and stopped into the best dress shops. Milena had Arinadya try on a few wedding gowns and even let the paparazzi get a decent view from the front window of the store. Arinadya studied Milena's skilled manipulation of the media hounds; they followed her everywhere, but she never lost control of them. They got the pictures she allowed them to get. They knew when to be seen and heard and when to remain discreet. They obeyed her silent orders from afar. As the women continued their day of shopping, Arinadya paid close attention to the way the princess carried herself in public. There was a way about her that kept the hordes of admirers at bay; as Milena wished it to be. An icy glare and a slight flare of her nostrils was enough warning for any cameraman to know his presence was not welcome at that particular moment. But when she wanted their attention, they were always ready in the shadows, eager to get her picture.

Arinadya had to learn this technique, or at least build this kind of rapport with the public on her own. It was important she be left alone when she needed space, otherwise she would go insane.

They were having a highly successful shopping spree. Many purchases were made and after their third stop at an expensive wine gallery, Milena phoned for someone to come and collect what they purchased thus far. From then on, two men followed them with duffel bags and a cart to carry any other purchases the two women made. Another two hours passed before Arinadya noticed the complexion and stamina of the princess started to falter. Any color that had been in her pale face at the beginning of the day was gone and her eyes looked tired. Milena's breathing became heavier and she wasn't talking as much.

Arinadya did not want to make the princess feel uncomfortable so she did not ask her if she was okay, but she could tell something was wrong. Before Arinadya had more time to wonder about the state of her well-being, Milena abruptly parked herself on a vacant park bench.

She smiled up at her as if she felt perfectly fine.

"I hope you don't mind that I have to cut our day short. Mikhail made me promise that I would have you back to him by 5 p.m. He wants to take you out to a fancy dinner."

"Of course." Any curiosity she had about Milena's sudden lack of energy disappeared and was replaced with the dread of having to spend another evening with the prince.

The car drove around the bend of Kronverkskiy Road, picked up the two women, and brought them back to the Winter Palace. Milena gave Arinadya a brief goodbye and headed straight to her bedroom. Arinadya waited for Mikhail to make his entrance for their date. He made her wait 15 minutes before appearing at the top of the grand staircase. He took his time as he made his way toward where she waited on a stiff couch in the foyer beneath a grandiose chandelier made of fine crystals. The light shimmered off them and onto her face, causing the spots of luminosity to dance across her body. Prince Mikhail smiled at her wickedly.

She stood so she wasn't at a disadvantage once he was upon her. He grabbed her chin and tilted her face up toward him.

Tenderly, he asked, "Did you have a nice day with my sister?"

"I did."

"Wonderful. Tonight will be just as good." He let go of her face. "I am taking you out to a fancy dinner. Milena had you buy a long evening gown, correct?"

"Yes," she answered, slightly annoyed that Milena had been working under Mikhail's orders.

"Put that on and meet me back here. The chauffer put all the purchases you made today in the spare bedroom at the end of the hall." Mikhail pointed down the long first floor corridor of the west wing and Arinadya made her way to the room with her dress in it.

She reemerged in a strapless gold gown that held tight to the shape of her body. The top pressed her breasts up, creating large cleavage, and the bodice of the gown was elaborately covered in golden beads. As she entered the foyer where the prince still stood, the light from the dim chandelier hit her again, creating a lightshow along the walls from its reflection off her dress.

Mikhail's eyes lit up; he was hungry for her. He swallowed a lump in his throat like he was suppressing an urge to rip the dress right off her. With much control, he extended a hand to Arinadya and escorted her through the large front doors of the palace and into his car. His show of restraint pleased Arinadya and she was already feeling more optimistic about their date.

Viktor drove them to Pelkin, one of the finest restaurants in St. Petersburg. It was known for its sophisticated interior and ambience that resembled life within an aristocrat's home during imperial times. Eating there was said to make you feel like royalty.

They got out of the car and made the usual walk through a herd of paparazzi. Mikhail enjoyed the chaos of the crowds more than Milena did; he did not have any secret way of warding them off. Instead, he reveled in the attention, absorbing every ounce that the masses threw at him. Once inside, Arinadya realized he reserved the entire restaurant for their date. The only other people in the building were the concierge and wait staff.

They were escorted upstairs into a private room lit by candles and a roaring fireplace. A jazz trio played in the darkness of the far corner of the room. As the waiter sat them at their table, the light from the fire illuminated half their bodies, leaving the other half in the flickering shadows of the table's candelabra.

"I don't mean to frighten you," Mikhail said after the waiter took their drink order and left.

Arinadya laughed. "Frighten? I am not the slightest bit scared of you."

Mikhail smirked. "Alright then. I guess I meant to say I don't like seeing you struggle with our arrangement. I would like to find a way to make you happier. I want you to be a willing and enthusiastic participant."

"Well, you could start by taking your aggression out on someone else. I can't live in hiding because your temper is continually displayed across my face. The solution is easy: If you don't want people to think you're a monster, then stop being one. I have a company to run and I need to be present on a daily basis." He stared at her blankly and Arinadya continued with a heavy sigh. "You've stripped me of all control. I have no voice, I have no say in anything that is happening, and it's overwhelming. I am trying to play along, but I have a very small fuse and all you've been doing is taunting me with lit matches. I don't want to fight this but I am not going to be your obedient slave, bowing down to your every whim and request."

"I see," Mikhail said thoughtfully. He didn't seem too concerned with how his behavior was pushing her to the brink, but he tried his best to pretend like he truly heard her. "I will work on it."

"You chose me. I didn't choose you. If you want to get me on board with the whole damned charade, you have to bend to my rules and wants as well."

Mikhail raised his eyebrows at her, intrigued by the reappearance of her strength. It had been absent for a while.

"I see a day out with my sister did you some good."

"Yes." Arinadya remained guarded. "It was a nice break from you."

Mikhail feigned a playful frown.

"You hurt my feelings." He did not care one bit if he was pushing her too hard or too fast, but he needed to keep playing like her feelings mattered. At least until the wedding. Arinadya needed to appear strong for the public, but behind closed doors she was his to treat however he pleased. One day she'd get it but now was not the time.

"On to better topics of discussion," Mikhail said with a fake smile. "As you know, Milena is excited to start planning the wedding. I'm sure she talked about it this afternoon."

"She did. She even had me try on wedding gowns."

"Fantastic. The date needs to move up. It has to happen sooner."

"Sooner? Why?" Her throat swelled from the pressure. The looming nuptials would end any sliver of freedom she had left.

He did not want to tell her of Milena's sickness; it wasn't any of her business.

"Political reasons."

"Because of this war you plan to wage on the condemned?"

Mikhail was relieved; she set him up with the perfect alibi.

"I need to have all my affairs in order before I make my first move. I need you to be my bride. Once I am married it will 'prove' to everyone that I am honorable and trustworthy, hence why you are so important to me." He flashed her an evil smile before continuing. "Not to mention the people of St. Petersburg already love you and once I have you securely on my side, I am positive I will be able to win the loyalty of those who were previously skeptical of me. They will see me as someone they can respect and my army will grow tenfold."

She was a toy in his games, a trophy for his arm. But she supposed she already knew that. She tried to remind herself that she could take the fabulous lifestyle and only deal with Mikhail when he was around. She had to assume she'd be left alone most of the time anyway, except for public appearances, which Mikhail would have to be on his best behavior for. She knew he would never love her, and she would never love him. This marriage was for power and status. It was for survival. She could have all she ever dreamed of and more with the last name Romanova.

"I will promise to treat you the best I know how," he said upon seeing her deep in thought.

Coming from him, it wasn't much of a promise, but she'd take it. She gave him a smile as the waiter came out with their glasses of red wine and a diamond-encrusted plate with two lines of silve on it.

The waiter left them alone with the musicians once more. The soft music bridged the silence between them, accompanied by the unsteady crackle of the fireplace. Mikhail took her hands and squeezed them with the intention of giving her some reassurance. Instead, he bruised her fingers. She took a deep breath and accepted his promise to try. Perhaps things would get better. Perhaps she could find a home in his world after all.

Chapter 18

Life at the white elm was moving slowly. No progress had been made on the two haemans they had in captivity, and as more time passed the more it seemed like they were losing the female. She was dying and they still couldn't figure out what they needed to do differently to help her survive the withdrawal.

Sevrick sat in the corner of the laboratory, watching Leonid work. Leo was there every day, monitoring the subjects and attempting new methods to see if any improved the rehabilitation process, but he continued to strike out. Ruslan and Alexsei were by his side now, reading off the vitals as he took hasty notes. A few years ago, a group of the Clandes managed to steal a significant amount of medical equipment from the city. With the help of a few solar panels they hid amongst the dense top of the white elm, Pasha, who was a skilled electrician in St. Petersburg before they all escaped, managed to filter electricity into the laboratory below.

Lizaveta sat next to Sevrick and together they watched the three men do the same failed techniques with no new results. Sevrick let out a heavy sigh, running through everything he knew about the rehabilitation process in his head. There had to be something they were missing. Some small detail that could change everything.

After a few moments of deep thought, Sevrick mumbled, "Their blood is just ruined."

Lizaveta furrowed her eyebrows at him and Leonid looked up from his notepad.

"What did you say?" Leonid asked.

Unaware he had spoken out loud, he repeated himself more clearly.

"Their blood is ruined." He looked around the room at the quizzical faces now staring at him. "They need new blood."

"A blood transfusion," Leonid said, though mostly to himself.

"Wouldn't a blood transfusion only make the withdrawal worse? Speed up their need for more drugs?" Alexsei inquired.

"In normal cases, yes," Leonid said, his mind racing. "But this is a new addiction. These are rare cases. The blood *is* the drug, so maybe we just need to swap it out for clean blood."

"There is still cocaine in their systems though," Ruslan pointed out.

"Yes," Leonid nodded fervently. "The minimal users, those whose only intake of silve cocaine came from the public water or those damned 'vitamins', can probably be cured with a simple blood transfusion. The level of cocaine is low within their systems, so it shouldn't be too hard to flush out." Leonid paused. "The real task is going to be healing the haemans who were snorting silve or injecting their blood back into their systems, especially the ones that have been marked. I still believe a blood transfusion will help jump start the process and heal the haemanism, but then we still have to rehabilitate them from the cocaine withdrawals which could become more intense due to the blood swap. I also don't know what factor the silve will play into all of this. It is a very strong chemical; Kirill is a brilliant chemist. I can only hope the blood transfusion wipes away the effects of the silve along with the haemanism." Leonid was deep in thought. "I don't know if that will increase their withdrawal or stop it, it's never been tried with an addiction like this. The main factor is the consumption of contaminated blood, so it's plausible to hypothesize that replacing their dirty blood with clean blood could solve everything."

"The only way to know is through trial and error. Do you have the supplies you need to conduct a procedure like this?" Ruslan asked.

"I need catheters and a few more IV's. I could always use more needles and tubes too. We need to keep everything as sterilized as possible."

"Alright. So there needs to be a hospital raid. I'm heading up to the living space to assign Nikolai and Zakhar to this task." Ruslan left, excited they had a new plan.

"I'll go update the other troop leaders and let them know our idea." Alexsei left as well. Only Leonid, whose nose was deep into his notebook, Lizaveta, and Sevrick remained in the laboratory.

The silence was awkward but it was better than talking. Eventually, Lizaveta broke it.

"If this works, will you go back for her again?" Her big, brown eyes were focused intently on Sevrick's reaction.

"Even if it doesn't work, I will. I will always go back for her."

Lizaveta silently took in his answer. She accepted defeat a while ago but could never seem to deafen the small part inside that still hoped. There was a tiny sliver within her heart that wanted so badly to have her affections returned. She kept reminding herself it was out of her control, but she could not silence this yearning, no matter how hard she tried.

"We used to be such good friends," she finally said. "I'm sorry I ruined it."

"You didn't ruin anything," he insisted. "We can fix it."

"I don't think so." Her eyes began to glimmer; her eyelashes were wet but the tears did not fall. "It has hurt too deeply for too long. I don't think you will ever realize how you affected me and I cannot be friends with someone who is blind to the hurt they have caused me."

Sevrick's face showed remorse for the first time. There was a barrier he placed between himself and Lizaveta and this was the first time he felt its presence. He shut her out, with callous disregard, as if her feelings would infect him. As if they were a disease he did not want to catch. It was crazy to shun her like a plague, she couldn't sway his love for Rina, but he supposed dealing with her pain was too much on top of his own. It was easier to ignore. They were good friends once; he never meant to make her feel unimportant.

"I'm sorry."

"It's not your fault," Liza said, standing up and gently placing her long, dark brown curls behind her ear. "I knew better."

She left before he could say anything else. Without looking up from his notebook, Leonid spoke.

"Hopefully that was enough to remove the blinders you've been wearing."

"What is that supposed to mean?"

Leonid removed his nose from the book and pushed his reading glasses to the top of his pallid blond hair.

"For the past five years, ever since you got here, you've been walking around unaware of your effect on people. You have tunnel vision, seeing only Rina in the light at the end. Sometimes I think you don't even recognize the friendships you've established here."

"Yes I have. You all are like family to me," Sevrick insisted.

"That may be true. But more days than not, you go into zombie-mode. Nothing anyone says can shake you out of it. And trust me, I get it. Nina and I lived what you are going through, and not even to the full extent of the torment you've been experiencing. But you can't forget that life will always go on." Leonid paused, his expression sympathetic but firm. "It doesn't mean you have to forget Rina or stop trying, but you can't push aside the people who have been caring for you through it all."

"That was never my intention," Sevrick became flooded with regret. These people were his family; he never meant to make any of them think they weren't as important to him as he was to them.

"All I am saying is you need to take more notice of where you are. If you're here with us, be here with us. Not lost inside your own head with memories of the girl you once loved."

Sevrick took a deep breath. Leonid was right. He knew it was a rare occasion that he was ever truly present in the moment. The guilt read clearly across his face. His friend continued, switching the subject to lighten the mood.

"Anyway, this is a great idea you came up with. I was so engrained with the knowledge that blood transfusions intensify an addict during withdrawal that it never even crossed my mind. But it could work. This is a whole new epidemic we are dealing with."

"Yeah, I really hope it does."

"If it does, we can save Rina," he said, reassuring his friend that he hadn't been encouraging him to give up on her. "It may be harder because you said she was marked, but we'd have a much better shot at it."

Hope filled Sevrick's chest once more.

"There is nothing I want more than to save her."

"I know. I am on your side. I've been in her shoes and I am grateful every day that Nina saved me. Once we bring her in and cleanse her blood, I'm sure she will be grateful to you as well. It's a terrible world in St. Petersburg and I can't even imagine how much worse it has gotten. But I can assure you, there is nothing more freeing than being released from haemanism. It is suffocating. And I think most of the haemans won't even realize how beat down they are by the addiction until they are released from it."

"There are moments when I can see the desire to escape in her eyes, but those moments come and go quickly and her eyes fog over any glimpse I catch of the girl I once knew." Sevrick shook his head. "But those moments still happen. Every time I see her. There is still a chance I haven't lost her forever, I am positive of it."

"I believe it," Leonid smiled supportively. "Let's hope Zakhar and Nikolai head out tonight. The sooner we get those supplies the better. I don't know how much longer these two haemans will last. I'd rather not have to start over with new test subjects."

Chapter 19

Nikolai and Zakhar wasted no time making their way to the city. Since it was going to be a quick and potentially easy raid, they decided they didn't need any others to join them. The hospitals in St. Petersburg were mostly vacant; only a few haemans on their deathbeds were checked-in as "patients". In reality, they'd never be cured; they were left in the hospitals to die. The idea of rescuing these haemans and trying to rehabilitate them at the white elm had been tossed around in the early years, but after attempting to kidnap these poor souls, and realizing how stubborn and opposed they still were to being anything other than haeman, the Clandes ceased the attempts. It wasn't worth the risk to their safety. Since these haemans were on their deathbeds, there was a good chance they wouldn't have survived the rehab anyway. It was reasonable to assume their organs were already damaged beyond repair.

It was 3 a.m. and the hospital was barren. The medical staff no longer worked night shifts so it was easy to take the supplies they needed. Zakhar found the supply cabinet and grabbed all the items Leonid listed. He looted the entire supply of catheters, IV's, needles, and tubes from this particular closet. Then he scoped out the rest of the items in the closet: boxes of band aids, multiple bottles of peroxide and rubbing alcohol, piles of folded bed sheets, spools of suture thread, tubes of topical antibiotic ointment, gauze, and a small clear box of surgical tools. He took it all.

While Zakhar made the raid, Nikolai kept an eye on the hallway. There wasn't a sound besides the occasional wheezing and coughing from the dying haemans in the rooms nearby. Nikolai ventured out of the shadows of the dark supply closet and into the hallway. Right across from where he stood guard was a patient room with an old haeman man inside. He looked to be about seventy years old and the sickness this addiction caused was running rampant on him. His skin was pale and flaking, his hair appeared to have fallen out unnaturally leaving clumps of brittle patches in random spots, and his bones protruded violently all over his body. He had thrown his blanket on the floor, leaving his skeletal body exposed. Only a thin layer of skin covered his bones, no muscle or fat left. Nikolai observed the sickly man through the window of the door he peered through.

The old haeman tossed and turned in his bed, uncomfortable in his tattered body. The sight of him made Nikolai ill. He was tempted to open the door and talk reason with the old man, but chose not to.

Nikolai's internal debate regarding whether to save the old man, who was probably too withered and fragile to survive rehab, or leaving him to die stopped when he noticed the old haeman staring at him from his bed. He had stopped moving and was lying still as stone with his mean gaze fixed directly upon Nikolai through the window. Nikolai only had time to notice that the whites of his eyes were now red before the decrepit haeman began screeching and flailing about in his bed again. He said no words, only shrill screams came from his mouth. His arms and legs flew violently against the mattress, but he remained in place; there would not be a chase. The haeman was tightly strapped to the hospital bed with a thick leather belt across his chest and pelvis.

Nikolai's heart raced as the haeman futilely protested him being there. He took two steps back from the door when the old haeman reached for a button above his head and slammed his fist against it. Immediately, the entire hallway came alive with sirens and flashing lights. Nikolai's heart froze. Zakhar exited the supply closet confused, a look of alarm on his face.

"What the hell happened?" he demanded of Nikolai.

"That old creep in there saw me watching him and hit some button!" Nikolai said frantically.

"What does it mean?"

"I think it means *run*."

They sprinted down the hallway toward a fire escape. If haemans were coming to investigate, going out through the front door was a bad idea. They ran at full speed through the fluorescent-lit hallways, Zakhar lagging a few steps behind with the large duffle bag of supplies over his shoulder. There was no staff around but they could hear the haemans thrashing about in their beds as they passed numerous patient rooms. The alarms sent them all into a state of pandemonium and their piercing cries were spine chilling. There were no nurses to attend to them at this hour but the alarms were clearly signaling the royal militia to the hospital.

Upon reaching the last corner, Nikolai slowed his pace until he came to a complete stop and then carefully inched the back door open. The alleyway was deserted.

"Coast is clear," he whispered and Zakhar followed him into the darkness. It was four in the morning and besides the blaring sirens emanating from the hospital, the city was asleep. They were nervous the noise would wake the neighboring area full of haemans but as soon as the door shut behind them, the noise became inaudible. Both men sighed in relief.

They wasted no time getting as far away from the hospital as possible. They stuck to back roads and alleys as they maneuvered their way toward the suburbs. They were about a kilometer away from the tree line when Nikolai stopped dead in his tracks, causing Zakhar to run right into him.

In front of them, about ten blocks away, was an enormous billboard. It was so big it blocked most of the sky from their vantage point. On it was a picture of Prince Mikhail with his typical devilish smile. His hands were covered in blood and he was pointing a finger toward Karelian Isthmus; the forest beyond the city of St.

Petersburg, the home of the Clandes. The billboard was positioned so the prince was pointing in the perfect direction. The billboard was even altered so his arm and finger were off the main frame and extended beyond it.

Beneath the large picture of the prince was a declaration of war so haunting, they shivered as they read it.

BLESSED BE OUR VEINS BY WHICH WE RID THIS WORLD OF MISUSE

Chapter 20

10 years earlier

It was the last day of high school and Sevrick Bykovsky was surrounded by friends. He was graduating with honors and moving on to study criminal justice at St. Petersburg State University. With his grades, he could have gone anywhere but he did not want to go far. His mother Dafna was sick with no one to take care of her except him. His father ran off when he was only four and he had no siblings. His extended family lived across the country in Yakustk so the two of them were always on their own. A year ago, his mother became very ill with stomach cancer. She was only forty, and since this disease was uncommon for someone her age, they did not catch the cancer fast enough to eradicate it. Now the doctors had her going to the hospital for continual preventative surgeries and treatments to slow the rate at which the cancer was taking over her body. It was tiring for Dafna and heartbreaking for her son.

"SEVRICK BYKOVSKY."

The principal said his name into the microphone and Sevrick stood up to take his turn. He could see his mother in the crowd, sitting on the bleachers and watching him with a huge smile across her face. He left his group of friends, walked on stage, and received his diploma. She waved at him from a distance and blew him multiple kisses. Without shame, the young man smiled and blew her a kiss back. Dafna caught his kiss and placed it over her heart. He loved her more than he loved himself. Tears of pride rolled down her cheeks and she used the bottom of her headscarf to wipe them away.

The crowd cheered as he shook the principal's hand and walked off the stage. He was adored in his community, beloved for his kindness and perseverance. Despite how handsome he was, he never let it affect how he treated others. Most times, he was barely aware of his own good looks. Sevrick did not care much for such shallowness; he had a hard life and knew there were much deeper things he craved from life than the pettiness that generally consumed the other attractive people his age. He picked his friends based off their virtues. He surrounded himself with people who valued life as he did. And most of all, his world was consumed with getting his mother healthy again. He did not know how he could go on without her if she did not beat the cancer. She was all he ever had and he did not want to lose her now.

The principal continued calling students on stage to receive their diplomas. Sevrick was supposed to sit back down in his assigned seat amongst his classmates, but instead he made his way into the crowd of spectators to sit with his mother.

"Hey, mamochka," he smiled at her and placed his long arm around her. She immediately rested her tired head into the nook of his shoulder. Her eyes were heavy and lined. It had only been a year but the cancer aged her tremendously. Though it frightened him, he knew she was still young and could muster up the energy to beat it. Especially if he was by her side, giving her the extra strength she needed.

"I am so proud of you," she said, grabbing his hand and kissing the back of it.

"Thanks," he responded, happy he had her with him to share this moment. She held onto his hand tightly as they watched the rest of the ceremony together.

As students continued to file on stage and receive their diplomas, his mind wandered. He held his mother tightly and scanned the crowd out of boredom. There were hundreds of people there; St. Petersburg was a big city with a regional high school that had thousands of students in attendance. In his grade there were nearly a thousand students graduating. Families filled the bleachers and cascaded onto both sides of the lawn that surrounded the stage.

Sevrick examined those who sat nearby to see if he recognized any family members of his friends. He was lost in a sea of foreign faces when he saw her. A few rows down and to the right of where he sat was a girl he never saw before. A girl so beautiful, he was having trouble averting his gaze. She had bright auburn hair, freckles all over her apple cheeks and a perfectly framed nose. Her smile illuminated the space between where she sat and where Sevrick watched her in awe. She was giggling at something a younger girl next to her said. When she turned to face the younger girl, Sevrick could see her bright blue eyes catch the sun's reflection.

His mother let out a loud, hacking cough, and the beautiful redhead turned to see where the noise came from. Sevrick was still admiring her and she caught him in the act. She gave him a shy smile then turned back around to face the ceremony.

Who was she? Why hadn't he seen her before? Was his school really that large? Adrik Tarasov's name was called on the loud speaker and the red headed girl and her family began to cheer extra loud, hooting and hollering Adrik's name.

Adrik, also red headed and freckled, walked up to get his diploma and Sevrick watched the girl clap and smile brightly as he entered and exited the stage. She must be his younger sister. Would Adrik introduce him? Sevrick didn't know; he had never been friendly with Adrik before. Plus, how would he even ask? *I noticed your sister at our graduation and I would love to take her out.* Sevrick shook his head. No, all that would get him was a nice punch to the face and a warning to stay away. Sevrick sighed, unsure of this new dilemma he faced. He was never too interested in having a relationship because he always had so much on his plate with school and taking care of his mother. But there was something about this girl that drew him in; he had to know her.

Dafna could feel Sevrick's occasional wistful sighs and recognized them as deep contemplations of matters of the heart.

Something she could recall feeling long ago in her younger years. She looked up at her handsome son who was longingly watching a pretty girl a few rows ahead of them. She looked at the girl carefully and could see the aura of positivity surrounding her as she laughed and joked playfully with her surrounding loved ones.

"She's very beautiful," Dafna said, hoping to get her son to open up so she could help him decipher what he was feeling.

"Yes, she is. I've never seen her before today."

"Well it's a good thing you're going to a college nearby. She looks a bit younger than you, so that gives you plenty of time to find out who she is and if you like her."

Sevrick looked at his mother quizzically; they never talked about girls before so it was a strange topic. She continued.

"You know, I am aware that I've become a burden for you. All these years of you holding down a part-time job to help with the household expenses hasn't been easy on you and taking care of me once I got sick has changed your life completely. I want to see you happy. I want to see you thrive and find your calling in life. And most of all, I would be overjoyed to watch you discover love. I don't know who that girl is down there or if she is right for you, but you've never taken much interest in dating before. If you don't give it a try, you'll never know."

Sevrick nodded. It was odd to get permission to start dating from his mother; he knew he didn't need it, but somehow what she just said released a weight that had been preventing him from pursuing anyone previously. Or maybe he really just hadn't been interested before. This was the first girl he ever saw that he felt inclined to know beyond friendship.

"Go talk to her," Dafna suggested, "Walk down there right now. Bite the bullet and find out what it is that's pulling you to her. She might reject you or she might feel it right away too."

"I can't just go down there and burst in on her with her family. It's something I need to do in private, not with an audience."

"Then catch her as we are all leaving. All you need is a five minute conversation to see if what you are feeling is real and reciprocated. If it is, you get her number and set up some time to get to know one another."

Sevrick sighed again, but this time it was relief. His mom was right. He didn't need to go through her brother or anybody else to meet this girl. He was eighteen and could be a man about it. He could walk right up to her and get to the bottom of it on his own.

The graduation ceremony was coming to an end. The principal was now calling out the last of the students and Sevrick was ready to make his move. The final student was called, the principal gave one last congratulatory comment, and the crowd began to disperse. Families started to filter through the bleachers so they could get to their students. Sevrick gave his mom a kiss on the forehead.

"Wish me luck. I'll find you after I talk to her."

His mother smiled back at him.

"I'll wait right here for you."

Sevrick took a deep breath and began jumping over rows and darting through the crowd to get to where the girl shuffled through with her family. The crowd was slow moving but she was a decent distance from him. He politely made his way through the masses, trying not to shove or push anyone aside too aggressively. When he finally reached her his heart stopped for a brief moment. As he was gathering his courage and preparing to tap her on the shoulder, she turned around and saw him standing there.

She smiled brightly at him. "Hi there." Sevrick was at a loss for words, so the girl continued, "You're Sevrick right? I'm Adrik's younger sister; he's in your grade. I'm a year below you guys."

"Yeah, I'm Sevrick and I know him. I saw you sitting a few rows in front me and I realized I never met you before." His deep blue eyes intensified as he grew even more interested in this girl.

"Yeah," she smiled, knowingly. "I saw you looking at me. My name is Arinadya but everyone calls me Rina."

"It's very nice to meet you, Rina," Sevrick was still in awe of her. She radiated confidence and there was a deep-rooted sweetness to her. "I'm not sure if you are already seeing someone, but if not, I would love to take you out on a date sometime."

Rina's eyes lit up at this suggestion and a giddy smile formed on her face.

"That sounds like fun."

Sevrick's heart trembled with excitement. He took out his cell phone and Rina gave him her phone number. The crowd around them seemed to disappear during this exchange. The space between them was electric and their initial chemistry was undeniable.

"Okay, Rina, I will give you a call and we can set up some time to go out," he smiled at her, his head on cloud nine.

"I look forward to it," she smiled back. Her eyes held his gaze for a few seconds and she smiled like her heart was afloat, too. In this moment, Sevrick knew his initial feelings were justified.

Rina turned back around and re-entered the crowd, shuffling toward the exit with her family. He watched her drift away from him and the noise from the crowd surrounding him reappeared.

Chapter 21

It had been almost two weeks since Sevrick went to see Rina and this length of break was more normal than the frequency he had recently been traveling into the city. It was typical that he would wait a month or two before heading back to check on her, but with all that was happening, Sevrick was much more anxious and eager to get Rina to agree to let them heal her at the white elm. When Zakhar and Nikolai returned from their raid, they informed the whole troop of the billboard they saw in the city. It was a declaration of war and Prince Mikhail had it plastered on a sign for all to see.

Sevrick had to sit alone in his room for an entire day before he could face his friends again; he couldn't control the panic attacks that continually snuck up on him after hearing this news. The prince was already stealing the woman he loved and now he was initiating war on the people who were family to him. The Clandes and other survivors truly posed no threat to the prince. They were at a disadvantage because their strength would never match up to that of the haemans, so why was the extinction of the survivors necessary?

Upon regaining control of his emotions, Sevrick re-emerged from the solitude of his dark bedroom and faced the day again. He had to save Rina, he could not waste any more time. The materials Zakhar and Nikolai stole for the blood transfusions proved to be life changing. The transfusions worked and the haemans that had been dying in rehab were now thriving as functioning members of the troop. They had moments where their bodies were still too weak to do much, but overall they were on a productive road to recovery. They even had good attitudes about the whole ordeal. After saving the first two haemans, the Clandes captured two more and completed successful rehabilitations with them as well. Four newly recovered haemans now lived at the white elm and all four were excessively grateful for being saved. They currently had three new haemans under sedation in the lab and their progress seemed to be going just as smoothly as it had for the previous four. Members of the troops were all taking turns donating blood, and since there were so many of them now, Leonid had a large collection of all blood types. Luckily, he only needed to give each haeman about four units of blood before their body began to adapt and the clean blood began diluting the toxic blood.

The time to save Rina was now. Her marriage to the prince was approaching fast and he needed to make her see reason before then. The moment she moved into the palace, Sevrick's mission to save her would become even more difficult.

He thought to ask if anyone wanted to go with him to St. Petersburg but he wasn't sure who to bring. Leonid was busy rehabilitating the haemans and Zakhar and Nikolai had journeyed to the city only a few weeks ago. Sevrick didn't think it was fair to ask either of them to go again. Elena already went with him once and Lizaveta was too emotional to bring into a situation like this. Ruslan and Alexsei were occupied with the expansion of their underground home. They already had added three new extensions. At the rate they were going, they could have enough room for the rest of the survivors before the end of winter.

Sevrick couldn't ask Pasha or Oksana to go with him; they were too old and the journey would be hard on them. Sofiya had to stay to watch Agnessa. And Isaak, Kira, and Maks were too young for this trip. He could ask Nina, but she was usually elbow deep in the expansion project or helping Leonid in the laboratory, so he didn't feel it was right to pull her away from such important tasks. Sevrick sighed, it was probably better that he go alone. Nobody wanted him to go back again anyway and every time he brought it up they found ways to convince him to wait. He bet if he did ask any of them to go, they'd all protest and tell him not to make the trip. Making the trip in secret was probably the only option.

Normally, having to go alone wouldn't bother him, but this trip was the most crucial visit of them all. He *had* to get Rina to leave with him this time. He couldn't let her stay behind any longer.

Sevrick went to his bedroom and packed a travel bag. As he was leaving, the only people sitting in the living space were Oksana and Pasha.

"Hey there, where are you off to?" Pasha asked as he noticed Sevrick's full backpack.

Sevrick sighed, he supposed telling them the truth wouldn't cause any harm. They wouldn't stop him from going and he'd be gone before they got the chance to tell the others.

"I'm headed into the city. I'll be back in about four or five days."

Oksana looked at him with concern in her old, wise eyes.

"You're going back for that girl again, huh?"

"You really ought to bring someone with you," Pasha added. "Things between us and the haemans are heating up. It couldn't hurt to have some back up in times like these."

"I considered it but everyone is tied up in other important matters. And most of them would be mad if they knew I was going; they think I need to get over it."

"Why don't you take me along?" Pasha asked. "I don't care that you're going after that girl again and I don't have too many jobs being thrown my way. Oksana here can vouch that I'm good company."

"It's a long journey," Sevrick said concerned. "Plus, I tend to use the time there and back to reflect in solitude. I took Elena once and completely ignored her the whole time. I felt terrible afterwards."

"Alright, suit yourself. But the offer still stands if you change your mind. It can't hurt to have a friend by your side."

"I appreciate it." Sevrick walked toward the large mahogany door that led to the exit hallway.

He gave them a nod of acknowledgment and left his underground home. Hundreds of people trained in the field but none of them noticed, or cared, that he was leaving. He made his way into the forest and kept up a brisk walk for as long as his energy would allow it.

He managed to make it to the city's edge in a day and a half, stopping to sleep only once. He left the white elm early in the day so it was afternoon when he arrived at St. Petersburg. He would have to wait until nightfall before he could make his way through the alleys to Rina's apartment, so he took a brief nap in the underbrush behind the tree line. By the time he woke up the sun was setting and he was able to maneuver his way through the shadows without being noticed.

Upon arriving at the back alley of her apartment, he made his usual climb up the fire escape and established himself outside her kitchen window. He peered in through the glass but the apartment was dark. She wasn't home. Sevrick lifted the windowpane, which Rina never locked, and let himself into her apartment. He crouched in the shadows, prepared to wait as long as necessary.

Hours passed. He was alone and unsure of when he'd get to see her. It was almost 2 a.m. before he heard commotion at the front door: the sounds of a fight. Fists slammed against the door as both Rina and the prince shouted at each other.

"Open the door and let me in," Prince Mikhail demanded, trying to control his temper but failing.

"I want to be alone tonight," Rina insisted. "Go home or I will cause a scene." Her voice became quieter when she made this threat. Sevrick wondered if a crowd was forming around them to watch this debacle. Surely a fight wouldn't be good press with the wedding looming over them.

No more words were exchanged; he could only hear a small scuffle outside, the clinking of keys, and the sound of the front door being unlocked. He remained motionless behind the kitchen counter, but could see what was happening from its edge.

Prince Mikhail had Rina in a tight embrace with his lips locked to hers. It wasn't a kiss; it was a muzzle. A sneaky way to silence her. She was in one arm and he opened the door with the other. Rina was fighting him off but the prince was stronger than her and he managed to make it look like a loving embrace for the crowd outside her apartment that watched intently. As soon as he shut and locked the door behind them, Mikhail grabbed Rina by the neck and threw her across the room. She landed on the glass coffee table causing it to shatter. The shards cut her, leaving her covered in blood.

"What is wrong with you?" she cried out.

"Don't you *ever* embarrass me like that in public again."

"I told you in the limo that I needed a night to myself. Yet you continued to try and force your way in after I said no," Rina's voice shook. Sevrick never heard her sound so weak before.

"Part of this little arrangement we have going on is that you no longer have the right to refuse me. You cannot say 'no' to me. I control you now."

Rina's temper was rising. She took a deep breath then spit in the prince's face. Mikhail let out a roar of fury before yanking Rina off the glass-covered floor by her hair and tossing her to the opposite side of the room. Rina looked like a rag doll as she hit the wall and fell. Sevrick's body began to shake with rage and it took everything in his power not to reveal himself in an attempt to fight off the prince.

Mikhail walked to where Rina's body lay crumpled against the ground. He stood over her and raised his fist above her head.

"This will be the *last* time you disobey me."

"You're drunk, stop!" Rina screamed at him but it didn't work. His fist came down hard against her cheek, causing her to whimper in pain.

"You need to learn your place. I own you now. Learn to accept it or else these lovely exchanges between us will become rituals."

"You mean they aren't already?" Rina managed to sneer as blood poured out of her nose and into her mouth.

"You're right." Mikhail paused in thought. "You really have been a naughty girl, haven't you?"

Rina was drinking all the blood that came from her nose, trying to regain her strength. But it wasn't working fast enough and Mikhail was now on his knees, unbuckling his belt. Before he removed his own pants, he reached a hand under Rina's skirt and ripped her underwear off.

"You're lucky I am so into you. My lust has overcome my rage." Then he pinned both her hands down against the ground and began to kiss the exposed skin above her breasts.

Sevrick could no longer control his fury; he was blinded with hate. He stood up from behind the counter and aimed his tranquilizer dart at the prince, who was too engrossed in molesting his former fiancée to notice. He pulled the trigger and the dart hit the prince in the thigh. Then he fired again, shooting him in the hip. To Sevrick's surprise, the prince didn't even feel the darts pierce his skin. He continued groping Rina until the sedative kicked in and caused him to fall into a heap on the floor.

Rina slowly stood up, still licking up the fresh blood that continued to pour down her face. At first she looked at Sevrick in shock, then her expression shifted to one of mischief. Her rejuvenated high was taking over.

"That was very bold of you. Unwise, but bold," she said, her courage slowly returning.

"It was bad enough to see him beat you. I couldn't let him rape you too," Sevrick explained, though he no longer saw Rina, only Arinadya.

"You should not have come back. I warned you numerous times." She slunk toward Sevrick, slowly and meticulously, like an animal hunting its prey. The cocaine-laced blood was taking over her brain, dramatically heightening her senses and reactions. "It was very, very unwise at this stage in the game."

"I know what you told me in the woods, but I have new information. I really can heal you now."

Arinadya slammed her fist against the marble counter top, cracking the stone beneath. She took a deep breath and composed herself once more.

"I am inclined to let you live for what you just did, but part of me also wants to rip out your throat for coming back after I told you to stay away."

For the first time, Sevrick was truly frightened to be around Arinadya as a haeman. Every other time he could feel Rina's presence, but this time was different. As soon as the prince went down, any notion that Rina was there in the room with him disappeared. Her bright blue eyes went dark.

She was a few feet from him now and her emotions were quickly becoming erratic from all the blood dripping into her mouth. Her vision was blurred and her peripherals were smothered in red.

His nerves were on edge as Arinadya came to stand right before him. They both breathed heavily, staring at one another without saying a word. Sevrick was staring down the monster, not the girl he once loved. He was holding his breath and she was biding her time, both anticipating the other's move. As discreetly as possible, he tried to reach for the gun he had foolishly placed upon the counter top after shooting the prince, but Arinadya didn't miss a beat. Her eyes immediately darted from his hand to the gun and she grabbed his throat and slammed him up against the wall. Sevrick struggled for air but her tight grip let no oxygen through. Her mouth curved into a wicked grin.

"It's been quite some time since I've had any control," she whispered into his ear as she squeezed his throat a little tighter. Her vision was now filled with red fog. "But oh, how sweet it is to feel strong again." Her eyes became brimmed with tears she was unaware were there; the blood's intoxication numbed their presence.

Sevrick's eyes began to close. As the light behind them dimmed, Arinadya let out a guttural howl.

"Fight back, damnit!" Her voice cracked as she screamed; furious that this was too easy, that this was not satisfying her need to be in control. All this time spent oppressed beneath Mikhail's will, she needed a fight she could win for a change. She needed a valiant opponent to crush and this was not satisfying her desire. It was not curing her desperate need for retribution.

The man she held in her grasp had become faceless; the redness of her fury washed out his features. A loud buzzing sound filled the inside of her head and the room started to spin around her and her victim. They spun in circles and the red fog became red streaks obstructing her sight, bleeding across her vision. Blood covered everything and she was choking on it, suffocating on her ruined life. The evil world she had created for herself was now shifting its devious head toward her demise. The blood covered her, falling over her like an endless night sky. There was no end. There was no way to stop it. And then the buzzing grew louder. So loud she missed the moment her conscience was ripped from the depths of her skull. She felt it happen but she could not stop it. She cried out in horror as she realized her mind no longer belonged to her; the demons living within her veins had finally taken that from her, too.

With all her might she willed the room to stop spinning. The man in her grip was on his last breath. She knew she should let him go but the demons had their claws pierced deep into her brain and wanted her to end his pitiful life.

"Give it back," Arinadya screeched at the demons within her, begging them to let her regain control of her mind. She hurtled the man out of her grasp and into the edge of the sharp marble countertop. He hit the pointed corner, slicing the edge of his eye and bruising his skull, but Arinadya noticed none of this. The red lines moved loosely now, staining her vision in unruly patterns as she frantically flailed about the kitchen, swiping at her own head, trying to beat the demons out of her brain.

As the effects of the blood she drank began to lessen, the buzzing grew dimmer. The room came to a sudden halt and she found herself sitting on the kitchen floor, blood drenching her body from the bottom of her nose down to her stomach. Her beige satin blouse looked like a crime scene and her hands were shaking.

In front of her she saw the prince lying unconscious in the living room. How did that happen? She remembered their fight and him beginning to undress her, but her memory after that was now foggy. She knew she didn't match the prince in strength; she could never overpower him.

Overwhelmed, she took deep breaths. Her vision was still returning to her, coming back in slow strides. The blurriness of the kitchen began to fade, and out of the corner of her eye she saw another body. She turned to face it and saw Sevrick lying on the ground, unconscious, with a pool of blood around his head.

One thousand different emotions engulfed Arinadya at once, the strongest of them being guilt. All the years of pain she caused him came flooding back to her and she could not bear it; it was too much. She destroyed this man emotionally; she could not let him die too. She needed to save him. The demons within her tried to numb these ancient emotions from resurfacing but her determination triumphed, silencing them for the time being. The prince could not see Sevrick here; the prince could not even know he existed. If this horrible act she committed against her ex had any upside, she hoped her brutality would be enough to keep him away. Maybe he would finally believe the girl he once loved was truly dead. Maybe he would finally give up and live a happy and safe life without her.

But now she questioned, for the first time, if that girl within her was really gone. She wondered if maybe, in the deepest corners of her soul, a younger version of herself still hung on to life.

The demons reappeared inside her mind, threatening to take hold of her thoughts again if she did not stop these fantasies. And Arinadya knew they were right; she was ruined long ago. Even if the girl Sevrick once knew still lived somewhere deep inside her heart, there was no way she'd be able to climb through the ruins unscarred. She'd be damaged. The journey to the surface would destroy her.

She grabbed her coat and put it on. She took a thick wool blanket and wrapped it around Sevrick until he was covered enough to stay warm with his own body heat. He was twice her size, but it didn't matter. With her haeman strength, she picked him up like a baby.

Before leaving her apartment, she placed Sevrick down and shot Mikhail in the ass with the tranquilizer gun one more time for good measure. She removed all three darts from his body and hid the gun under a couch cushion. She picked Sevrick back up and left her apartment.

It was five in the morning and a heavy snow had started to fall. Arinadya didn't know what her plan was, but knew she had to get Sevrick help somehow. Taking him out of the city was her first priority; assessing his injuries would be next.

She got him through the suburbs quickly. In one of the backyards she cut through she found an old wooden sled large enough to place Sevrick's body on to pull him through the snow. It was much easier to transport him like this and she arrived at the edge of the forest in no time. She stopped upon reaching the tree line. How could she go any further with him? Perhaps she could take him deep into the woods in hopes of another condemned finding him, but that didn't guarantee his survival.

She clenched her teeth and groaned as she fought back tears. She didn't know what else to do. Then she saw something within the trees, a reflection. They were the eyes of something, but she couldn't tell if it was an animal or another human. She took a step closer and an old man stepped beyond the tree line to reveal himself. He walked toward her, unafraid and unyielding.

"Are you the woman he loves?" the old man asked directly.

Tears filled her eyes. "Not anymore."

The old man nodded and then looked down at the condition of Sevrick. His face was swollen and he still wasn't moving. A look of disgust came across the old man's face.

"Is he dead?" She shook her head. He sighed in relief, then continued. "Have you done this to him?"

She choked on her words, but nodded. The tears now streamed down her face and the old man examined her with a bewildered expression; he never saw a haeman cry before. But Arinadya couldn't hold it back. Years of remorse for what she did to their love hit her all at once and Arinadya couldn't control the way her grief escaped its confines.

"Promise me you won't let him come back again. I hope this was enough to make him realize I'm a monster now, but in case it wasn't, remind him. Don't let him return to me." She felt a deep sting pierce her heart, a pain she never expected to feel again.

"I won't. You have hurt him enough already," he looked at her sternly. "And I'm not even referring to the bodily harm you have caused him."

"I know," Arinadya said, accepting all the blame.

The old man walked up to where she stood with Sevrick and grabbed the rope of the sled. Without saying another word to her, he pulled the sled carrying his body into the woods and disappeared from sight.

Arinadya fell to her knees, ashamed of what she had become and overwhelmed by all the human emotions that were inundating her after seven years of suppression. How could she have let herself become such a monster? How could she have hurt the one person she loved more than herself?

All the feelings were coming back and she had to make them stop. She could not escape her fate now. The prince would hunt her down and kill her if she tried. So Arinadya numbed the pain the only way she knew how. With the simple click of a button, her serpent watch pierced her wrist. A small dose of blood trickled from her skin, which she licked up quickly. It only took a minute before she began to feel right again. The guilt began to fade and her demons happily took control of her senses once more.

Chapter 22

Pasha pulled the sled as fast as he could through the forest. Nature was being unkind and began dumping heavy snow underfoot. The sun was slowly rising but the storm showed no signs of slowing down. Pasha was over sixty years old but had the spirit of a man half his age. He would get Sevrick back to the white elm and they would give him the medical attention he needed.

Pasha looked back at Sevrick bundled up and laying motionless on the large sled. Oksana had begged Pasha to follow their comrade into the woods. She didn't like that he was trekking to the city on his own, and it didn't take much convincing to agree that it would be good to watch Sevrick's back. But once he crossed the tree line and entered the haeman suburbs, Pasha decided he could not follow him any further, so he waited for him to return. Seeing his unconscious body delivered back to the forest by a haeman was the last thing he ever expected to happen.

The girl had beaten him close to death and then returned him to the forest's edge because some piece of her conscience came back to life. She felt remorse and guilt for what she had done, which was very unusual haeman behavior. Pasha had never seen or heard of anything like it before. Part of him now understood why Sevrick continued to fight so hard to save her and bring her back. At some point in time, their love must have been a force to be reckoned with.

Despite the drugs and the monster that had taken over her mind, she still managed to feel something. The sorrow she wore on her face seemed genuine as she realized she might have murdered the only person in the world that still loved her unconditionally. Her revelation was a miracle. Without it, she would have never brought him back to the forest's edge and would have left him in a gutter to rot.

He was grateful that he followed Sevrick. If he hadn't, he wasn't sure how far the haeman would have brought him into the forest. He could not pretend to make guesses at what her actions would have been, but he was glad he was there to take control of the situation.

Luckily, Pasha had taken a lengthy nap near the forest's edge while he waited for Sevrick to return. The energy he reclaimed from that slumber was proving crucial now. Like an ox, he towed without pausing for rest. His joints ached but he refused to stop. He didn't know how bad Sevrick's condition was and one minute might be the determining factor in saving his life.

The snow stopped at noon. As night cascaded over, the docile clouds covered the moonlight, leaving him to blindly navigate through the darkness of the trees. He pressed on. He wasn't sure if anyone ever made this trip without stopping at least once, but that was what he planned to do now. He couldn't tell how far he was from home but hoped he could make it back in one day instead of two.

He was unsure how much time passed, every minute in the darkness felt like an hour. It was impossible to guess, but as more and more of it went by, his body began to reap its effects. His lungs began to itch and a wet cough developed at some point during the night. His head throbbed with a deep-seeded migraine and his throat burned. Pasha wasn't sure what was coming over him but he kept the pain at the back of his mind. He had no time for it; he could deal with his own wounds after Sevrick's were attended to.

With his brain turned off to everything except the rhythmic and steady pace of his own breathing, Pasha trudged through the snow with boundless energy. When the open field of the white elm was suddenly visible in the distance, he wheezed with relief. The scouts were patrolling the perimeters and someone would help him. He saw Ruslan in a tree, taking his turn to watch over the forest's border for rouge haemans.

Pasha called out his name, his voice cracking from the effort. Before he could call out again, he was consumed by a long, rattling cough.

Ruslan's head snapped up. Pasha's pace slowed as Ruslan jumped down to help, not noticing Sevrick on the sled.

"Oksana told us where you went. What happened?" Ruslan asked, concerned with Pasha's current state. The old man collapsed before he could answer and Ruslan took in the enormity of the scene when he saw Sevrick lying lifeless on the sled.

"Was it that girl?" he asked, already knowing the answer.

"Yeah," Pasha panted from his knees. "She did this to him. She brought him back to the forest's edge in this condition."

Ruslan sighed, he had prepared for the day when Sevrick was forced to learn the hard way.

"Will you be alright if I take him first?" Ruslan asked Pasha, knowing Sevrick needed immediate medical attention.

"Of course I'll be alright," Pasha snapped between gasps. "Take him to the lab." Ruslan took the ropes of the sled and sprinted toward the white elm.

"I'll send someone out to help you," he called to Pasha over his shoulder.

Pasha could hear what Ruslan said but the words passed in a blur; the sound of his own heart pounding was too loud. He tried to slow his breathing but he could not calm the pace at which his heart raced. The adrenaline from running non-stop through the woods still ran rampant through his body and Pasha felt his old heart working overtime to keep up.

Suddenly, he could feel his chest tighten and a sharp pain resonated through his entire body. Without a sound, Pasha placed his hands over his heart and fell face-first into the snow.

Chapter 23

Arinadya raced back to her apartment. She hoped Mikhail was still knocked out but was prepared with an excuse in case he wasn't. He drank a lot of whiskey at dinner so it wouldn't be hard to convince him that he passed out drunk.

Quietly, she opened her front door. Mikhail was still slumped over on the floor. A heavy weight lifted off her shoulders; she wouldn't have to explain why she left because he would never know.

After tidying up the kitchen and erasing any evidence of what took place the previous night, she picked him up from beneath his armpits and dragged him into her bedroom. Without too much exertion, she managed to toss him onto her bed. She then stripped down to her nightgown and climbed in with him. In an attempt at feigning affection, she snuggled up next to him so when he woke up, he would think nothing was wrong. He would think he just drank too much and forgot how he made it to bed. He would not think anything was out of order. He would never suspect what really happened.

Now she waited. She hated that his arm lay over her side, dead weight against her skin. She hated his touch. His whiskey breath rhythmically touched the back of her neck, making her squirm with loathing each time it did. But he could never know about Sevrick so she had to make him believe her lie. She had to play nice so he didn't get suspicious. She swallowed her pride and counted the minutes until the prince awoke.

A few hours passed before he began to rustle from his tranquilizer-induced slumber. It was morning now and Arinadya turned beneath his arm to face him.

"Good morning," she said, giving him a small kiss on the lips.

Mikhail opened his eyes, blinking a few times rapidly. He couldn't make sense of his surroundings or how he had gotten there. "What happened?"

"What do you mean? We fought, fucked, then went to bed. The usual. Don't you remember?"

Mikhail was confused. "I remember fighting and then messing around in the living room, but I can't remember anything after that. Or how we wound up in bed." His eyes were half open. He was still fighting off the remaining effects of the tranquilizer darts.

"That's probably because you drank too much whiskey at dinner last night. You were in rare form. I'm not surprised you blacked out."

Mikhail let out a grunt, accepting this as fact. He didn't have the energy to continue scouring his mind for memories he would never get back. "Did I behave myself?"

"No," Arinadya said, pointing to her left eye. Her left arm was covered with gashes from him throwing her into the glass coffee table as well. Mikhail forced his eyes open wider so he could truly register her face; she had mostly been a blur up to this point. He could now see the monstrous black eye he had given her. The entire left side of her face was swollen, causing her to look temporarily disfigured.

"Damnit," he shouted, "the wedding is next weekend." He jumped out of bed with haste and punched a hole in the wall.

"Putting a hole in my wall won't solve anything."

He ignored her and paced the bedroom, trying to think of a solution. She could not attend their wedding looking like Frankenstein. He also could not postpone it because all the arrangements were set in motion and Milena would kill him.

"I guess we will have to see how it heals this week. Maybe the swelling will go down and your makeup team can disguise whatever marks are left on your face. Your arms are of no concern. In fact, those cuts will look perfect by next Saturday."

"Right," Arinadya said, still avoiding eye contact with him. "As long as no one finds out how I really got them."

He gave her a glare filled with warning.

"How could they? Only you and I know how you got those marks."

"Right you are." She was losing her patience. She had to play nice with him but wasn't sure if all the strength in the world could hold back the urge she felt to call him out for what he had done. She wanted the world to know he was a monster. She had to be alone before she lost it completely. "My head hurts. I think it would be best if I had some time to myself to heal. I want to look perfect next weekend."

"I agree. I will leave you now. I'll have my people come to check on your progress during the week."

Of course someone from his devoted crew would come to check on her, not him. It was the little things that bred the most resentment in her. She knew he would be secretly rendezvousing with other women all week while she had to stay locked up in her apartment, away from the public's view while the black eye *he* gave her healed. The unjustness of the situation infuriated her. She could not tolerate this treatment forever. The prince diminished everything she ever stood for and she was sure one day his complete disregard toward her would backfire on him. He ignored her warnings pleading that he treat her better. He seemed to think she'd adjust to his behavior when in reality, it was only a matter of time before it caused her to lash out.

So for now, she played along. She had no other choice. The prince would have her killed if she attempted to escape or defy him publicly; it was easy to make a murder look like an accident these days. Plus, she still had hope that she may find some alternate joy in her new role. She could not deny there were appealing perks. From the start, she loved the lavish lifestyle she was now able to lead. As time passed, the adoration from the public grew on her too. In small doses, she found it to be quite exhilarating. It was nice to be idolized by other women for her style, the same way she used to idolize Princess Milena in the magazines.

Mikhail put his shirt back on, buttoning it over his pale and scarred skin. He ran his hand through his curly brown hair and looked around the room for his shoes. His hazel eyes still seemed to be fighting off remnants of the tranquilizer compound but he did not suspect any foul play. Arinadya doubted he ever would, he didn't think much of her skills or cleverness, so she was sure he didn't think she was capable of pulling off or getting away with the events that happened last night.

He left her with a brief kiss goodbye and a sense of relief washed over her. She had a week to collect her thoughts. A week to get her mind right. A week to calm down from the chaos Sevrick managed to stir within her once more. By Saturday, Arinadya was positive she would be back to her regular self and ready to marry the prince. Despite her doubts about him, she knew the rest of her existence as a royal would be extravagant, a life she believed she deserved. She worked too hard and sacrificed too much to accept anything less than extraordinary, even if she had to sacrifice some elements of her own happiness to get it.

Chapter 24

The week passed quickly. Arinadya used the time to nap and ice her face. A few of Mikhail's personal "doctors" came over after he left on Sunday with a concoction to heal her wound quicker. They gave her an injection of a medicine she'd never heard of, but by Friday the swelling had all but disappeared. She was amazed. Her eye wasn't even blood shot anymore. All that remained was some scarce bruising around the rim that the makeup team would be able to cover up easily. The entire left side of her face remained tender to the touch but an onlooker would never know that she had a disfiguring black eye only a week earlier.

A council member stopped by to update the golden tattoo down her spine. She had killed two more people and her count was now 24. A hushed part of her heart hoped Sevrick wasn't her 25th. Even if he was, he would never count toward the tally on her back because she would never tell them of his existence. There was a good chance she'd never learn the outcome of that night, but hoped he wasn't a secret addition to her kill count; she could not bear that extra burden.

Milena stopped by on Thursday to check on the treatment of her eye and to talk over last minute details with Arinadya. The conversation felt rushed and a bit forced, like the princess's mind was elsewhere. She was with Arinadya for barely an hour before she left. Arinadya didn't know what the rush was but could tell something was causing her to act frantically.

Then again, she didn't care to know what the hurry had been. She was grateful to only be inundated with wedding details for one hour rather than a couple days, or months. This wedding was nothing but a headache, an irritating means to an end. Surely it would be glamorous and exciting, but the build-up was tiring. She could only imagine how hard it would be to uphold the pretense of love and happiness for eight hours on Saturday. It was going to be a struggle.

It was Friday and she was enjoying her last few moments of peace before the royal style crew burst into her apartment to pretty her up for the pre-wedding day festivities. The scars on her arms from being shoved through the glass table healed nicely. They were now raw, pink lines. They covered both her forearms and made her appear much more intense in her blood collection than she truly was.

She made her last cup of coffee as a free woman. By the time she took her final sip, the style crew was banging on her front door.

Arinadya got up from the stool at her kitchen counter and opened the door. Milena led the troop of stylists in and they set up shop in her living room. Izolda headed straight into her bedroom with an arsenal of clothing options draped over her arm. Gavriil set up his station and plugged in his hair dryer, straightener, and curling iron. He lined up his armory of hairsprays and gels on the new coffee table Mikhail shipped to her earlier in the week. This one was not made of glass.

Milena and Olesya headed straight for Arinadya's face. Olesya grabbed her by her chin and yanked her in close so she could examine the state of her eye. Arinadya thought it was healing nicely but Olesya clicked her tongue in disapproval.

"That brother of yours," Olesya directed her frustration at Milena, "always making our jobs harder."

"I told him to calm down," Milena spoke to Arinadya. "You really must have pushed the wrong button this time. He promised he'd be on his best behavior with the wedding so close."

Arinadya pulled her face out of Olesya's grasp, agitated that she was being blamed for his wrongs.

"It's not always my fault, you know."

"Of course not," Milena faked a tone of understanding; she did not want to set Arinadya off into one of her highly unpleasant moods. "But you know how he is now and you ought to adjust accordingly. Like I've explained to you before, if you can't love him, learn to love and appreciate the benefits you receive by being with him. You cannot forget how lucky you are to be chosen for this role. It is a gift, show some appreciation."

Arinadya didn't say another word. In the beginning she thought Milena would be her ally, someone on her side. But as time passed she realized just how attached the royals were. They were evil cohorts and she couldn't trust either one.

Olesya shooed Milena away as Gavriil came over with a bottle of hair dye.

"Me first," he exclaimed, excitedly. Gavriil was bi-polar, Arinadya learned this when she met him on her first shopping spree. He had been happy all afternoon, then in the blink of an eye, he began punching walls and breaking windows at a local salon because they didn't carry the shampoo he liked. Arinadya was stronger than him but attempted to keep the peace in his presence. His antics gave her migraines and she didn't want her hair stylist to end up on her kill tally.

"Why the hair dye?" she asked, wondering why they wanted to change her signature hair color.

"Special request from the prince. The base color will remain the same. He just wanted it a bit darker. He asked for your hair to have the resemblance of fresh blood."

Arinadya rolled her eyes; it was all part of his elaborate game to recruit followers for his pointless war. In his master plan, she was just another pawn. Arinadya was sure he would enlist her and the princess to recruit the women, and expect them to make this war seem fashionable somehow.

She didn't care anymore. She was over it. His agenda was of no concern to her. She would play her role and eventually pave her own way in this new lifestyle. She would make goals of her own once things settled down.

Gavriil took her to the bathroom and began to place the foils in her hair for the lo-lights. He heated them with the hair dryer then rinsed it all out in the tub. The dye stained the porcelain, leaving a blood-like trail. Seeing it reminded her of the mess she spent hours cleaning off her white-tiled kitchen floor a week ago. No matter how hard she scrubbed, she couldn't erase the trauma she caused Sevrick; the cracks would forever be stained with his blood.

They went back to the living room and he finished her hair. The sunlight from the windows poured in and its warmth felt good on her body.

As soon as he was done drying it, everyone in the room gasped in awe. Arinadya looked at herself in the mirror and was amazed too. Her natural bright strawberry hair was still there but now it was layered with subtle streaks of crimson. The way Gavriil did it, the transition from light to dark was smooth and resembled the flow of fresh blood.

Her blue eyes looked brighter than ever with the lo-lights creating a dark frame around her face. Arinadya admired herself in the mirror, very pleased with this new look. He continued his job, styling her hair into an up-do for the night's festivities. He knotted it into a thick braided headband that went across the top of her head. Behind that, he created a messy pouf bump and then tied the rest of her long thick hair into a large bun. He wrapped a white, wide-laced ribbon into her hair to hold the bun in place with a neat bow beneath the mound of hair.

Gavriil messed around with his creation, teasing spots here and there to create an image of controlled chaos, and eventually took a step back to admire his work.

"Perfection," he cooed, his smile so wide it showed off his surgically sharpened teeth all the way to his back molars. "She's all yours."

Arinadya walked over to Olesya's station and sat down on a kitchen stool. Olesya unfolded a tall lamp and let it shine brightly onto Arinadya's face as she applied a heavy coat of makeup. The woman's neon green eyes darted back and forth, checking to make sure everything was being dispersed evenly. She scratched the top of her wild blonde hair a few times as she got caught up on Arinadya's bruised eye.

"Good thing we have a mask you will be wearing tonight," she said, her hot pink lips smacking together as she talked. "Let's hope this bruising fades by tomorrow."

She took out a pair of black, feathered eyelashes and glued them to her subject's eyelids. The feathers and heavy eyeliner camouflaged all remnants of the bruise. She then took out a white lace mask that stuck to Arinadya's face with adhesive. The mask had wide, lace cut-outs that clung to her face like it was part of her skin. The details swirled and flowed across her forehead and down her cheeks.

"Last step," Olesya muttered under her breath as she took out a tube of lipstick. She smeared the red rouge on Arinadya's lips, covering them with three coats. She then placed an overcoat gloss meant to make the color last.

"You're done here. Once we get you dressed we'll be on our way." Olesya gave her a shove toward Izolda who held up a white cocktail dress for Arinadya's viewing. She put it on and examined herself in the mirror. The dress was backless, dipping down into a V; its lowest point touched the top of her tailbone. The edges of the V were sheer with flecks of diamond particles stitched into the lining. Her boney back was framed with sparkles and her golden tattoo was the focal point. The front of the dress was strapless, strong adhesive held the bodice of the dress in place, all while managing to create the illusion of busty cleavage. Arinadya had the curves but with all the weight loss, it took a bit more trickery to create the image of voluptuousness she used to sport effortlessly.

The entire dress was designed to appear see through, when in fact it was skin colored fabric covered in wide set lace; the same pattern as her mask. Her long legs, which had become another one of her signature features, were showcased nicely since the dress cut off at mid-thigh.

"Good job, guys. Should we be on our way?" Arinadya was over the fuss of getting ready and wanted to get this night started so it could be over. Tonight was the rehearsal dinner and family crowning ceremony. Normally, this was a private event but nothing was ever private with the prince; he always had to put on a show for his adoring fans. The media would broadcast tonight's events and there would be crowds watching the whole ordeal take place.

Milena gave the final approval on Arinadya's look and they escorted her into the limo. As they were preparing her for the festivities, they all managed to get themselves ready when they weren't working on her. Izolda wore a long black gown that was low-cut down the front. It showed off the thick scars around the flesh of her breasts. Her brown hair was tied in a low ponytail, accenting her sharp chin nicely. The necklace she wore had a crystal pendant that contained an ounce of her own blood.

Gavriil had on a royal blue suit with a frilly white undershirt beneath the coat. His bleach blonde hair was shaved close to his scalp and he sported fake contacts that made his irises completely black.

Olesya put on a short pink dress with a fluffy skirt; it matched her lipstick perfectly. Her light blonde hair was braided to the side and had bouncy curls beginning where the braid stopped. She was gossiping with Milena in the limo as they moved forward through the streets.

Milena was dressed in a lavender evening gown that flowed like water. The straps had golden brooches covered in diamonds and the waist of her dress was laced up in the back with ribbons, showing off her extremely slight figure. Her makeup was done perfectly; large fake eyelashes with lavender tips, smoky purple eye shadow, and plum lipstick. She already wore the famous Vladimir tiara. It was large, made up of teardrop pearls dangling within each diamond-encrusted hoop. Her light brown hair was long, curled, and covered in clip-on amethysts, thanks to Gavriil. Her mane sparkled like a starry night sky.

Nobody paid much attention to Arinadya in the limo. She wasn't even sure where they were going, but instead of asking the chatty style crew or the standoffish princess, she decided to wait and see.

As they reached Marsovo Polye Square, she realized the answer to her question. Hordes of haemans surrounded the park, fighting each other for a space near where Mikhail was situated. The royal militia cleared a path within the mob of bodies for the limo to pass through. They drove to the center of the square and entered a section surrounded by high gates. After the limo was safely through, the guards locked the gates behind them and opened the car door.

"You will exit last," Milena said as she shuffled past. The princess waited her turn as the style crew exited to minimal applause. When Milena exited, the crowd burst into cheers, hooting and hollering, all vying for her attention. Milena gave a curt smile and walked up onto the elevated stage, taking her seat at the table next to Mikhail.

It was now Arinadya's turn. She took a deep breath and accepted the outstretched hand of one of the guardsmen who assisted her out of the limo.

As soon as her foot hit the pavement, the masses erupted into a roar so loud, she lost her balance for a moment. The guard steadied her stance and she regained her composure. The animalistic cries from the swarm of eager haemans was unnatural; they sounded like frenzied beasts of the wild, restless with desire. But for her? It was disconcerting; she did not want the haemans of Russia to have an unhealthy obsession with her. She looked up at the prince. He was thrilled that she was getting an overwhelming reception and that his minions loved her so thoroughly. Then she looked over to the princess who wore a scowl foul as murder. She was so upset by the public adoration her brother's bride was receiving that she lost all semblance of her normal, uncaring façade. Her eyes were green with envy and Arinadya cursed inside her head, *Perfect, now she really won't have my back.*

Though somewhere deep within her, she got a tiny bit of joy out of watching the princess squirm. Somewhere along the line, she had stolen Milena's role as the female archetype for Russian haemans. She couldn't help but feel elated that she surpassed the status of her former idol. She had landed far beyond the goals she set for herself years ago.

Arinadya walked up the steps of the elevated stage and sat in her seat on the other side of Mikhail. A tall, barbed-wire fence protected them from the masses. As she sat, the prince rose and a guard walked over with a microphone. At the sound of the crackling speakers the massive crowd hushed and waited with bated breath for the prince to speak to them.

"Thank you for joining my family and I for our pre-wedding festivities. As our audience tonight, you will see an array of spectacles. As we eat our dinner, the Rekulin Circus will entertain you."

The aerial artists emerged from the midst of the crowd, attaching themselves to wires hung above the square. They wore long ribbons and twirled in circles as acrobats did flips across the wires they spun from. Mikhail continued to speak, "Following the summation of our feast, President Dobrynin will begin the traditional crowning ceremony. I'll ask for your complete silence during this part of the night." The crowd had a low hum of murmuring as they watched the circus performers dangle above them.

"Lastly, as a reward for all your loyalty and support, I have arranged a concert for your viewing pleasure. The artist will remain a mystery until the end of the night, but I promise you it's worth the wait." He then switched the microphone off and took his place at the center of the long dining table.

Enchanting circus music began to play. It filled the air and provided a magical ambience for the carnival extravaganza. Large cages were pushed through the crowds carrying angry tigers, bears, and wolves. The haemans taunted the animals as they passed, cackling with laughter and sticking their hands into the cages, unafraid of the animals drawing blood.

Once the cages were in place, the haeman animal trainers perched themselves atop the bars and prepared to perform their act. Each one sliced their arm, consumed a massive amount of blood, and then got into the cage with their ferocious animal. Once inside, it was a fight to the death. The surrounding haemans watched in awe and horror as each of the animal trainers won the battle against their beast. It was a show of power, signifying that the haemans could conquer nature's strongest monsters. These performances made the crowd go wild.

Back on the stage, safely confined by the enormous caged fence, the royal family ate their dinner in peace. They could hear the circus music and the occasional roar of excitement from the crowd, but it didn't interrupt their silent dinner. No one talked. Everyone just moved the food around their plates, occasionally taking a bite, and sipping blood from their goblets. The rim of each cup was razor sharp, so every member of the dinner party was able to fill their cup as they wished, fulfilling their own needs.

Arinadya didn't know many people at the table except the royal siblings and her style team, who were seated at the end of the long table due to their social unimportance compared to the others. The table was filled with Mikhail and Milena's extended relatives and the friends they brought into the spotlight with them after being discovered in the slums ten years ago. These individuals were crooked and untrustworthy. It was an uncomfortable environment, even for someone who considered herself to be one of them now. But these people came from another world than her. Even though they were adopted by society as royals, they still belonged to the underworld. No amount of wealth or cultural acceptance could take the deep-rooted wickedness out of them. She could feel their innate evilness spread through the air around her. Occasionally, she could feel them staring at her from various locations along the table. She tried not to look but often couldn't help herself. As she caught the glare of her assessors, they did not look away in shame of being caught. Instead they held eye contact with her, trying to make her look away first; a twisted mind game of power and control. Just when these nasty relatives of Mikhail thought they won, Arinadya casually placed her hand upon the prince's and smiled back at the perpetrators, a swift and solid reminder that she ranked above them now.

As the dinner concluded, the untouched plates were taken from the table. The circus music gradually softened until it became silent and the performers disappeared into the crowd. The haemans heard the transition and refocused their attention back to the royals beyond the high circular fence. President Dobrynin grabbed the microphone and spoke to the masses.

"The crowning ceremony will now proceed." An extended version of Reinhold Gliere's "Arietta" began to play from the speakers scattered throughout Marsovo Polye Square. A charming melody with dark undertones soothed the crowd as the ceremony began.

Milena stood up from her chair and exited the stage. She appeared to walk into a storage room beneath the platform, hidden from view. Mikhail was already wearing his replica of the Great Imperial Crown of Russia. It retained the traditional form of two open hemispheres lined with pearls and topped with a blood-red ruby. Unlike the original, though, this crown held no cross.

He took his bride-to-be's hand and walked her around the dining table to the front of the stage where President Dobrynin stood. The prince wore a tender smile that was foreign to Arinadya; the sight of it made her stomach squirm. Milena came back onto the stage carrying Queen Alexandra's Kokoshnik tiara. It was fringe-styled, with dozens of platinum bars covered in hundreds of flawless grade-A diamonds. The bars cascaded downward in size from the peak that sat in the center.

Arinadya's chest tightened as the tiara sparkled under the spotlights cast on the ceremony. The crowd rustled impatiently; she could tell they wanted to cheer but they remained quiet, obeying Mikhail's earlier demand for silence. The cameras that were stationed on each post of the octagon cage swiveled around maniacally, trying to catch every moment of this night. And while the stationary cameras moved via haemans who were in a distant control room, the four handheld cameras were operated by on-site haemans who diligently captured their targets all evening. One had been assigned to the extended family, and the other three were tasked with following every move Mikhail, Arinadya, and Milena made. One of the cameramen was crouched down low with his camera pointed up, circling the spot where she stood with the prince. She tried to ignore him. The videos and pictures from this night would be part of history and she didn't want to look foolish or awkward.

Milena finally approached them with the radiant tiara. Mikhail let go of Arinadya's hand and President Dobrynin moved the microphone toward his mouth so he could speak to the crowd without touching it.

"Tonight, Arinadya gets her first true introduction into the royal family. Tomorrow, she becomes my wife. As I place this crown upon her head, rejoice with us. Tonight is a victory for all haemans to celebrate."

He picked up the tiara and as soon as it was placed atop Arinadya's fiery blood-red hair, the crowd exploded with excitement. The energy they radiated was contagious and she couldn't help but smile as he grabbed her face and planted a long kiss on her lips. This riled up the crowd even more. They loved it. Mikhail was giving them exactly what they wanted.

He then put an arm around Arinadya's shoulder and pulled her in tight. With his other arm, he threw a fist into the air, signifying his great accomplishment. He got the girl, his people were happy, and soon, he would win his war.

The prince took her hand, grabbed Milena's with the other, and escorted them off the stage. The rest of the sullen extended royal family followed suit behind them, no noise or smiles from any of them.

As the royal party left the stage, the haeman hard rock band Krov'in entered. The mere sight of them sent the crowd into a frenzy. Haemans began grabbing at the cage surrounding the stage and shaking the barricades. The band was unfazed; they put their set together in less than a minute and began playing. Their music echoed through Marsovo Polye Square, filling the night air with chaos.

Mikhail, Milena, and Arinadya were already in their limo, making a swift getaway from the mob. As soon as they were out of public view, all façades were dropped. Milena resumed her normal scowl and Mikhail began issuing orders. He needed water, wanted a warm towel, and couldn't focus without a backrub. Arinadya rolled her eyes, glad he had minions to do these demeaning tasks for him.

He barely looked at her the entire trip home and the princess had fallen asleep so she was terrible company as well. Once they reached her apartment, Arinadya got out of the limo as quickly as possible. If she was to put on a happy face again tomorrow, she needed as much time away from them until then. Before she shut the limo door behind her, the prince spoke.

"Enjoy your last night in this apartment. After tomorrow, you'll be moving in with me." He gave her an unnerving smile. She couldn't decipher his intent. Either he believed this was news she'd be excited to hear or he was taunting her. She slowly nodded and shut the door. She would not pretend to be happy about it but she knew this day would come.

Upon entering her home, she made sure to lock the door behind her. If this was her last night alone then she wanted to enjoy it with no interruptions.

Chapter 25

Saturday morning came too soon. Arinadya was still fast asleep when the style crew arrived and began banging on her door. When she finally got up to let them in, they barged through, bringing their chaotic energy into the apartment with them. Milena was absent from the group and the icy message it sent was not lost on Arinadya. The princess did not like the adoration the haemans of Russia held for her; it was written all over Milena's face during last night's pre-wedding ceremony. The princess's choice to abandon her now meant she had never really supported her as much as she pretended to. She shook her head, trying to forget about the fact that her new family members were already dismissing her.

"You look like hell," Izolda commented as she walked past. Olesya immediately put three lines of silve out for Arinadya on the coffee table.

"Snort up, missy. You need to be a vision of perfection today."

Arinadya happily snorted the silve and began to feel better instantly. The silver powder left residue on the edges of her nostril. Hastily, she wiped her face clean, took her place in Gavriil's chair, and let him fix her hair. The high from the silve cocaine helped the tedious prep session fly by. Before she knew it, she was standing in front of a full-length mirror, admiring the work of her style team.

Her long red hair was left down with voluminous, loose curls. Her Kokoshnik Fringe tiara sat perfectly upon her head and Gavriil attached a collection of platinum chains that varied in length to the back of it. Each chain had a few diamonds on it and the platinum strands fell nicely into her curly hair, shining sporadically as she moved.

Olesya put false, jet black eyelashes on her that were very long and thick; they made her eyes look extra blue. She wore foundation to even her skin tone and blush to highlight her cheekbones. Her plump baby doll lips were smeared in red lipstick, her signature color.

They put her in a platinum collarbone necklace that draped over her shoulders and across the top of her chest. It was decorated with diamond-covered chains that looped and fell symmetrically around the top half of her body. It was elegant and highlighted the dainty bones of her neck.

The wedding gown she wore was strapless with a sweetheart neckline that tapered down into a tightly pulled corset. The bodice had white-on-white paisley embroideries stitched into it and the fabric had a gloss finish. The back was cut low, showing off her golden spine tattoo. The bottom of the dress was enormous. Besides the one front slit that would show a little leg when she walked, it completely engulfed the lower half of her body. It was gathered and bunched in sections, creating a flowing effect. There were diamonds and pearls sewn onto the bottom half of the gown as well. The designer of this dress took crimson ink and let it bleed into the fabric. The effect was subtle but brilliant. It was an elegant nod to haemanism.

Arinadya took a step back from the mirror, in awe of her perfection. The scars on her arms were an incredible addition. So much so that she hated Mikhail for adding such a beautiful final touch to her wedding day look. She was the perfect haeman bride. She turned to face her style team.

"I am ready to go." A smile appeared on her face, one that hadn't happened naturally in years. Maybe it was seeing herself look so perfect in the mirror, maybe it was the idea that she had finally made her mark in the haeman world, or maybe it was just the drugs causing this euphoric feeling. Regardless, Arinadya couldn't stop the elation that coursed through her now. Her style team looked at her with shock but accepted this happy version of her personality and escorted her out and into the stretch limo.

The ride to the Winter Palace was not far. Once they were a block away, the crowds appeared. They filled the streets and obstructed their path. The royal militia was on duty and they eventually cleared a path for the limo to drive through. Once they got through the gate, the crowd was behind them and they were able to drive to the front door unobstructed.

Though the crowds of civilian haemans were not permitted into this area, plenty of media hounds and paparazzi were. The moment the limo door opened for Arinadya, flashes began to fire and she was blinded by the relentless cameramen trying to get the winning shot. Her good mood began to fade but she forced herself to maintain the smile she had been wearing at her apartment. She kept up a good pretense until she was safely inside the palace with the door shut behind her. She shut her eyes and took a deep breath, only to be greeted by another swarm of paparazzi. Her heart contracted as she hastily regained her composure and resumed the façade.

Mikhail stood at the top of the Ambassador Jordan staircase, looking down on her with a fake expression of pride. He did not truly care for her but he did a good job pretending he did.

She smiled courteously back at him before making her way up the right side of the staircase to meet him. He took her hand, his skin cold against hers, and led her into St. George's Hall. This room had centuries of history within it and she could feel the former Romanov spirits coursing through the air around her. This hall had been the principle throne room for the Tsar's of Russia throughout the ages until the Imperial family moved to the Alexander Palace for seclusion and security after the Bloody Sunday massacre. This happened in 1905; by 1918, the dissolution of the royal Romanovs had begun. The Russian Civil War separated the country and the

Bolshevik authorities were ordered to execute Nikolay Alexandrovich Romanov, the last Tsar, and all of his immediate family. Yakov Sverdlov, Chairman of the Russian Communist Party, ordered this unlawful murder in order to prevent the rescue of the Imperial family from approaching White Forces. The entire extended family was murdered the following day as well. It was rumored, and proven to be true, that two of the Romanov children escaped. Mikhail, Milena, and their extended family had the DNA tests to prove they were true descendants. Now that they regained their family's royal titles and took back the kingdom, they had free reign over all the palaces. Mikhail had all museums removed from the remaining palaces, including the Hermitage Museum that used to exist within the Winter Palace, in order to maintain privacy under his new regime.

St. George's Hall was beautiful in its grandeur; it made sense the prince would be married here. Rows and rows of benches covered with gold trim and flowers lined the room. Spectators filled the seats, watching the couple intently with their dead haeman eyes. Arinadya did not know many of the guests at her own wedding; Milena had been in charge of the guest list, which mostly consisted of the other royals and hundreds of haeman socialites and celebrities. There was a small portion of the guest list that was hers. A few people from her office had been invited. Boris, Luca, and

Tanya sat in the back row, fidgeting with excitement at the company they were in.

Arinadya did not focus on the crowd of unfriendly faces watching her; instead she kept her gaze on the altar the two thrones sat upon. They reached the steps and ascended, taking their seats on their appropriate throne: Mikhail in the seat of the Tsar, Arinadya next to him in the smaller chair.

The Russian Orthodox Church had been reformed to include haemanism, and the leader of the religious revolution officiated their wedding ceremony. His name was Damir Mazarov and he wore an expression that was hard as stone. He spoke into a microphone to begin the proceedings.

"Do you, Haeman Mikhail Romanov, consent to this marriage with Haeman Arinadya Tarasova?"

"I do," Mikhail answered confidently.

"And do you, Haeman Arinadya Tarasova, consent to this marriage with Haeman Mikhail Romanov?"

"I do," her voice was low but clear.

"Do you both hold true to your beliefs in haemanism, using the gift we've been given by God as he intended us to?"

"We do," they responded in unison.

"And do you both promise to hold this union up to the standards of a haeman lifestyle? One of great strength, passion, and perfection?"

"We do."

"And lastly, do you both vow to help the other in upholding their commitment to the Russian Haeman Orthodox Church, promising to help the other if they ever lose their way?"

"We do."

Minister Mazarov then lit a candle and held it in front of him at arm's length.

"Let light be your guide when the road gets dark," he walked over to Mikhail and Arinadya, who both had outstretched hands. He poured the hot wax into each of their palms and then placed their hands together, interlocking their fingers and letting the wax dry between them. He then put another candle beneath their grasp. Its flame was dangerously close to their skin and began to melt the wax that had dried and bonded their hands together. As the hot wax melted and dripped from their hands, the minister poured more hot wax over their grasp from the first candle. The waterfall of wax continued falling into the top of their clasped hands and out the bottom. The wax burned their skin but neither flinched. Their pain tolerance was so high they barely felt their skin begin to blister.

"Let this show that no matter the trials you encounter, no foreboding flames can scorch your bond." Minister Mazarov removed the candles from above and below their grasp. The wax between their hands hardened once more, leaving their hands glued together. The minister motioned for them to stand. Hand forcibly in hand, the royal newlyweds stood and walked to the top of the front step of the altar.

Minster Mazarov walked behind them and stood in the space between their bodies. He placed a hand on each of their wrists.

"This union of marriage is now official," he ripped their hands apart, the dried wax fell and clumped on the ground beneath them. "Let them kiss and complete this ceremony of marriage."

Mikhail grabbed Arinadya by the shoulders. With mighty force, he held her face and leaned in for the kiss. For the first time, the crowd made noise. They clapped vigorously and some even cheered. It was a much more subdued crowd than the one that had surrounded them at Marsovo Polye Square.

She took the prince's hard kiss, devoid of any tenderness, and put on a happy smile once it was over. They walked back through the mildly excited crowd and into the hall. They ducked into a side room while the crowd of guests exited St. George's Hall and made their way to the reception.

After the crowd passed, Milena got the four-person bridal party together and led them into the small throne room, known to most as Peter the Great's Memorial Hall. Once in the room, Arinadya realized this was the location of the wedding photos. Unlike traditional pose-and-shoot photos, this room was equipped with state of the art photography equipment and had a style team so large, she felt like she was walking onto the set of a high fashion photo shoot.

The bridal party consisted of Mikhail, Arinadya, Milena, and Mikhail's best friend from childhood, Kirill. Kirill was tall and humorless. He never smiled and always wore a look of utter disdain. He didn't really like anyone except Mikhail and Milena, so he rarely spoke. Arinadya only met him once before this day but he only said "hi" and "bye" to her on that occasion. Today was no different. She wasn't even sure if he had made eye contact with her yet. A heavy drug user and one of the three originators of haemanism, Kirill was Mikhail's right-hand man. His underground roots were seeded deeply within him and his lack of grace and etiquette were wildly apparent during events like this. She supposed that might be why he chose not to speak. It was hard to tell. All she knew for sure was that he'd never have her back if things went wrong with Mikhail. No one would. Arinadya was very aware of how alone she was in this new world.

The photo shoot commenced. Besides looking like a professional shoot, it was orchestrated like one as well. They were positioned and instructed to pose like supermodels, creating high fashion editorial-type shots to be distributed for all of Russia to see. She was sure a few photos would make it into the global media as well. The rest of the world didn't know about the haemans, not yet at least. Tourism was under a strict regime. The royals made the process of crossing borders next to impossible to complete so that it drove vacationers away and kept Russians confined to their homeland. For foreigners wishing to enter who made it through the labyrinth of requirements, they were only allowed to stay at specific hotels and visit certain places once they entered the country. All international business was done through the Internet, or the Russians did the traveling. Mikhail was very careful with the secret of his new world, but he would surely let a few of the better wedding pictures, the bloodless ones, make it to the desks of editors in the United States and Europe. Arinadya didn't know how this new breed of human had been kept secret for ten years, but somehow the rest of the world was still blind to the massive evolutionary changes Russians had bestowed upon themselves. She wasn't sure if Mikhail purposefully kept this development a secret in order to maintain an upper hand over the rest of humanity, or if he was biding his time, waiting for the perfect moment to spread his reign throughout the rest of the globe. Either way, he was the most powerful man in the world, even if the rest of the world wasn't aware of it yet.

Once the wedding fashion shoot was complete the bridal party made their way down to Armorial Hall for the reception.

Milena and Kirill entered first to enormous applause. The crowd had livened up a bit after bathing in silve and liquor during the break between ceremonies. The two took their seat at the head table and then the conductor of the Russian chamber orchestra announced the arrival of the bride and groom.

"Ladies and Gentlemen, please raise your glass in honor of the newlyweds, Arinadya and Mikhail Romanov!"

All the guests raised goblets full of blood toward the sky and cheered as the royal newlyweds entered the room. They let out cheers of approval and sipped from their glasses as the newly married couple took the center of the dance floor. The crowd hushed as the musicians began to play Rimsky-Korsakov's "Scheherazade." The eerie instrumental began slow, giving the bride and groom a mellow tempo to accompany their slow dance. After two minutes of full attention, Milena and Kirill joined them on the dance floor. Another minute passed and the rest of the royal family took their places on the ballroom floor, slow dancing to the opening sequence of this symphonic suite. The middle of the song picked up in tempo and the essence of the song shifted from grim to whimsical, transforming itself into a magical melody with the foreboding undertones maintaining their presence in the underscore. The woodwinds gained strength as did the harp and violins. The rest of the guests grabbed a partner and joined the royals on the dance floor. The couples spun in unison, moving across the floor like sweeping ghosts. Everyone's faces were gaunt and emotionless as they twirled and rotated positions throughout the hall. From above, the crowd moved in perfect synchronicity, like the dance had been rehearsed many times before. This classical Russian music moved everyone naturally, as if each chord steered their bones. No instructions were needed because the melody took them where they needed to go.

The prince held his new bride close. Their bodies touched but there were no sparks between them. No inexplicable electricity binding them to one another. Their skin was cold, as were their hearts. This was not a union of love, nor was it meant to be. This was a wedding meant to manipulate the public, to improve Mikhail's image. This entire wedding was merely an extravagant series of fanfares and festivities masking his true intentions. His elaborate charade of tenderness and devotion was convincing to outsiders, but Arinadya maintained her distance. Her guard was high and she dreaded the moment this day of make-believe happiness would come to an end. She was unsure what terrors awaited her on the other side.

The reception continued on with ease. Tradition after mindless tradition ensued, all led by the overly ambitious Milena. Arinadya was not sure why her new sister-in-law had taken such an extreme interest in managing every detail of this event. For the past month, Milena acted like the royal wedding dictator, bossing people around and making insane requests. Luckily, she mostly left Arinadya out of it. Milena instructed her to show up, look pretty, and act happy.

By 10 p.m. the party shifted from an elegant affair into a chaotic one. The hall was now bursting with utter debauchery; booze, drugs, sex, and violence filled the air. The intoxicated guests lost all control over their behavior and their mindless actions transformed the atmosphere. There was nothing pretty about this wedding anymore. It had turned ugly in the most desirable way. The complete lack of inhibition made everyone seem more attractive. More fun. More exciting. Temporarily eliminating the void they all desperately craved to fill. Arinadya was highly intoxicated as well, but she was not allowed to join in on the madness. Mikhail kept her close to him as the party took on a life of its own. As she watched the depravity with an outsider's perspective she understood how Mikhail achieved his kingdom. Even though their behavior was deplorable and disgusting, they were so confident in their bad decisions that it made them seem acceptable. She could understand why others wanted to emulate them. Somehow, this tragic mess had the power to manipulate the insecurities of outsiders and their fear of missing out. It toyed with their mind, clouding their ability to stay away.

Midnight struck and the bells throughout the palace chimed loudly, as they had been set to do on this eventful night. The party was over and the drunk and disorderly haemans filed out of the palace, as they were no longer welcome to stay.

The palace was quiet once more; only the wait staff shuffled about, cleaning up the mess the party guests left. Arinadya could feel the cavity beneath her chest swell in anticipation of what would come next. The pleasant expression Mikhail wore throughout the entire day rapidly disappeared. He sat down at a random table and dropped his head into his hands.

"What a fantastic success," Milena squealed, her happiness was genuine, a rare emotion for any haeman, especially her.

Mikhail shushed her. "I can feel my brain pulsing within my skull. I cannot have you running about, shouting nonsense."

"Do you not think today was a victory?"

"Of course it was. Everything went perfectly. But it's over now and I need quiet."

"Fine." Her nostrils flared in annoyance. She wanted someone to gloat with but her brother wasn't having it. She looked to Arinadya, who did not care one ounce for the "success rate" of their masterfully crafted pretense of a wedding. Milena shook her head with disgust at Arinadya's jaded facial expression and stormed out of the room.

"Where will I be sleeping tonight?" Arinadya asked, hoping the answer wouldn't be with him. Mikhail looked up at her with a fatigued expression.

"I never knew pretending to be happy could be so exhausting. I will have to remember never to plan a day-long public event again."

"Why do you even bother pretending? Everyone in Russia is haeman now too. They are all just as volatile and angry as we are."

"You don't get it. It doesn't matter that collectively we are a wild, unstable pack of humans unable to control our urges, emotions, or actions. We are above them. They need to believe that we *can*. That is why we stood apart from the rest of them when the party became out of control. They cannot consider themselves one of us, even the high-ranking individuals who let loose tonight. We must always stand apart." He paused, "They need to understand that we are stronger than them, not only physically, but mentally. It is essential in order to maintain the balance."

"You mean to maintain your control over them. To keep your place on the pedestals they've made for you in their minds."

"Exactly," Mikhail smiled. "I need them to worship me always."

"You do realize that it is borderline insane to assume you can control other people's thoughts."

"Insane if you fail. Genius if you succeed." His eyes caught the flicker of a nearby candle. The light illuminated them for a moment, revealing the evilness he held within his soul.

Arinadya nodded, unimpressed with his narcissistic need to control everyone around him.

"Where will I be sleeping tonight?"

Mikhail returned his gaze downward at the bloodstained tablecloth.

"I have no interest in you tonight. Find a spare bedroom to sleep in. I will have someone settle you and your belongings in tomorrow."

Arinadya blinked her eyes once in acknowledgment then left the room without another word. As soon as she was out of his presence, she let out the breath she had been holding since the guests left. She had one more night of freedom, one more night without him next to her while she slept, one more night without fear of his touch.

She ran down the long corridor, her white gown trailing behind her and catching flight from the speed at which she moved. Upon reaching the opposite side of the palace, she took an empty room that was furthest from where Mikhail slept.

The moonlight poured in through the window. With the lights off, she hastily removed her gown, tossing it into a corner. With more care, she took off her tiara and placed it upon a dresser. She went into the bathroom connected to the room, removed the fake eyelashes, and then splashed her face with cold water. Her mascara ran like black rain down her cheeks, making her look even more tormented than she felt. She did not feel any urge to clean her face; it felt nice to be imperfect for a change. No one was there to tell her she looked terrible. There were no hands of stylists coming at her from all directions to try and fix her. She was in control and it was her choice to let the makeup remain smeared down her face. She stared at herself in the mirror, admiring the horrifically honest mess she had become. Arinadya believed it was the truest reflection of her soul she had ever seen. She got into bed and wondered if the thick black makeup would stain her face, leaving permanent tattoos of sorrow on her cheeks. It was only a matter of time before this metaphor became her reality. She was a shadow of her former self, a monster who wept black tears because there were no pure parts left in her soul to cry out.

Chapter 26

It had been eight days since Pasha dragged Sevrick through the woods and to the safety of the white elm. Eight long days that Sevrick remained trapped in the recesses of his mind. He had moments where he would slip in and out of consciousness, giving the rest of the Clandes hope, but even when he squeezed someone's hand or groaned at the mention of Arinadya's name, he always wound up slipping back into an unresponsive state. Leonid did his best with what he had to keep Sevrick alive, but as the days continued, the Clandes grew less and less sure that they were taking care of him properly.

After another day of watching Sevrick lay on his cot unconscious, Leonid lost his composure.

"I am not a doctor." His eyes were wide and his white hair was wet with sweat from deep anxiety. "I don't know how I got this role but I have no experience with this stuff."

"Your mom and dad were both doctors. You got your undergraduate degree in pre-med. You know a lot more than the rest of us do," Nina said calmly, rubbing the back of Leonid's neck. "Stop putting so much pressure on yourself, nobody expects you to save the world. Everybody knows Sevrick is in bad shape and no one will blame you if he doesn't survive this. You're just better prepared for this role than the rest of us. Sevrick's best shot is with you."

Leonid's breathing was heavy. He was failing to convey how unprepared he felt for the task. Sure, his parents had been doctors. Sure, he got through four years of pre-med classes at St. Petersburg State University. But he also spent most of his time hiding out in the sewers with Mikhail, Kirill, and the rest of their crew. His priorities were all mixed up during that time in his life and he wasn't sure how much knowledge he truly retained. The drugs were all he cared about and they always trumped his family, classes, and future. For his entire high school career, his extracurricular activities consisted of hanging out in the Russian underworld with Mikhail and Kirill, doing drugs and causing mischief. His parents forced him to go to college but that didn't stop him from continuing to hang out with his closest friends. As he took his classes at the university, he began sharing his newfound knowledge with Mikhail, which eventually led to their discovery of haemanism. When the government sought out Mikhail and Milena ten years ago, Leonid was just finishing his third year of college. He finished his last year of school during their first year as royals and after graduating, Mikhail immediately brought him into his royal posse. The entire time period was a blur to Leonid and the only memories that truly stood out were the insatiable cravings for his own drug-laced blood and those involving Nina. He had no concrete recollections from the classes he took, and very few from the clinical internships he did. The knowledge was stored somewhere inside his brain and he hoped it resurfaced as he needed it.

Ruslan sat with his nephew Isaak in a far corner. Alexsei had insisted that Leonid teach his son what he knew, so he took the teenaged boy on as an apprentice. He tried to teach him the little bit of knowledge he remembered from his hazy days as a haeman college student.

The room was quiet. Sevrick was unconscious on one cot, a recovering haeman lay sedated on the second, and Pasha was on the third, still unresponsive. They were unsure if he would ever recover from the heart attack and pneumonia that resulted from his run through the woods. Leonid was doing his best to keep him alive.

Ruslan and Isaak made no noise as they sat across the room from Nina and Leonid. Leonid was in Nina's arms as she whispered words of encouragement, trying to build up his confidence. Leonid's breakdown began when Ruslan carried Sevrick into the lab eight days ago. Then Alexsei followed close behind with a convulsing Pasha. The sight of both men unconscious sent him into a panic and he had been shaky and emotionally unstable ever since. It was the first time any person that wasn't haeman had to be taken care of in the lab, and the pressure of possibly failing was getting to him. With the haemans it never felt as crucial to guarantee their survival, but Sevrick and Pasha were part of their family. If either died, Leonid wasn't sure he could live with the guilt.

The only noise in the room was Nina's whispers and the low hum of the few machines that were set up. A few moments passed before Elena and Nikolai entered. They had ventured out into the city to spy on the royal wedding. Getting a good view was easy because all the haemans had been obsessed with getting as close as possible to the nuptial rituals all weekend. The outskirts were abandoned. On Friday, they found a spot on the roof of an abandoned building near Marsovo Polye Square. They witnessed the normally private rehearsal dinner take place in the middle of the square for all to see. They watched in disgust as the royals sat on the stage surrounded by a large and probably electrocuted fence while the rest of the regular haemans surrounded the feast like wild animals, desperate for a taste of the high life. The massive crowd was abuzz with dangerous energy as the creepy haeman circus performed for the masses. They reveled in the murder of innocent animals and let the brutality feed into their excitement. The whole ordeal was disturbing and uncomfortable to witness.

On Saturday, Elena and Nikolai snuck to the top of one of the newly built skyscrapers that bordered the city and the suburbs. The construction on this particular building wasn't finished, so they climbed up the scaffolding while the rest of the haemans flooded the streets that surrounded the Winter Palace. They climbed high enough so they could see the palace from afar. They got a brief glimpse of Arinadya as she exited her limousine and entered the palace, but that was all they could see in person. The rest they observed on the enormous screen that was set up in Marsovo Polye for the rest of the haeman community to watch. The square was jam packed and they could only imagine the nastiness taking place within the crowd as haemans bumped into one another and lost their tempers.

Nikolai and Elena wanted to witness the events of the wedding firsthand so they could tell Sevrick about it when he woke up. Sevrick would be miserable but if they could tell him they saw the wedding happen with their own eyes, maybe it would give him some closure. Sevrick trusted them, and since he wasn't capable of witnessing this wedding himself he would have wanted them to do it for him. Lizaveta wanted to go but Elena advised her not to. If Sevrick knew Liza went, he'd automatically assume the intention was out of bitterness and he would be resistant to receive any closure from it.

"How is he doing?" Elena asked. Lizaveta walked into the room a few moments later. She immediately went to Sevrick's side and placed her hand inside his.

"The same," Leonid answered. His face was tired and lined. "He occasionally fidgets but still hasn't woken up completely. Just small indications to let us know he might be on his way to regaining full consciousness."

Lizaveta looked down at Sevrick with concern. His dark brown hair was matted with sweat and his face was growing more facial hair than he'd normally allow.

"I hope this is enough to help him get over Rina."

At the mention of her name, Sevrick squeezed Lizaveta's hand with force and groaned loudly in agony. His hold on her was so tight that Liza let out a tiny scream in pain and Nikolai helped pry her hand out of Sevrick's grip. Tears filled Lizaveta's eyes at the realization that even unconscious, Sevrick still loved Rina with profound strength. Not being able to stand another moment of this torture, she left the room in a hurry.

"I guess we shouldn't expect him to be out of love with she-who-I-will-not-name when he wakes up," Nikolai said. "It's going to take some time for him to fall into hate with her."

Sevrick was rustling on his cot, fidgeting incessantly from discomfort. Leonid propped him up and placed another pillow behind his neck. At his touch, Sevrick began to breathe frantically. The room became tense as everyone wondered if this was a good sign or a bad sign. Leonid released his hold of him and then Sevrick opened his eyes.

Completely disoriented, Sevrick looked around, trying to grasp where he was as his eyesight adjusted to the dim light in the lab.

"Do you know who I am?" Leonid asked, trying to determine if Sevrick suffered any memory loss.

"Leo," Sevrick's voice was hoarse due to lack of use for a week. Leonid sighed in relief.

"And do you know who you are?"

"Yeah. Sevrick Bykovsky." He looked around at the room full of concerned faces. "What happened?"

"Why didn't you tell anyone where you were going?" Elena demanded, not feeling very sorry for him anymore.

"I told Pasha and Oksana."

"Yeah? Well thank God you did. If you hadn't you'd be dead," she said, furious.

"What do you mean?"

"Pasha saved your life," Ruslan spoke now. "He followed you through the woods to make sure you were alright. When you left the safety of the woods, Pasha waited in the forest for you to return." Ruslan paused, unsure how to continue the story.

"I remember what happened up until I went unconscious. I know Rina did this. I just don't understand what happened after that."

Nikolai stepped in to explain.

"Well, after Rina beat the shit out of you, she returned you to the forest's edge. Luckily, Pasha was still there waiting for you because he hauled you all the way back to the white elm on a sled. He made the trip in one day, didn't stop at all."

"Rina saved me?"

The entire room became tense as each individual felt different emotions: anger, frustration, pity.

"No. Rina almost *killed* you. *Pasha* saved you," Elena said before anyone else could. "And *you* might have killed him." The room went silent at this. Nobody truly wanted to blame Sevrick if Pasha died, but it was hard not to associate him with it, especially while he was still trying to defend the haeman.

"He's dead?" Sevrick asked, his eyes wet with remorse.

"No. We just aren't sure if he will make it. We think the pneumonia is preventing his recovery from the heart attack. Dragging you back to the white elm through the woods was too much for his body to handle." Ruslan's voice was heavy.

"I don't understand why she didn't just leave me for dead."

"She felt some weird and twisted haeman guilt. If I were you, I wouldn't confuse her moment of clarity for a true feeling. Nothing she felt was real. We have no idea what she would have done with you if Pasha hadn't been there to retrieve you. My guess is she *would* have left you for dead at the forest's edge," Nikolai said.

"You don't know that," Sevrick said, unsure why he was still eager to defend her.

"What is wrong with you?" Elena shouted, not really wanting an answer. "You almost died because of her, Pasha *might* die because of her, and you *still* refuse to let her go. You were in and out of a coma for eight days. When will you learn your lesson?"

"It's been eight days?" Sevrick had not realized he was knocked out that long.

"Yeah, eight horrible days," Leonid said. "I thought we were going to lose you."

He could see the deep pain on Leonid's face and then realized he was being selfish. These people cared about him and he had put them through torment the past week as he lay on his deathbed. While they were worried about him being okay, all he could worry about was Rina. He wanted to put his Clandes family first, but his heart was fighting him.

"I need to see Oksana. I need to apologize. I don't know how to make this right, but I will find a way. I will stay by Pasha's side until he gets better. And I can go to the city to get whatever supplies you need to heal him more effectively."

"You're not getting out of that bed anytime soon," Leonid said with authority. "This is the first time you've fully woken up in eight days and I don't trust you won't slip back into that damned coma at any given second."

"I'll stay in bed today, but I am not under house arrest." Sevrick did not want to be treated like a child even if deep down he understood why none of them trusted him at the moment.

"Yeah, well you don't call the shots right now," Elena said, hands on her hips. "You betrayed all of us when you went back to the city alone. You knew we would've said no or insisted someone accompany you, which is why you only told Pasha and Oksana. It was wrong and you know it." Sevrick felt like he was being scolded by his mother.

"I am extremely sorry for what happened to Pasha. I will never forgive myself for causing him pain and I will do my best to make it right. But I did not do any of it on purpose. I did not expect Pasha to follow me all the way to the city. He shouldn't have and I should have died. That's how it should have happened. If I died it would have been my own fault. I can own that and be okay with it."

"You don't think about anyone else but yourself." Elena's temper was rising. "Don't you realize you are *our* family now too? That maybe *we* don't want to lose you? How heartbroken all of us would have been if you died? Most of us lost our real family members and loved ones years ago and now all we have is each other. If we can't even care enough about each other to think about how our actions may affect those who love us, then we are just as bad as the haemans. Just as selfish and heartless. It's hard to be patient with someone who is supposed to be my friend but doesn't have any consideration for me or the other people I love. Get out of your own damned way. You're missing the life that's right in front of you."

She stormed out of the room. Sevrick was speechless and ashamed. Everything she said was accurate; he had been solely focused on saving Rina instead of putting his efforts and attention into his new family.

"I'm sorry," he said. "I thought I could have all of you and Rina too. I never realized I was putting our Clandes family second."

"It's okay, we get it," Leonid said. "We have all wanted to save loved ones from our previous lives. The only difference is that we let go much sooner than you. We all accepted that there are certain people we may never be able to save."

"We also didn't let ourselves get so consumed by it," Ruslan said. "When I tried to save my wife, I did all I could. While I spent countless hours trying to get her back, I made sure to dedicate any moment I wasn't with her to my own survival. I never forgot about my own health or well-being, and that's where you differ from me and every other survivor. You don't care how torn up or destroyed you become while trying to save that girl, as long as you eventually do."

"I don't know any other way," Sevrick's eyes filled up with tears. "She was my everything. My only family. My only love. If I cannot save her then I have failed her."

"Sev," Nikolai spoke again. "You need to let her go. While you were out, she married Prince Mikhail."

Sevrick's heart stopped at this news. He knew the day of the wedding had been approaching but somewhere deep in the back of his mind he didn't really believe it would happen.

"When?" he asked, his voice as tiny as a whisper.

"Saturday. Two days ago."

The room began to spin; he could not control the speed at which his heart raced. His mind became cloudy as one hundred thoughts moved like blurs through his consciousness. A weight that was heavier than he was able to hold landed straight upon his chest, making it hard to breath. He was suffocating. Drowning in the reality he had been fighting off for years. The loss of Rina was always imminent but he never let himself believe it could really happen. But now it did. He let the monster win.

"Are you okay?" Nikolai asked hesitantly.

"No," Sevrick gasped, the word came out as a sob. He began convulsing through heavy weeping and Nikolai and Nina immediately sat on the bed and held him in a tight embrace. "She was my everything. She saved me at my weakest moment and then I couldn't do the same for her."

Nina whispered to him, rocking the group hug back and forth, "Let it all out, it's okay. It's okay."

"It's not okay. I am a horrible person for letting this happen. Rina, the real Rina buried beneath the haeman, would be so disappointed. She would be heartbroken. She must think I gave up on her."

"No. She knows it's safer for you to be far away from her evil side. She would be happy you wised up and stopped risking your life. She knows you tried. She does. You did everything you could." But Nina's words went unheard.

"I let the monster win," Sevrick cried. "I let the monster win." Then he slipped back into a state of unconsciousness, knocking himself out with his own overwhelming grief.

Chapter 27

9 years earlier

Dafna's cancer progressed rapidly; she had been in the hospital for two months and they were releasing her today to live at home with hospice. Sevrick drove their rickety old station wagon while Rina sat in the back with his mother, holding her hand and speaking to her tenderly.

"We are going to take good care of you," Rina said softly.

"I am so happy my Sevrick has you," Dafna said, kissing the back of her hand. Her eyes were watery as she looked at Rina with contentment; her face at ease knowing her son had a wonderful girl to be with once she was gone. The love she saw between Rina and Sevrick had always been undeniable. They were together one year and Dafna could see they were soul mates.

Sevrick heard them speaking from the driver's seat but didn't say a word. He happily listened as the two women he loved bonded.

The car jerked to a stop in front of their small house on the poor side of the city. They helped Dafna into the house and then into her bed. Rina gently tucked her in under the fluffy covers and then sat next to her on the mattress, placing a hand upon her shoulder.

"Can I get you anything?" she asked, her eyes wide with concern, eager to do all she could to make Dafna as happy and comfortable as possible.

"Could you get me a water, dear?" she requested. Rina smiled and stepped away.

As soon as she left the room, Dafna refocused her attention to Sevrick who was sitting in a rocking chair next to the bed.

"I absolutely adore her," his mother said. "She is good for you."

"I know. I never knew I could love someone as much as I love her."

"I am very happy for you." Her grin went from ear to ear and tears filled her eyes. "What you have with her is special and rare to find."

"I wish you were healthy so you could enjoy it with us. There is so much to come in the future and I want you to be part of it all," Sevrick said, his face grief stricken; he could not imagine life without her.

"You will be just fine without me. I will always be watching you from above."

Rina reappeared at the doorway with the glass of water. She gave it to Dafna and sat back down on the bed. Then the three of them spent the entire night talking about fond memories Dafna had from Sevrick's childhood.

Two weeks went by with hospice caring for Dafna at home. Sevrick and Rina stayed with her the entire time. Rina's parents were in America with Adrik as he attended Columbia University in New York City. They expected Rina to follow suit and get accepted into a college in America, but Rina had other plans. While her family was determined to escape Russia, she wanted to stay. As appealing as the freedom in America seemed, Russia was her home and it was where she had someone who loved her. She also could not shake the feeling of abandonment from her family. They could've waited one more year to leave, or at least until she graduated, but instead they left her in their rental home with a lease that expired one month after her last day in high school. She felt trapped in their little plan and it was unfair to assume she wanted to follow them to America. Adrik was their ticket out, not her.

Sevrick assured her she didn't need to worry. That he had enough money saved up for his own college funds and if they both worked hard enough, they could pay for hers too. He promised her he would take care of her and she did not have to fall in line with her family's plans if she did not want to. And without words, he showed her everyday how strongly he loved her. No matter the mood, the issues, or the hardships, his love was unconditional.

She continued her high school education and moved her belongings into Sevrick's home so she could help take care of Dafna. The two weeks since she came home were tough; she was getting sicker and deteriorating right before their eyes. Her body had become alarmingly frail and she had trouble speaking without expending a tremendous amount of energy.

Sevrick cried every night. They usually spent the evenings talking with his mother and telling her funny stories until she fell asleep. Then immediately afterward, Sevrick would collapse into Rina's arms in the family room and sob until he passed out. His mother was the only person he ever had throughout his entire life and to lose her was like losing a part of himself. So Rina was his rock; she was his anchor in this maddening sea of despair and suffering. It was not easy for anyone, but Rina was the force that kept everyone sane.

It was only three weeks into hospice care when Dafna passed away. As Sevrick was telling her about a date he had with Rina in the park, he could hear her breathing change. He stopped the story and grabbed his mother's hand.

"Mom, are you okay?" His eyes were wide with fear.

"I think it's my time," she said in a whisper.

"No," Sevrick broke down but he could see she was at peace. Rina grabbed her other hand, silent tears streaming down her face.

"Sevrick," Dafna said. "You have a long and wonderful life ahead of you. I could not be more proud to call you my son. I don't know how I did it, but I raised a selfless, genuine, and compassionate man despite the tough hand I was dealt. I love you more than I ever loved myself."

"Mom," Sevrick whimpered. "Please don't leave me."

"I have to. But you are in good hands." She slowly shifted her gaze to Rina. "You managed to find the most beautiful woman in Russia, inside and out. Knowing you have her by your side is all I need to be okay with leaving you in this life."

"I love you so much." He held her delicate hand to his lips. His tears fell onto her skin as he kissed the back of her hand.

"I love you too," her breath rattled as she spoke. She smiled at him one last time, then exhaled her last breath. Sevrick leaned over her now and held her tight, sobbing onto her lifeless body. Rina quickly walked around the bed and placed a hand on his back. Her touch was soothing and helped him regain his composure. He stood up and kissed his mother one last time on the forehead. Tears rolled down his cheeks as he made the call to hospice to let them know she was gone.

Rina held his hand as he said the words out loud.

"My mother just died." She could feel his body tremble between their clasped hands. He hung up the phone and waited for the coroner to arrive and retrieve Dafna. Rina held him tightly and through the tears he whispered into her ear, "I am so grateful to have you."

"You will always have me."

Sevrick kissed her on the neck and held her close. "Thank you for being so strong."

"Of course. You'd do the same for me." She smiled at him; its radiance put a tiny sliver of hope back into his heart. If he had her love to help him through, he knew he'd make it to the other side of this sorrow one day.

Chapter 28

Haeman nurses surrounded Milena as she lay on her deathbed. They hovered over her like vultures; paid to save her, but eager to see if she would die. Mikhail was banned from the room because his constant outbursts were a serious distraction for her caretakers. Every time his sister coughed up blood or expressed any discomfort, he flew off the handle, punching holes in the walls and breaking whatever was within his reach. After he launched a chair through the window, letting in a frigid draft of air, they insisted he leave.

He begrudgingly obeyed, surrendering only because he knew it was best for Milena. She was too fragile to be exposed to his explosive temper. He didn't trust himself with her and neither did anyone else. She was dying and he could not control his rage. It scorched his insides like a wild inferno, setting a flame beneath his icy heart. His army was set to find Leonid but most of them were still traveling from across the continent to fight. Nobody liked to fly because the closed confinements always led to murder, so the roads were in a constant state of heavy traffic. Because of this, the majority of haemans traveling to St. Petersburg found other means of transportation: walking, running, horseback riding, bicycling. They traveled in large haeman herds, trekking across the massive continent toward St. Petersburg. They had boundless energy and they moved with intention. As they traveled, their vision was clouded in red from the silve in their veins. Their motivation was the desire to get the blood of the condemned on their hands. The anticipated massacre put a jump in their step as they moved menacingly toward the city.

Mikhail was growing impatient. While haemans gradually began to fill the city streets, he had to sit idly back until they all arrived. He went to a lot of trouble to scout the haemans from Far East Russia, convincing them they had to participate. If he began this mission without them after forcing them to make the terribly long and tedious journey, they would be furious and possibly revolt. He could not have any haeman go unaccounted for; they were all essential. Not because he needed them for this particular mission, but because he needed their loyalty and allegiance in the missions yet to come. Mikhail had big plans for the future of his empire and he needed every haeman on board if he planned to succeed.

Haemans were scattered through all of St. Petersburg, sleeping on benches and scattered along the sidewalks. The mood was tense as they all tried not to kill each other before being sent off to battle. Their emotional restraints and will power typically did not hold and the royal militia found themselves breaking up fights regularly. It was easier than ignoring the brawls and being forced to pile up corpses for removal.

Kirill suggested Mikhail move on with the plan and make a promise to the haemans who hadn't arrived yet that they'd be part of the next battle, which would be much bigger. Every day that passed, the prince grew more anxious. His sister was getting sicker by the minute and if they didn't find Leonid to discover how he reversed his haemanism, they wouldn't be able to come up with a suitable cure in time.

After his last blowup in Milena's bedroom, he gave himself a few hours to think it over. Finally, he came to the conclusion to reassign this first mission as a small, targeted strike; one to set the following attacks in motion. He would only need a select team rather than the entire fleet of haemans to participate. The rest of them would get their chance to battle in the coming weeks.

Mikhail sent a few of his top men into Marsovo Polye Square to address the crowd. They explained the new orders and after a few outbursts of complaints, the crowd settled down and accepted the new plan. The royal militia then scoured the masses for the 200 haemans that would accompany them on their hunt for Leonid.

As his militiamen did this job for him, Mikhail stormed around the palace, talking to himself and smashing antiques. When he reached Arinadya's alternate bedroom, which he had been making her sleep in a lot lately, he burst through the door to find her passed out in bed.

She was still recovering from a recent beating. The day Milena was officially confined to bed rest, Mikhail took out his frustration on his new bride, bruising both her eyes and the entire left side of her torso. She was looking a little better now as she lay fast asleep.

Mikhail sat on the side of her bed, watching her slumber blissfully unaware of his looming presence. He took her hand and placed his fingers around her wrist, holding her tightly in his grasp. In her unconscious state, she did not fight him. He smiled and silently wished she were this calm and compliant while awake; perhaps then their relationship would be less volatile.

She began to toss in her sleep but the prince kept hold of her wrist. He placed a hand on her bare inner thigh and she moaned. At first the words were inaudible. Then he heard a name.

"Sev," she muttered, but it was hard to understand. Mikhail kept touching her leg, coaxing the name out of her subconscious. "Sevri—" she moaned. "Sevrick." Her voice was sleepy and unaware of its misgivings.

Who was Sevrick? The anger he felt all evening in Milena's room was now multiplied. There wasn't another man, Mikhail was positive of it. Arinadya had not been allowed to leave the palace since their marriage and there was no man named Sevrick working within the palace. Perhaps another man during their courtship? He did not believe so. She was a prude. If she did not desire sex with him then he did not believe she'd go out looking for it with someone else. But what if he was wrong? What if she was making a fool of him in the many hours he let pass without seeing her, without monitoring her every move?

"Sevrick," she said, her moan more like a whimper this time. "Help." A single tear fell from her eye as the nightmare she was having became reality. Mikhail's rage boiled over at the mention of this foreign name again. He grabbed a fistful of her long red hair and yanked her upright.

"Who is he?" he demanded, screaming and spitting in her face. Arinadya was confused, still half-asleep.

"What did I do?" she cried, unsure what caused this assault in the middle of the night. His grasp was tight as he shook her, hurting her neck in the process.

"Sevrick? Who the fuck is Sevrick?" At the mention of his name, her heart contracted. A deep fear emerged from the depths of her soul and she fought back the urge to show her recognition of this name.

"What are you talking about? You're crazy." She tried to fight Mikhail and loosen his hold of her but that only made him angrier.

"You said his name in your sleep, you stupid whore. I came in to check on my wife and I hear her whispering another man's name at my touch."

"Came in to check on me? Don't pretend like you give a damn about me, you callous bastard. The only time I've seen you since our wedding day were on the occasions when you came to me horny or full of rage. I'm sure you stopped in to 'check on me' in order to get in a quick rape."

"Who the fuck is Sevrick?" His eyes were lined with hysteria. He had one thing on his mind and he was going to get an answer. He threw her back onto the mattress and held her down by her throat. Arinadya just stared back up at him defiantly, exhausted with his antics.

Mikhail's voice shook with fury. "I'll ask again nicely. Who is Sevrick?" His grip on her neck tightened but she did not fight it.

"I don't know anyone by that name," she answered with calm confidence. "The subconscious works in funny ways. I probably made him up in an attempt to replace you, even if it was only in my dreams. I wish now that I could remember what I was fantasizing about in my sleep." Arinadya had no emotion in her eyes. "I bet it was nice."

"I don't believe you," he growled, his eyes wide in the dim moonlight that filtered through her window.

"I don't care if you believe me or not. That's the truth. You're wasting your energy with this bullshit. Freaking out because I said a random name in my sleep. Get over it." Arinadya's gusto was back; she was tired of being bullied, tired of feeling weak. "Or, if you can't let it go because you're a neurotic control freak, maybe you can send your haeman army after my imaginary lover. I assume that's what the psychotic thoughts crossing through your mind right now are telling you to do. I'm sure your haeman army would really appreciate running through all of Russia hunting down a ghost." A spark of madness entered her eyes. "And if I'm lucky, maybe a pointless mission like that would finally be enough to make them turn on you. Could you imagine? Thousands of emotionally unstable haemans finding out their beloved prince wasted their precious time trying to track down and kill a person who didn't even exist? Might just be enough to free me of you once and for all."

"What is wrong with you, you stupid bitch? You're supposed to be on my side. I gave you the title of my wife. Of royalty. And you thank me by wishing death upon me? I should kill you here and now."

"Then do it. I'm not afraid of you." She kneed him in the groin and broke free of his death grip. She sprinted in a blur to the opposite side of the room and chugged her morning dose of drug-laced blood. The chemicals hit her instantly, leaving her feeling strong and powerful. Her confidence was high and streaks of red smeared across her vision, making the impending fight seem less intimidating.

"Come to me, husband. You never know, I might match your strength now."

He laughed at her, condescendingly.

"You wish. I don't think it's wise that you tempt me. If you make me angry enough, I may not be able to stop myself from enjoying your murder."

"That's exactly what I'm hoping for." She meant it. She knew he would wind up killing her eventually and she'd rather he do it now than make her suffer through years of his unrelenting torment. She was a miserable shell of her former self. She was no longer human and no longer sure who she was as a haeman. Mikhail was slowly stripping her of her identity. She considered running away but when they inevitably found her and dragged her back, the torture would be worse. And even if she did get away, what kind of life was there for her on the other side? She was a monster straight from the depths of hell, and there was no room for creatures of the dark in the world outside of haemanism. She was a murderer who wore her kill count on her back. She walked around for years with no shame for what she had done. Her kills were celebrated as achievements. A person like her could not be trusted around innocents, nor did she deserve to be.

Mikhail lunged at her but she did not back down. She threw the bottom of her palm into the center of his chest, knocking him back. The prince tilted his head, accepting the challenge, then dove with a fist extended toward her face. She caught the fist and returned her own, but he caught hers as well. They were in a dead lock. Her initial burst of strength was already wavering; there had not been

308

enough drugs in her morning concoction. Mikhail could feel her beginning to tremble as she held him back.

"You will never be stronger than me," he whispered. "I would never allow it." Then he twisted her arm behind her back, locking her in his grasp. She twisted violently, trying to break free, but his hold on her was too tight. As he slipped a hand beneath her nightdress she tilted her head back and bit his neck, taking out a chunk of skin. His blood poured down his shoulder, mixing into her blood red hair.

Outraged, Mikhail threw her into the glass window, causing it to shatter. As she fell, a piece of jagged glass sliced her skin open from her left hip up into her armpit. It wasn't terribly deep, but it was enough to slow her down significantly. She stayed on the ground. He put pressure on the side of his neck to stop the bleeding.

"Look what you've done to me!"

"That's rich, coming from you."

He began to walk out of the room to seek medical attention, but she stopped him.

"Where are you going?" Her voice was full of outrage. "Finish what you've started!"

"Don't be foolish, I'd end up killing you."

"That's what I want," she screamed back at him. His face shifted into revulsion at the realization that she meant it when she said it earlier.

"You're sick in the head," he spat out, lowering his guard.

"Just kill me," she pleaded, her voice frenzied. "Just do it already. You're bound to kill me eventually, let it be now. Let me go."

A look of profound disgust lined Mikhail's face. His narcissism could not understand what Arinadya saw in inviting death. He saw it as quitting, as the ultimate failure, something he could not have tied to his legacy.

Arinadya saw it as the only way to escape, to be free, and to find herself again. She no longer wanted to be haeman and she could not be human. If she was human, the weight of everything she had done as a haeman would haunt her forever. The burden upon her shoulders was all her own and she knew there was no way to ever truly get rid of it. She could not go back, and she didn't even think she wanted to. If she could not be haeman or human, then death was the only way to end this.

"I planned to keep you around for a while actually." Mikhail refused to entertain her insane pleas for death. "Despite your fight, I rather like you." He didn't like her; he just needed her because the entire haeman population idolized her, probably more so than they ever did Milena. A good portion of his army came to St. Petersburg on behalf of Arinadya, not Mikhail. Certain groups within the haemans felt more devotion toward her. He'd lose them if he lost her.

"Well, I despise you."

Mikhail took a deep breath, aware that he should not engage her any longer or it would not end well for anybody. Instead, he turned it all back around on Arinadya.

"I already told you a million times to stop fighting me and this relationship. You being miserable is your own doing, not mine. You haven't even tried." Then he stormed out of the room.

At his disappearance, she broke down in tears. She couldn't take it anymore. Haemans were not supposed to harbor emotions but ever since the prince's forced courtship, she felt smothered in despair. As much as she wished she could keep the feelings away permanently by being high all the time, her daily allowance of silve wasn't enough to accomplish that. Mikhail made sure nobody got more than he did.

The gash on her side would certainly scar. The beauty she used to find in the little marks scattered along her body was gone. The old scars she made were now overshadowed by the ones Mikhail gave her. The novelty of the tiny painless markings disappeared as soon as their maker became the prince and not her. Now they disgusted her. He left his permanent mark upon her many times over, and whenever she saw them in the mirror she cringed. The scars made her think of him. It made her feel encased within the wounds he had inflicted upon her, trapped beneath his unyielding hold. But while Mikhail left horrifying scars upon her skin as constant reminders of his power over her, Arinadya was burdened even more by the ones that weren't visible to the eye, the ones she had unknowingly given herself over the years, carved deep into her heart because of what she had done to Sevrick. She knew those were the scars that would always haunt her most of all.

The moonlight still filtered through the broken window. She looked down at the long, jagged pieces of glass all over the floor. She could easily end this now and escape from the cruel world she created for herself. She picked up one of the glass daggers and held it close to her face, examining its sharp edges. It would be swift and uncomplicated. It amazed her how simple a solution this could be. But while the outcome of this was the most logical way out, Arinadya could not do it. Not like this. She would not put another scar upon her body that Mikhail could take credit for. If she was going to end it all, it would be on her own terms. And it would be for herself, not anybody else. She was tired of having choices made for her and having no control over her life. She had to take it back. This was her way to reclaim the reins of her own life and crash this ship once and for all. Once she was gone, her soul would be free from the years of abuse she placed upon herself. She would be free from Mikhail's emotional and physical torment. She would be free from this addiction that ruined everything she once loved about herself. And most importantly, she would be setting Sevrick free from her.

Chapter 29

A few days passed and Sevrick was now able to get out of bed and walk around without assistance. The gash above his eye still had stitches in it, so it was covered with a large square piece of gauze and medical tape.

Sevrick was amazed at the progress the Clandes and other survivors made on the underground fortress. Its expansion was so large that the Primos could now live beneath the ground too. Everyone anticipated this project would take months to complete, but with all the extra hands it had taken half that time. Two new living spaces were created as well as two new exits from the underground fortress that led out into the depths of the forest near the homes of the Scots. These new entrances were disguised within the dense forestry and would prove useful if they were attacked and could not enter through the main entrance at the white elm. The Lads said they were happy with their home by the lake; it was out of the way and unlikely to be investigated by the haemans. But the Scots decided that once all the Primos were settled they would like to dig extra tunnels and create more room for their own people. Their tree homes were on the opposite side of the open field where the white elm sat. They lived right along the forests edge and while the haemans would most likely not see their homes that were craftily hidden amongst the trees, the concern that they might, if they were looking hard enough, concerned Scarlov. They had no protection if they were spotted and he felt it would be best if he moved his people underground as well. It was the only way to ensure their safety, especially since the news of Prince Mikhail's billboard declaring war was discovered. Nobody knew when the strike would happen, but they all agreed being underground was their safest bet. Despite all their training and attempts to be prepared to fight, every survivor knew it would be a massacre if they tried. They weren't ready and they did not have the weaponry necessary to defend themselves against a slew of jacked up haemans.

As the weeks passed, Ruslan, Alexsei, Scarlov, Lyov, Vladimir, and Oleg, leaders of each respective group, decided they were going to need outside help. The survivors had been in hiding too long without the rest of the world being aware of their dire situation. They needed powerful reinforcements. Once the underground fortress was complete, they would send groups out beyond the heavily guarded borders of Russia. If they could make the rest of the world aware of the terror that engulfed their country, maybe they could find a way to finally save their homeland from these monsters. Having the power of other nations on their side would hopefully prove to be enough when the time was right to fight.

So far, the royals and the government masterfully hid the terrifying truth of haemanism from the rest of the world. In fact, they encouraged many nations to celebrate the reinstatement of the royal family while keeping their secret contained. They built up their publicity in other countries just as they had done in Russia, leaving out any signs of haemanism. Mikhail was clever, providing only the information he wanted outsiders to know. He generated excitement about Russia's new regime within the people of other lands, getting them on board and making them fascinated with their royal lives from afar. Besides the devout groups of minions he crafted out of innocent and naïve Russians, he also managed to create a loyal following outside of Russia, amongst the media hungry Americans and the culturally thirsty Europeans. They treated the Russian royals like their own. Sevrick was sure they all celebrated the wedding right alongside them through their televisions and computers, though the version they saw was surely edited to only hold content these foreigners would find socially acceptable.

It disgusted Sevrick that Mikhail was getting away with these atrocities. He turned Russia into a nightmare and nobody was stopping him because nobody except his fellow haemans knew what he had done.

Sevrick enjoyed exploring the new sections of his expanded home. Everyone he came across was a stranger and nobody asked him questions he wasn't ready to answer. It felt refreshing to be around people who didn't judge him for what happened to Pasha or think he was crazy for loving a woman who almost killed him.

Sevrick wandered through the new tunnels to investigate the progress that had been made. There were two new living spaces created for the Primos. After walking through long corridors that connected them all together, he eventually reached the work area for the third room being built. There were four rooms total for gatherings and many new hallways off the main corridors that held bedroom coves.

When Sevrick got to the construction site for the fourth overall gathering room, he saw they were making this room even larger than all the others. There were wood beams providing ceiling support throughout the room, making sure the weight of the earth above did not collapse on them. Sevrick watched their progress, impressed that he and his fellow survivors adapted so well to the conditions forced upon them. Sevrick wished he could help but his head still ached and his vision occasionally fogged over from the trauma he received.

As he quietly watched the workers use their pick axes and shovels to carve out the frozen dirt walls, Sevrick's mind wandered toward the recovered haemans. He had not seen any of them during his walk and they saved quite a few already. Sevrick headed back toward the laboratory and when he arrived, he saw there was a new tunnel off that room. He walked down this dark corridor and peeked into one of the bedrooms. Inside was a middle-aged recovered haeman woman sleeping on the floor with only a pillow. Sleeping amenities were scarce and many people slept on the hard floor until a raid could be done for pillows and blankets, but it bothered him that the haemans were being kept away from everyone else. The laboratory was off the beaten path. It was located down a long hallway off the original gathering room and the haeman's hallway was extended off that, extremely far from any of the other survivors or rooms where everyone could be together.

Sevrick shook his head in disapproval and as he was about to leave, the woman woke up.

"What are you doing here?"

"Sorry," Sevrick was caught off guard. "I wasn't spying. I was giving myself a tour. I hadn't seen any of you through the natural flow of tunnels in the fortress so I was just wondering where all the recovered haemans were now living."

"Yeah, we are pretty far from the main living quarters."

"I'm sorry they put you all over here." Sevrick felt genuinely bad that they were being treated as outcasts.

"Don't be sorry, this is what we wanted. We collectively asked them to make our housing as far away from the rest of you if it was possible."

"Why would you want that?" he asked, confused.

"Because we don't belong with you. It's hard to explain to someone who never lived as a haeman, but we have dormant evil within our souls. We all have done things we can never erase. Evil acts that were celebrated and treated as accomplishments. It's a terrible burden to live with and it's hard to feel comfortable around so many kind and genuine souls, knowing you yourself were once proud to be a monster."

Sevrick was at a loss for words; he never saw it that way before.

"But you are healed now and no one here judges you for having once been a haeman."

"That's because no one here knows the horrors we committed *while* being haeman. If they knew, they wouldn't be so quick to welcome us into their home."

"Maybe you're right, but trust me, we are very aware of the evil that comes from haemanism. Why do you think we went to such extremes to hide from it?" Sevrick spread his arms wide, indicating the massive lengths everyone had gone to in order to build their elaborate underground home. "We know you were once bad, we can imagine you've done terrible things, but we went to great lengths to save you in order to give you all a second chance. You don't need to let what you've done define who you will be."

"Maybe it will just take some time for me to believe that. I am going to have to forgive myself before I can trust myself around innocents again. I don't feel worthy of forgiveness. None of us do, and until we can move past that, it's better we cope amongst ourselves."

"Well, my name is Sevrick. I want to help you heal. I will give you all space but please come to me if you ever need to talk."

"Thanks Sevrick, I'm Polina. We are very grateful to be rehabilitated; I haven't been able to see this clearly in years. But it will take time to find solace in who I used to be."

"I understand. Just know that you and all the other people who were rehabilitated are not alone. We cleansed you of the haemanism but the help doesn't stop there. You are a part of this group now and you shouldn't feel ashamed to take part in this large, unconventional family of survivors."

"Thanks, I appreciate it. In time I am sure it will all feel right again." She smiled at him, her bright green eyes kind and full of remorse. The light that came through from the air ducts above cascaded on her, illuminating her lined face and graying brown hair.

"Before I go," Sevrick knew he should not be inquiring about this but he could not help it. "Did you know the new princess?"

Polina's eyes lit up. "Arinadya? I did not know her personally but I was infatuated with her before you guys shot me down and rehabilitated me. Though she is much younger than me, I idolized her. She is so strong. She kept the prince in his place. Every haeman adores her."

Sevrick sighed. He did not know what he wanted to hear.

"I used to be engaged to her. I loved her once upon a time."

Polina's eyes widened, shocked at this revelation. But then her face turned sympathetic, understanding his loss in this situation. "I'm sorry."

"It's alright. She chose haemanism over me. I have to learn to let it go." He said these words very unconvincingly.

"Yeah. She is very far into that lifestyle. I can't imagine her wanting to be anything else." Polina's tone sounded like she still held some fascination for Arinadya. "But if you ever did get her back, you'd really screw up what Prince Mikhail has going on out there."

"What do you mean?"

"Every haeman loves Arinadya now, probably more than they care for Mikhail or Milena or any of the other royals. Mikhail made a mistake when he picked her to be his bride. He didn't realize that his army of devout followers would eventually like her more than they liked him. I bet if she jumped ship, a lot of other haemans would rethink what they were doing too. I know I would have."

"I've tried for years to get her back. I made my last attempt about two weeks ago and she gave me this," Sevrick pointed to the large, bloody gauze that covered the top of his eye, "and left me unconscious for a full week. I was the last one to think I'd ever give up on us but I think I have no choice now."

"You're lucky she didn't kill you." Polina appeared impressed. "Or give you an injury that serious sooner. I imagine she must have had a pretty deep love for you to retain control and spare your life through all these years. Being a recovered haeman, I know how hard it must have been for her to dig up old reasons to let you live. Haemans suppress. They do not feel anything and when they do, they do what they have to in order to erase that feeling. And generally that means murdering whoever is causing you to feel."

"Well, maybe I didn't make her feel anything. I know she buried our love pretty deep. Maybe she never killed me because I didn't evoke any kind of emotion out of her anymore."

"I highly doubt that. They suppress, they don't forget."

"I don't know. I can't worry about it anymore. She is where she wants to be so I need to move on with my own life too."

"I think that's best," Polina agreed.

"Okay, I'll leave you be. But don't forget to come find me if you or any of your friends need anything."

"I won't forget the kindness," she smiled one last time at him and then rested her head back on her pillow.

Sevrick left with a heart that felt swollen inside. Seeing Polina suffer, even after being saved from the haemanism addiction, overwhelmed him with grief for Rina. He missed her terribly and wished that it had been a recovered Rina he got to console. The more he thought about it, the more he needed to get away and let fresh air cleanse his mind.

Chapter 30

Sevrick quickly returned to his bedroom and put on his winter jacket. He made his way through the white elm and into the open field without being seen. Unsure where to go, he walked without a destination in mind. His thoughts swirled around memories and images of Rina he had stored away in the recesses of his brain. As hard as he tried, he could not shake her. He could not silence his love for her. He was not crazy enough to go back to the city now, but his heart ached knowing his last chance to save her had passed.

He walked through the forest aimlessly, trying to eradicate the relentless thoughts of his lost love. She still coursed through his veins like she was a vital part of his existence.

Before he knew it, he was deep into the woods. The trees looked familiar and he realized he was near the lagoon he followed Rina to many weeks ago. This was where he needed to be. The snow on the ground began to seep through the toes of his boots as he continued on with new purpose.

The lagoon was a place he believed Rina ran to in attempts to find peace. A place to escape what she could not control. A place to let go. He hoped to do that here too. It was time for him to finally let go, once and for all, and this was the perfect spot to reflect upon his thoughts and find closure. His heart tightened as he reached the last row of trees and took a step into the small opening.

The lagoon's water was shallow and clear. The forest to the right of it was dense and the rocky cliffs to the left had such height they cast a shadow of menacing authority over the lagoon. Sevrick did not have a chance to appreciate the beauty of this spot the last time he was here because he had been too focused on Rina. But this time, he was able to take it all in: the crystal clear water that shimmered as it moved; the luscious green forestry that cradled the lagoon along its edges; the small mossy beach that offered a soft entrance into the water; the great cliffs that overlooked the lagoon, protecting it from the volatile ocean beyond. As he scanned the progression of the cliff's height, his eyes reached the edge of the highest spot. A shape stood out amongst the skyline. Were his eyes playing tricks on him or was that a person up there? To Sevrick, it looked to be a body: someone was standing dangerously close to the cliff's edge, inviting disaster.

Panic flooded his body and he quickly, but calmly, made his way up the incline. The walk was rocky and demanding on his recovering body, but he ignored the pain. These cliffs were dangerous; no one should be standing so close to their edge. Once he was halfway, the clouds in the sky shifted and let the sun shine through for a moment. In those few seconds, the rays hit the top of this stranger's head, setting fire to their skull. Sevrick blinked twice, adjusting his vision as the body more clearly became that of a woman. As the sun set her hair ablaze, the strong red tones flashed brightly in the light the sun offered. Then the clouds reclaimed their dominance over the sky and the person stood there like a shadow once more.

Sevrick's mind became frantic. Despite his body's disapproval, he began to run. He ran as fast as he could and when he was only a few feet from the woman, she turned to face him. It was Rina.

"What are you doing?" he screamed, out of breath and in pain.

Rina's eyes were filled with tears. She said nothing and turned back to face the wide and mighty ocean beneath her.

"Answer me," he shouted, his voice shaking with fear and anger.

"I'm doing us both a favor."

Sevrick did not understand what she meant.

"The winds up here are strong. You will fall."

"Not if I jump first." Rina's voice had no color to it, no animation or emotion. She sounded like the life that used to burn inside her had been stripped away.

"What are you talking about, are you nuts? Why would you jump?" His intention to let her go vanished as he realized she was toying with death.

"Because I want to die." She turned to face him again. "I have no soul. I have no purpose. I have made a mockery of my life and the potential I once had. I don't know what I am or how I came to be so lost, but I cannot be found. There is no place left on this earth for someone like me."

"Stop it!" Sevrick could not fully comprehend what was happening. This was not his Rina, but it wasn't the haeman Arinadya either. He did not know who she was right now but it was by far the worst version of her he had ever experienced. Sevrick had known great fear in his life, but none as formidable as this. "Rina, stop and think. Take a step away from the edge and think about what you are saying."

"I don't need to think anymore. All I have done for the past few weeks is think. And think. And think. And it has driven me mad!"

"Then take a step back and *stop* thinking. You have thought yourself into despair."

Rina turned away from him again.

"It may be despair, but it is by far the clearest feeling I have had in years."

"Remember beyond that. Beyond the addiction and before everything turned to hell. You were happy once. I swear that you were."

"I don't know what happy feels like anymore." Her eyes remained upon the ocean that crashed against the jagged rocks below.

"Look at me and you'll remember," Sevrick pleaded but she would not engage him. "Look at me goddamnit!" Rina's face scrunched up tight, fighting back tears as she turned and made true eye contact with Sevrick for the first time. He took a step toward her.

"It's okay to let me help you." He tried to embrace her but Rina recoiled from his affection. She took a step backward and her heel hung ominously off the cliff.

"Don't touch me!" Arinadya could not handle the flood of emotions attacking her from every angle. "Stay where you are!" Sevrick halted his movement the moment she moved closer to the edge. Arinadya's eyes were wide and Sevrick could see for the first time how intoxicated she was. Her pupils were dilated and she kept twitching her nose, as if to itch it without touching it. Sevrick had to be more careful with his approach; Arinadya was not in a stable state of mind.

"Okay, I am sorry. You just need to know you are not alone."

"Oh, but you are wrong. I am very alone. I am so alone I cannot bear my own company anymore."

"Then what I meant is that you don't *need* to be alone anymore. I am here for you. I always have been."

The tears Arinadya had been fighting fell with anger. "Why? After all this time, why haven't you just forgotten me? I have been terrible to you. Look at your face!" She threw an arm in his direction, indicating the large piece of gauze covering the stitched gash above his eye.

"It was your addiction that did this to me, not you. And if you gave me the chance to help you beat your demons, you could feel right again. You could be your old self again."

"That girl is dead."

"You're wrong."

"She was silenced by the monster in me years ago. She is gone, Sevrick. No normal human soul could survive beneath the crimes I have committed. Even if she was still trapped inside me after the addiction began, she shattered to pieces the moment I proudly made my first kill."

"She may be shattered but the pieces are still in you. You just need help putting them back together."

"No. Stop trying to save me. Stop trying to recover the girl you once loved; what you are looking at now is all that is left of her. An empty shell with the face of your Rina."

"Don't you remember any of it? Any of the love we shared? None of it still lives in you?"

Arinadya twitched at this question, rubbing her nose as her high continued to course through her veins. "It doesn't matter what I remember, none of it can ever be how it once was."

"Can't you try?"

"I don't want to. I don't want my old life and I don't want my new life. I don't want any of it. I just want this nightmare to be over, once and for all. Then I will be free and so will you."

"What kind of delusional thinking is that? I will be free of you once you're dead? Don't you see what's happening? This can't be a coincidence that you wound up being here on the same day I came here to forget you. It's a clear sign that we aren't meant to be free of each other. Whether you jump off this cliff today, die in ten years by Mikhail's side, or pass peacefully as an old lady that I am lucky enough to call my wife, I will never be free of you just because you died first. Your memory would haunt me forever, no matter how it happened. I will never 'be free' of you."

Arinadya took a deep breath, trying to control the rush of panic she was feeling. Another deep breath and she lost it. She began to sob, shaking from the depths of her soul.

"I am a monster. Can't you see?" Arinadya's eyes were crazed. "I am nothing but a ghost of who I used to be."

"Stop letting this addiction define you."

"I should have been stronger. I should have gotten out when you did."

"You cannot change the past but you can salvage the future. You don't need to end it this way. I promise I will help you get through it."

"This is something I need to do on my own. I can't have you carrying my burdens anymore."

"You didn't let me down when I needed you most. I would not have survived the death of my mother if it hadn't been for you. It's your turn to lean on me."

"She would be so disappointed in me," Arinadya sobbed.

"She would be more disappointed if you quit now."

"I cannot imagine being able to live a life outside of haemanism and be okay with all the things I have done. I can't just pretend like they didn't happen."

"Of course not, but it is possible for you to still move forward and live your life the way you want to again. We've already rehabilitated multiple haemans. They are struggling with their own guilt but they are getting better every day. They are happy to be healed. You may have done some awful things as a haeman that you will have to carry with you through life, but it is not who you are. If you could only see that you are worth more than the errors you have made, you would see it is possible for you to forgive yourself."

"I don't think I will ever be able to forgive myself for the horror I have been."

"In time, you will. I forgive you."

"You shouldn't," silent tears poured down her face. "Out of all the terrible things I've done, what I did to you was worst of all."

"I forgive you. In fact, I forgave you a long time ago."

Arinadya shook her head violently, refusing to believe he could possibly still love her.

"You are a fool. Stop letting your love for me blind you. I am a monster and one day you will wake up feeling nothing but hate for me. When you look back on all of this with hindsight, you will be disgusted. It is inevitable; one day you'll see how effortlessly I destroyed you without any remorse."

"But you feel remorse now," Sevrick tried to rationalize.

"I don't want to feel *anything* now. I am so tired of feeling. I wasn't supposed to feel anything as a haeman yet I still managed to become riddled with misery. I am exhausted and I am ready to be done."

Arinadya's high was not wavering. Her behavior was erratic and her judgment was impaired. Sevrick could not upset her any further or he was certain she would jump. He was not sure how to handle the situation from here except to be calm and hope she calmed down too.

"I am not here to change your mind. I cannot pretend to know all the answers but I do know that the rehabilitation system we established where I live works. We have cured at least a dozen haemans already. We could cure you too."

"I don't need to be cured. I need to be put down."

Sevrick shook his head, choosing to ignore her insistence that death was the only solution.

"I'm just saying there is hope. You have a chance to try. I don't know how you will recover after the drugs are out of your system or if you'll be able to forgive yourself one day. All I know is that you have the opportunity to give this life another shot."

Sevrick's words were not helping; they were only giving her more anxiety. She turned to face the ocean again. Her heart was racing and her head was spinning. Nothing made sense anymore. None of it felt right. Sevrick shouldn't have been here, but he was. She had been so sure of what she was going to do until fate brought him to her again. Now she stood with her toes over the edge of the cliff, second guessing herself and the certainty she felt only an hour ago. Ups and downs, highs and lows. Arinadya was overwhelmed once more. Her heart beat uncontrollably as the weight she planned to finally let go of got significantly heavier. The drugs still coursed through her veins, gushing freely through her body, making everything foggy. She could not see straight through her blood stained vision. Nor could she hear anything except the ocean crashing against the rocks below and the blood that rhythmically pulsed within her skull. She had to jump. It was the only way to stop the incessant pounding in her head. Sevrick thought he cared but she knew he would be better off without her. He had to be. She offered him nothing but heartache.

Without awareness of what she was doing, Arinadya's right foot lifted off the ground. She held it suspended over the open space in front of her. From behind, she could hear Sevrick shout in objection. As the words left his mouth, Arinadya's heart went into overdrive. It was working too hard. Her throat felt like it was closing and the fresh oxygen around her became hard to swallow. She was not sure if it was this new apprehension toward what she was about to do or the drugs that were causing her body to malfunction, but her thoughts went fuzzy as the pain increased. She no longer knew why she was there or what she was doing with her foot over the edge of a cliff; all she could feel was the intense pain that resonated through her body.

Without warning, she passed out. The pain was too much and her body shut down in an attempt to shield her from it. It took a few seconds for her vision to go completely black and in her last moment of awareness all she saw were the hungry waves crashing violently against the sharp rocks below.

Chapter 31

Sevrick dove to catch her as she fell. He grabbed her limp arm just in time, holding her back from plummeting to her death. Her weight hung over the edge but Sevrick kept her safe, pulling her back onto the solid ground beneath them. She collapsed to the floor in a heap, knocked out from the fear and the pain she was feeling. Sevrick was still in great pain himself but he ignored it. He picked her up and carried her like a baby through the woods. The exertion raised his blood pressure, causing the gash above his eye to begin bleeding again. It bled through the gauze and dripped down his face as he ran with Rina in his arms. They weren't far from the open field and he knew they would make it back to the white elm soon. Her red hair swayed in the breeze as she lay limp in his arms. Her lips were purple and her skin pale.

Halfway through the journey back, the sky opened up and began to flurry. The snow kissed Rina's lips as it fell upon them. She was so cold that each flake lingered for a few moments before melting. Sevrick reached his hand around her neck and through her hair to feel her pulse; she was still alive.

As he approached the white elm, he saw no one outside. Everyone was diligently expanding the living space below the earth. They didn't know how much time they had to finish it before the haemans attacked, so they worked in shifts to hurry its completion.

He placed her on the ground delicately and then maneuvered himself through the roots that surrounded the white elm. He thought it would be hard to get them both underground since the entrance was so elaborately hidden, but to his relief it was much easier than anticipated because she was so much smaller than him. His heart raced as time ticked on. Part of him worried she might be dying while the other half worried she might wake up and try to fight him. He needed to get her to the lab where she could be restrained, examined and, most importantly, healed.

He raced through the living space where a few of his fellow Clandes were taking a break from carving out tunnels. They saw him run past with Arinadya in his arms but did not have time to register who she was before he was out of the room and headed down the laboratory tunnel.

He burst through the plastic curtain that hung over the lab entrance and placed her on a vacant table.

"Strap her in," Sevrick demanded, out of breath. The blood from his eye dripped into his mouth and he spit it on the floor.

Zakhar and Leonid helped strap the haeman princess to the table. Lizaveta stood up in horror.

"Are you out of your mind?" she exclaimed, horrified that Sevrick brought her into their home. "She will kill us all."

"Not if we begin healing her before she wakes up," Sevrick said, confident.

"We told you not to go back. What is wrong with you?" Lizaveta demanded, tears in her eyes.

"I didn't go back. I walked to a spot in the woods where I had seen her once before and she happened to be there again."

"Why is she unconscious? If you forced her to come back with you she will be resistant to the healing process." Lizaveta would not back down.

"None of the other healed haemans came willingly. We tranquilized them and they are all fine. So stop. Leave if you are going to keep berating me." Sevrick was out of breath and Lizaveta wasn't helping him feel any better. She stormed out of the room without saying another word.

"How did this happen, Sevrick?" Zakhar asked, concern in his eyes.

"I didn't go back to the city, I swear. I followed Rina to this lagoon once, a few months ago. I needed fresh air so I went on a walk and she happened to be there again."

"She just married the prince and she lives a life of luxury now," Leonid looked skeptical. "Why would she be out wandering through the woods?" Zakhar cut in before Sevrick could answer.

"Why is she unconscious?"

"She fainted. I don't know why. I think from fear."

"Fear?" Leonid asked. "What was she afraid of?"

"Death."

Zakhar raised his eyebrow in question.

"Haemans don't fear death."

"I guess they do when they are bringing it upon themselves."

"What do you mean?" Leonid's voice became low; his curiousness was overcoming his doubt.

"When I found her back at the lagoon, she was standing at the edge of a large cliff that overlooked the ocean. She was going to jump," Sevrick's voice shook as he spoke. "She wanted to kill herself. She said she did not belong in either life, human or haeman."

Leonid let out a heavy sigh and got his instruments to check her vitals. She still had a regular heartbeat, and although her breath was now shallow, she was maintaining her respiratory functions.

"I think she will be alright, it appears she just fainted. It was probably from extreme fear but it's also possible she had a mini heart attack. I won't be able to determine that without doing an EKG and a CPK-MB test. And even then we'd probably have to wait to see if she had an episode again and then compare the results from the second episode to this one. I don't have that technology here so there isn't any way to know for sure. We will just have to put her on a strict diet and watch her carefully if she survives the rehab."

"She will survive it," Sevrick said stubbornly.

"Of course she will," Leonid said, realizing the harshness of his previous statement.

"Sevrick, come with me," Zakhar cut in. "We need to clean up that wound of yours." He put an arm around Sevrick's shoulder and guided him out of the room. He looked back once to make sure he wasn't dreaming all that just happened. But there she was, red hair shining beneath the harsh fluorescent lights of the laboratory. Leonid stuck an IV containing liquids into her arm to replenish her fluids. Eventually they would give her new blood to reboot her system. His Rina was finally back with him.

Chapter 32

Zakhar cleaned the blood off Sevrick's face and applied more ointment to the healing sutures. He made Sevrick promise that he would lay down and rest, then left the white elm to take his shift in the forest as a look out. Zakhar was stationed with Nikolai thirty meters into the forest. There were other scouts located even deeper into the woods. Ever since the haeman followed Sevrick and Elena through the woods, scouts had been placed along the perimeter of the forest to keep an eye out for approaching haemans. After the incident with Pasha, more scouts were dispersed throughout the forest toward the city as extra precaution. Zakhar and Nikolai both agreed it would have been nice if those scouts had been in place when Sevrick got injured. Pasha wouldn't have had a heart attack if someone were there to help him drag the sled back to the white elm.

But now the forest was nicely decorated with lookouts in scattered locations to prevent the haemans from ever reaching the field again. This was how they caught the few haemans they rehabilitated. The scouts saw the haemans first, shot them with their tranquilizer darts, and knocked them out before they could be spotted. It was a great system and, to their knowledge, hadn't failed yet.

"Come on up," Nikolai waved an arm to Zakhar from the high tree branch he sat on. The tree was a tall and sturdy Norway spruce.

The branches were plenty and covered with green pine needles; it was an ideal lookout spot. Zakhar made his way up the tree with his VS-121 rifle slung over his back. Upon reaching the point where Nikolai sat, he got himself into a sturdy position between two tree branches.

"I just got done cleaning up the wound Sevrick managed to reopen."

"How'd he do that?" Nikolai asked.

"Well, according to him, he went for a walk in the woods and came across Arinadya at some lagoon. She was going to kill herself by jumping off a cliff but passed out before she could do it, and then Sevrick ran with her limp body through the woods and back to the white elm. The adrenaline got his heart working so fast his wound began to bleed through the stitches."

"Gross."

"Yeah, I know."

"That's strange, I didn't see him walking through the forest."

"He said it was a lagoon, so it must be off the gulf, and that isn't an area our scouts watch. He traveled a path we don't cover. We never thought the haemans would use that route to get to us, but apparently they could."

They both shrugged their shoulders. Sevrick would need to eventually show them the location of this lagoon so they could put scouts near it.

"So the princess, or queen, or whatever she is now, is knocked out in our home?"

"Yup. Leonid has her prepped for rehabilitation."

"I guess that's a good thing," Nikolai sighed. "Sevrick finally got what he wanted."

"Yeah, I just hope she survives the rehab like the others. And that she doesn't freak out once she's awake and healed. She was pretty deep into the lifestyle, I don't know if she really wanted to be healed."

"Well, if she was suicidal then she clearly wasn't happy as a haeman," Nikolai pointed out.

"That's true. I just think it will be a million times worse for Sevrick if she comes out of the rehab healed, but still doesn't love him. Or can't love him again. You've seen how the healed haemans have recoiled from the rest of us because of their guilt. If she recoiled from him after everything he's done to save her, I think he'd finally crack."

"What do you mean 'finally'? Sevrick's been cracked since we met him. Total loon, that one."

Zakhar laughed but maintained his genuine worry.

"Love can wreck you. I just hope Sevrick gets what he wants."

"You and me both," Nikolai agreed. He pulled out a canteen from his backpack and offered the warm water to Zakhar. The snow fell lightly on their heads, covering their jackets with a light dusting of snowflakes. The heated water soothed Zakhar's throat as he swallowed it, making his insides warm for a moment. Nikolai put the canteen back into his knapsack to keep it insulated and refocused his gaze on the ground below.

The earth before them was as quiet and stagnant as usual. For hours, the two watched the snow collect on the forest floor, covering the old with the new. It was boring but essential. The haemans were out to get them and they could infiltrate the forest at any time. There were no signs it was happening soon but it was better to be prepared. They did not want any survivor to be outside when the haemans attacked. It was decided recently that none of them were truly ready to fight. They needed back up, the kind they could only receive on a global scale. So they needed to remain hidden and alive until they could get extra support.

The day was shifting into night when a bird sang in the distance. Zakhar looked at Nikolai skeptically. The birdcall happened again in the exact same melody.

"Is that the call?" Nikolai's eyes were wide with fear.

"I can't remember. We've never had to use it before." Zakhar was frustrated and alarmed. "Why don't they just shoot the haeman and be done with it?"

But Zakhar's question was answered before they had time to wonder. A massive horde of haemans made their way through the trees below. It was a slow march but a menacing one. Why didn't they run? *They were looking for something.*

"What do we do?" Nikolai whispered.

"I don't know but we can't leave here. The haemans are blocking our way to the white elm and to the entrances in the forest on the other side of the field. I guess we need to wait it out."

"Great. We are going to end up dying at the top of a pine tree. Just how I always dreamed it would go."

"Oh shut up. I'm sure once the haemans find no one out there they will head back to the city."

"Let's hope they don't find anyone," Nikolai said, being more realistic.

Zakhar sighed, knowing this wasn't going to be a good night for any of the survivors.

Without hesitation, Nikolai repeated the birdcall in the direction of the white elm. He did the call four times before going silent again and praying the other scouts heard him.

Zakhar blinked a few times as he watched the haemans move toward the tree they sat in; they were so pale that they would have blended in with the snowy scenery if it wasn't for the bloody scars they wore on their exposed skin.

The tall tree shook as the mass of bodies walked below. A giant haeman man slammed the tree with his fist as he walked past, causing the tree to resonate dangerously. Zakhar and Nikolai readjusted their grips on the tree until it stopped shaking and then watched the group of haemans below.

They held their breath and remained as still as possible, making no noise while they waited for the parade of murderous haemans to pass.

Chapter 33

Kirill led the haeman troops through the forest. Mikhail stayed behind with Milena, who was on her deathbed. She only had a few more days to live so the prince insisted on staying with her. He hadn't left her bedside in days.

Kirill and two of his sergeants from the royal militia led the pack. With his sergeants Roman Vershinin and Sergei Greshnev by his comrade's side, Mikhail knew the mission was in capable hands.

Together, the three soldiers hand selected 200 haemans for the mission. These recruits had to be smart, strong, and in control of their tempers. If any of them accidentally killed Leonid upon finding him, Mikhail would murder the entire company.

"General Mikvonski, we are approaching an opening in the forest," Roman spoke. "Look ahead beyond the trees. What do you suggest we do?"

Kirill saw what he was talking about but did not see the issue. "Are you afraid?" he asked condescendingly.

"Of course not," he spat back defensively. "I am just trying to think tactically. We don't know what they've been doing out here the past few years. We may want to have a plan moving forward. I'd rather we not lose any haemans during this battle since we have much bigger ones ahead of us."

Kirill nodded. They needed to be wary about how many of their own they might lose to this fight. He wasn't too worried about it though; he couldn't imagine a situation where the humans outmuscled the haemans.

Kirill paused to address the crowd of eager followers. "You have all seen the picture of Leonid Federoff, correct?" The crowd grunted in unison, indicating they had. "Good. That is our *only* concern while we are out here. If any of the condemned get in our way, kill them. But *do not* kill Leonid. Mikhail will not react kindly to news that Leonid is dead."

A haeman shouted out from the middle of the crowd, "He's one of the condemned, he is a traitor. Why are we being tasked with his retrieval but not his murder?"

"That's none of your business," Kirill exploded. He took a second to regain his cool and address the question. "But what I can tell you is that I don't believe Mikhail will keep him alive long after we deliver him. His use is temporary to us but essential. That is all any of you need to know."

Collectively, the group of haemans mumbled at this tidbit of information they were given. They hadn't been told much about this mission except that they needed to find this guy Leonid and return him to Mikhail alive. Many of them were frustrated but obeyed due to the promise that bigger battles would come their way.

Kirill stewed as the group made their way to the edge of the forest. All he could think about was the picture of Leonid they had used to prepare the troops for this mission. It was from the day Leonid graduated from St. Petersburg State University. They had to crop Mikhail and Kirill out of the picture so the other haemans didn't ask questions. It used to be a good memory: they were best friends, they were young, and they were about to conquer the world. Kirill couldn't understand why Leonid chose to leave all of that behind. He resented him for the betrayal and wished he were allowed to kill Leonid himself.

The open space Roman pointed out was upon them but there seemed to be no sign of life. The massive horde of haemans entered the field and were greeted by silence. The only thing in their line of sight was a huge white elm tree and another forest that started a few kilometers beyond it.

"Spread out," Kirill demanded. "Form lines, two-deep, across the length of this field. We will comb the open space. Keep your eyes and ears on the alert for any indication of life." Then Kirill led them forward.

Sergei covered the space to the left of Kirill. He scanned the skies and the space in front of them as they continued their march forward but there was nothing to see, only vacant skies and an empty field. Then he heard a loud thud and the sound of people murmuring. He threw out his arm and stopped the part of the line behind him. Confused, he looked around for the source of this noise.

"Were you idiots just talking?" Sergei turned to the men behind him and asked with outrage.

"No, of course not," the man directly behind him said.

Sergei turned back around, annoyed and unsure of what he had heard. Nothing was in the sky and nothing was ahead of them. He looked at the ground, replaying the noise in his mind, but shook his head. *Impossible.* He motioned for his section of the line to continue walking and they caught up to the others.

Beneath the ground there was a collective sigh of relief as the haemans continued to move forward without further investigation. It was easy to forget about the many ventilation holes that led from the safety of their home into the field above. They could hear the haemans marching. They could hear the haemans when they conversed. They could hear everything.

Kirill led the group past the white elm tree. There was no trace of humans present in this part of the Karelian Isthmus so they continued to move forward. But as they approached the next set of trees that lined the start of a new forest, he saw something odd. The trees didn't look right. In certain parts they didn't seem to flow with the rest of the tall Scots pines that lined this forest's edge. He threw out an arm to stop the progression of the haemans behind him.

"Tree houses," he muttered to himself. Wordlessly, he got the groups attention and pointed out what he saw. They acknowledged and moved forward.

Five meters into the tree line, Kirill stopped them again, directly beneath the tree homes.

"Attention, condemned," he shouted up into the elaborate infrastructure of tree homes scattered throughout the pines. "We know you are up there and we suggest you listen closely. We aren't here to harm you. We are here to retrieve a specific individual. His name is Leonid Federoff. If you give him to us, we will leave without harming the rest of you."

Kirill was answered with silence. His temper flared.

"You have built lovely little monkey homes up in those trees, it would be a shame if we had to destroy them while ripping you all out of hiding. The solution to this is simple. All we want is Leonid." He waited again for a response but got nothing. "Your cooperation is crucial to your survival."

He turned around and silently motioned for the haeman behind him to scale the tree and determine if anybody was up there. The lowly haeman obliged and climbed the tree in seconds. Pills filled with cocaine and extra drops of the silve had been given to every haeman soldier on this mission. The additional drugs running through their veins were proving to be highly beneficial. Many of them weren't council members but were moving as if they were.

The haeman reached the landing of one of the tree homes. As he opened the door to the hut, a gunshot went off. The haeman was shot in the face and fell off the platform, plummeting to the ground right in front of Kirill's feet. The body landed with a thud and Kirill let out a guttural roar.

"Destroy their homes. Kill everyone. *Except* Leonid," Kirill growled.

Scarlov stepped out of his tree home wielding a semi-automatic Dragunov sniper rifle. Ruslan had lent it to him when he and the other adult Scots declined to hide beneath the earth with the rest of them after hearing the bird call. They knew the sheer amount of numbers would be too many; there wasn't enough oxygen down there for them all. The Scots children were sent to stay with the Clandes but the rest remained in their tree homes, hoping they wouldn't be found.

The Scots leader opened fire on the rapidly approaching haemans, hitting many and slowing down their progress. He needed kill shots though. He needed to stop them forever, not just temporarily. A few other men and women had semi-automatic rifles lent to them by the other survivors. The entire forest was alive with the blaze and roar of ammunition as the haemans entered the treetops.

The Scots were outnumbered. They had less than a hundred people to fight off a group twice that size. They knew the risk of hiding in the trees once the birdcall was received, warning them all that haemans were headed toward them, and it was collectively agreed upon that none of the other survivors could come to their aid. Everyone understood that being found meant death. The survival of the Clandes and Primos was too crucial to risk them fighting, especially since their chance of beating the haemans with such few numbers and minimal armory was grim. Scarlov and the rest of the Scots made this sacrifice for the greater good.

Kirill ascended the trees with ease, dodging bullets as he jumped from branch to branch effortlessly. He wanted to find Leonid. He had to.

He tore the doors off tree homes one by one, checking for Leonid and snapping necks systematically. He had gone through five homes before he noticed a man shooting down at him from the tallest of the tree homes. This was the highest point anybody lived, so the haeman figured this man must be important amongst the traitors.

Guns fired continuously. The haemans killed those without weapons first and then cautiously bombarded those who carried the heavy armory. Sergei successfully ripped out the throat of one woman who had been shooting down at them. Roman broke the spine of another machine gun operator. As Kirill climbed, he looked to the forest floor to see if he could gauge how many of his haemans died. There were about fifty corpses so far. He could live with that.

Scarlov saw the enormous haeman gaining speed in his direction. He tried to shoot him down before they made contact, but this haeman was too fast. He evaded every bullet. In moments, the creature had reached his balcony and swung over the railing with monstrous grace. Scarlov had no time to react before it snatched the gun out of his hands and broke it in two.

"The prince can't even fight his own battles?" Scarlov spat out with spite, knowing he could not get away.

"Don't speak to me as if I owe you an explanation."

"Kirill, I take it. I remember you from the days when I still lived in the city. I always felt bad for you, living in Mikhail's shadow. It was an embarrassment to all men, watching you grovel at his feet."

Kirill growled beneath his breath, containing his anger for a few seconds more.

"If you give me Leonid, I will call off the rest of my men and whoever has survived thus far will live to see another day."

"I don't know who that is," Scarlov said. Kirill knew he was lying.

"So you'd die for him?"

"I would always chose death over helping you."

"I hope you meant that," Kirill said, lunging at him and breaking his neck before Scarlov could even lift a hand to defend himself. He crumpled to the floor of his treetop home as Kirill stepped out onto the balcony.

"Has anybody found our target?" Kirill shouted out to nobody in particular. He got a resounding "no" in response as the haemans finished off the few humans who were left. Sergei happily threw a man by his neck off a high tree limb, sending him straight to the earth below. Roman grabbed two survivors and slammed their skulls together, then sent them into a death plunge as well. The ground was littered with dead bodies. Some were haeman, but most were the lifeless corpses of the condemned.

"Everyone gather down below. We've left our mark here."

"We did not find Leonid, what do we do now?" Sergei asked.

"We keep going," Kirill said, seeing the answer as obvious. He could tell his small army of haemans was tired but he did not want to stop. He could not return to Mikhail without Leonid.

"I am feeling weak, I need my vitamins," a haeman woman declared from the back of the group.

"Me too," another said.

Kirill looked at them all with annoyance but he knew their blood did not stay powerful as long as his did. Many of them were not on the council; they were weaker. But he was comforted that the first complaint was someone asking for vitamins and not cocaine; Kirill was unsure how many of these haemans were savvy to the truth. Happy to have avoided that potential fiasco and relieved that the council members among them were smart enough not to say anything about needing silve, he caved.

"We can return to the city for one night. You get exactly 24 hours to rest and refuel, and then I expect each and every one of you to be ready to fight once more. We will pack backup supplies so this issue never arises again." It would be good to return to the city and recruit more haemans for the return trip since he lost more than he had expected.

"Go," Kirill shouted at them. "We do not need to travel together." They ran, turning to blurs as they sped toward St. Petersburg. Kirill was left alone now, surrounded by countless dead bodies. His thoughts circulated around Leonid and what it was going to take to find him. Mikhail was going to be furious once he found out the army Kirill assembled had returned without their old comrade. Kirill was sure he could make it right; this one failure would not define his role as a leader. He just had to make sure the prince believed that too.

Chapter 34

When Kirill returned to the Winter Palace he entered into a scene of mayhem. Everyone was in a panic. Members of the palace staff were frantic, running through the corridors while the royal militia stood guard over every doorway.

"Filipp, what is going on here?" Kirill demanded of a young soldier watching an exit on the west side of the building.

"Milena died this morning and Arinadya is missing," the young haeman answered without emotion.

Coldness flooded Kirill's chest; Milena was the only person the prince loved more than himself. This was not good news.

"Where is Mikhail?"

"You do not want to see him now," Filipp warned.

"Why not?"

"He has already murdered a dozen members of the palace staff. He is not handling the death well."

"Of course he isn't, it was his sister. But I am his friend and he needs me. Tell me where he is," Kirill demanded.

"He is in the library with her corpse. He took the body from her bedroom and has been holding it hostage for the past eight hours. He has a pistol and is shooting anyone who tries to enter."

"Lovely," Kirill muttered beneath his breath. "Lend me your spare gun. Mine is in my chamber and I don't have time to retrieve it."

Filipp obeyed, pulling his personal Makarov pistol out of its holster. He handed it over then resumed his guard over the exit with his Kalashnikov AK-47 rifle positioned across his chest.

"Why are you guarding the palace exits?"

"Because of Arinadya. If she is still in the palace, we are making sure she doesn't leave. The palace staff is searching the grounds hoping to find her."

"I'm sure that's really helping the prince cope with his sister's death."

"Mikhail doesn't know Arinadya is missing. We haven't told him. Didn't want to make everything worse."

Kirill's heart began to race; Mikhail was going to be lethal once he found out this news.

"We are hoping to find her before he realizes she's gone. We don't know where she is, but if I were you I wouldn't mention it to him. I am positive he will shoot the messenger."

The large, meticulously carved doors to the library were shut and locked. Kirill knocked twice.

"Go away," Mikhail shouted from inside, his voice cracked with hysteria. He fired his gun, sending off a warning shot. "Leave or I will kill you."

"It's Kirill. I want to help." Everything went silent for a moment before the prince spoke again.

"Did you find Leonid?" His voice softened a bit.

Kirill took a deep breath, "No, not yet."

"Then go away."

"Let me talk to you. I loved Milena like a sister, too. We are all sad, let us grieve together."

"Nobody loved her as much as I did."

"You're right, but we still want to honor her legacy properly. You know she would want that." He was testing Mikhail's patience but the thick doors kept him safe from the prince's unstable grief. A few moments passed before Mikhail spoke again.

"Come in."

"Are you going to shoot me?" Kirill asked.

"No, of course not. Besides Arinadya, you're all I have left."

The deadbolt slid out of place. Kirill gritted his teeth.

He slowly cracked the door open, keeping his pistol in hand. Mikhail resumed his spot in a large chair with Milena's lifeless body strewn across his lap. He looked mad with his crown on his head and her blood on his hands. Kirill supposed it was fitting; the prince did start her on this addiction after all.

Blood poured out of every orifice of the princess's face. Nobody knew why, though her nurses suspected internal hemorrhaging. It was an atrocious sight. Mikhail was covered in her blood too as he held her and whimpered over her dead body. He delicately touched her face.

"She was the only light I saw in this world," he said through the tears. "I do not know how I will go on without her by my side."

"I know. She was so strong and so smart. All of Russia has suffered a great loss today. It will never be the same without her."

Mikhail nodded and waved Kirill to come closer. "She would have wanted to have a proper funeral. She would have wanted all of Russia to take part in honoring her life. We will do it with style and grace. She planned my glorious wedding so I will have Arinadya put together an opulent funeral for her."

Kirill nodded, holding his tongue. Now was not the time to tell him more bad news.

"I am sorry we did not find Leonid," Kirill changed the subject. The prince waved his hand to shoo away his guilt.

"It would not have changed anything. She never would have lasted long enough for us to alter the cure. Leonid is human again, Milena wanted to stay haeman. It would have taken us weeks to figure out a way to make that work."

Kirill nodded, relieved that he wasn't placing the blame on him.

"We can still find him if you want us to. We only came back to refuel."

"Yes, send Roman and Sergei back out with the rest of them. They can find him. There's no rush anymore. I need you here though. We have bigger plans to attend to."

"Alright. What is on the agenda next?"

Mikhail stroked his sister's pretty brown hair as he spoke, "The world will be devastated at the loss of Princess Milena. They truly adored her from afar. As we grieve, so will they. And in the time after her funeral, while the world has sympathetic hearts for us, we will infiltrate. We will travel, we will form underground societies, and we will plant the seed of haemanism. I plan to take over the world."

Kirill smiled for the first time in days. Mikhail had devout followers across the globe, people who were fascinated with his existence without truly understanding who he was at all. They were putty in his hands, ready to be molded however he desired.

"We will manipulate the media during our worldwide campaign to allow admirers to grieve alongside us. During our travels, we will do our part to recruit those in power within each location. Simultaneously, we will have street teams deployed abroad, spreading the word and know-how to impressionable youth and those willing to take part in laying the foundation within their area. It will take a few months to get it initiated, then another few months for it to kick in. And in a year or so, once haemanism has reached its full force in different areas, we will move in with our troops to eliminate those who are fighting against it. Once we eliminate the outliers, I will rule the entire world." Mikhail smiled through the tears and blood on his face. A look of despair still lingered in his eyes but he managed to push through it. He had done it with one nation, what was stopping him from taking the rest?

Mikhail gently tucked his arms under his sister's back and knees, then stood up, holding her like an infant.

"I wish she would have been here with me to take part in the next chapter of our reign. It would have been much easier with her on board. She was the main reason I was able to capture the devotion of the Russian females. It won't be the same without her."

"Of course not, but you will find a way. I am positive women around the world will continue to idolize her, possibly even more so now that she is gone. With the right light shed upon her life, she could live on for decades with a legacy women will try to emulate."

"Yes. I have no doubt she will live on through posthumous fame, I just wish she were alive to see all the wonderful things that are about to unfold. And to help me with this great task I am about to embark upon." Mikhail's nostrils flared as his anger returned from the reminder that he would no longer have Milena by his side. "I suppose I have Arinadya to fill Milena's shoes when it comes to persuading women to join."

Kirill nodded, still avoiding telling him that Arinadya disappeared. He hoped they already found her but was not optimistic. Mikhail looked down at his sister's dead body in his arms once more. His sorrow shifted into fierce concentration.

"Please take her from me. Bring her back to her sleeping quarters and have the palace staff begin preparing her body for cremation. I want the ashes placed in a platinum vase covered in amethysts. Those were her favorite. Call on Arinadya to arrange the funeral procession. Tell her I expect it to be perfect and stunning. Nothing less than what Milena gave us for our wedding." He paused in his train of thought. "Tell Arinadya she has one week to plan the funeral. After the ceremony is done, phase two will begin."

Kirill took a deep breath. He couldn't keep the truth from Mikhail any longer. If nothing else, he figured the news coming from his best friend might earn him loyalty points versus Mikhail realizing he had purposefully avoided telling him.

"I have to tell you something but you must promise to remain calm," Kirill said, taking Milena's body from Mikhail and preparing to use it as a shield.

Mikhail's fists clenched. "What is it?"

"After returning to the palace from today's mission, I was informed that Arinadya is missing." Kirill flinched as Mikhail's newly found calm shifted back into rage. He did not ask for the circumstances of her disappearance to be explained because he suspected that she ran off on her own accord. Not kidnapped or lost somehow. From the depths of his being, he let out a demonic scream. The entire castle became silent as the sound of Mikhail's tortured fury resonated through the halls for all to fear.

Chapter 35

"Restrain her!" Leonid shouted. The laboratory turned into a scene of pandemonium upon the sudden reawakening of Arinadya. She woke up with a scream, catching Sevrick, Leonid and Elena off guard. They had removed her restraints because her skin was raw from trying to break free and they were hoping to give the lesions a chance to heal while she slept. They assumed it was safe because a sedative had recently been given. To their dismay, she woke up while unbound and they now had to seize and control an unruly patient suffering from extreme withdrawals.

Leonid guarded the exit while Arinadya thrashed about the room, slamming her body against the frozen dirt walls and demanding in various levels of desperate cries that she be given silve. Her eyes were bloodshot as she clawed at her own skin, trying to draw blood. None came. Her fingernails were regularly trimmed to prevent self-harm. As she failed repeatedly to draw blood, her rage increased. She darted across the room, her speed still faster than the Clandes because the haemanism wasn't fully out of her system yet.

Elena made an effort to grab her as she darted past but Arinadya swiftly stopped her attempt with an elbow to the side of the skull. Elena fell down, knocked out from the strike. Furious, Leonid shouted into the hall beyond the laboratory for extra assistance.

Sevrick pleaded with Arinadya to calm down but she could not obey. Her mind did not belong to her at this moment; all she could process was her need to end the pain with more drugs.

"Give me silve. Let me heal myself," she screeched as she took a momentary break from her sprint around the room.

"You need to be patient," Sevrick said, catching his breath. "I know it doesn't feel like you are being healed but you are. You are on your way to feeling healthy again."

"This is torture," she cried at Sevrick, "you are killing me!" Angry tears spilled from her eyes and her face furrowed with an irrational look of betrayal.

She bit her forearm, finally causing herself to bleed. She let out a hysterical squeal of excitement as she feverishly licked the blood off her skin. In this moment of distraction, Zakhar ran into the room and helped Sevrick capture her.

Sevrick grabbed her arms and yanked them behind her back. Then he placed his weight against them and wrapped his arms around her, trapping her in his embrace. Zakhar immediately knelt to control her legs. With his arms wrapped around her ankles, he was able to prevent her from kicking anyone and escaping once more. Leonid took this opportunity to inject her with another sedative. He gave her a stronger dose this time, realizing her body's chemicals broke down the previous quantity too quickly.

After a few moments, her attempts to fight her new constraints ceased and she fell limp in Sevrick's arms. He gently picked her up and placed her back onto the hospital cot. They tightly strapped her back into the leather bounds, then looked at one another and sighed in relief.

Leonid ran to Elena's side. She was slowly coming to, reestablishing her bearings after the hard hit. She suffered from a concussion but would be okay. He would keep watch over her that night to make sure she did not slip into a coma while she slept.

"I've never seen withdrawals as bad as hers," Zakhar said. "Don't take these straps off again. It is bad enough to witness her episodes while she's contained, we can't risk her having another incident like that and managing to escape this room. It would put everyone in danger."

"We only took off the restraints to heal the wounds beneath them. We had no clue her body would eat up the sedative as fast as it did." Sevrick felt guilty that Elena got hurt. He couldn't seem to escape the harm he continually brought upon his friends. "It won't happen again," he promised. Zakhar nodded then helped Leonid get Elena onto a neighboring cot.

Two days had passed since Arinadya's unrestrained withdrawal. Leonid kept her sedated because it was important she didn't cause herself anymore stress from unnecessary outbursts. The blood transfusion required rest to work properly. They performed the procedure when she first arrived using Alexsei's universal type O blood. If it worked, the silve-laced blood would leave her system and she would be cured of the haemanism and blood lust. Then all they would need to tackle was her remaining drug addiction.

Sevrick stayed by her side through all the chaos that now engulfed the underground fortress. The loss of the Scots had been traumatic. Everyone heard the slaughter through the ventilation holes and it only instilled more fear into the hearts of the survivors. The Scots children were left orphaned, so the Clandes and Primos assigned them new family units and tried to make them feel welcome.

In addition to this, those in charge were zealously drafting up new survival plans. They did not know what would come next, but they spent their days and nights considering every possibility. Ruslan visited Sevrick in the laboratory a few times to update him on their progress. Their plans covered everything from planting false trails that led the haemans away from the white elm to assigning scouts locations closer to the city in order to be better prepared for the next invasion. But the only idea that could truly save them and their homeland was their plan to sneak across the borders of Russia and into neighboring countries. They finally felt the urgency to attempt this feat. Even though it would be time consuming and dangerous, it was the only strategy that could provide results. Once there, they would do everything in their power to gain the attention of those in charge so they could inform them of the atrocities that have been taking place in Russia. They would divulge the secrets the royals kept from the world.

The Clandes would need to find a stretch of border that was unprotected by these guards. They would need to be stealth about leaving the country. If seen, their entire mission would be blown because Mikhail would catch wind and intercept their attempts to ruin him. His charm was unstoppable, especially amongst the international media that already adored him.

Sevrick looked forward to the day that he could be part of this mission. Once Rina was healed, he could focus on setting things right. Slowly, his world felt like it was falling back into place. He looked down at her, slumbering peacefully under the sedatives. Her eyes were circled in purple bruises from exhaustion, her skin was splotchy from malnutrition, and her arms, torso, and legs were covered in raw sores from the many attempts she had made to break free of her bindings. She looked sickly, and Sevrick did all he could to muffle his thoughts that she might not survive this rehabilitation procedure.

Leonid entered the room, ready to attend to his patient once more. Enough time had passed, and today could mark the beginning of the next phase. Since she was so deep into the addiction before arriving, they were unsure if the first blood transfusion would be enough. The next time she awoke, they would be able to determine whether it eliminated the haemanism or not.

"It should only be a few hours before she wakes up again. We will be able to tell within the first few minutes if she is adjusting to the new blood properly."

"I hope she is. It's been hard watching her wake up in fits of panic, screaming and fighting the restraints that hold her down. She has been so hostile. I haven't seen any remnants of the girl I once knew these last few times she was conscious."

"Yeah, well, this should stop all of that," Leonid said. His words were optimistic but his voice was sullen. The haemans had come into the forest looking specifically for him. They all heard Kirill announce it to his men before they approached the white elm. He wasn't sure why but he knew it had something to do with him being cured. As they crossed over the field, he begged the rest of the Clandes to let him turn himself in so he could stop them from entering the Scots side of the forest. If he was able to prevent the inevitable suffering the haemans would cause, then it was worth it. Not a single comrade needed to die on his behalf, but no one would let him leave. Despite his efforts to fight his way out of the underground fortress, he was unable to get past his large friends. During the audible massacre of the Scots, they had to hold him down on the ground to restrain him from running. His agony and guilt blinded him from the fact that giving himself to the enemy would do more harm than good. Leonid's knowledge was an opportunity for the haemans to learn how to survive longer. With it, they might be able to maintain their fragile lifestyle through generations rather than decades. This fad would have a short lifespan if they could not find a way to reproduce and raise offspring who were healthy enough to survive infancy through adolescence. Having time to reflect on it all, Leonid realized his friends were right in demanding that he stay hidden during the attack on the Scots. It didn't change the guilt he felt, though. He walked around with heavy shoulders, doing his job in stony silence.

Sevrick sat next to Rina, holding her limp hand as he waited for any sign of her recovery. A few hours passed. He dozed off in his chair, still holding her hand in his own. When her fingers began to twitch, he shook himself out of his slumber. Her eyes were still closed but her fingers moved slightly within his palm and her eyeballs darted back and forth beneath her eyelids.

He rubbed the back of her hand, hoping to coax her awake. Leonid came to his side. As Sevrick was about to speak, she gasped and her eyes shot open. Her slow, heavy breathing contradicted the ravenous look she held. They took a step back as they wondered which girl they were facing now. Whoever she was this time, she was an entity neither man could define.

Thank you for reading *Haemans* – I hope you enjoyed it! If you have a moment, please consider rating and reviewing it on Amazon and sharing your thoughts with me via social media. All feedback is greatly appreciated!

Amazon Author Account:

www.amazon.com/author/nicolineevans

Facebook:

www.facebook.com/nicoline.eva

Twitter:

www.twitter.com/nicolineevans

Goodreads:

www.goodreads.com/author/show/7814308.Nicoline_Evans

Instagram:

www.instagram.com/nicolinenovels

To learn more about my other novels, please visit my official author website:

www.nicolineevans.com

Made in the USA
Middletown, DE
11 September 2017